THE NARROWING ROAD

Copyright © 2021 Kevin Slimmer

All rights reserved

The characters and events portrayed in this book are fictitious. Any similarity to real persons, living or dead, is coincidental and not intended by the author.

No part of this book may be reproduced, or stored in a retrieval system, or transmitted in any form or by any means, electronic, mechanical, photocopying, recording, or otherwise, without express written permission of the publisher.

ISBN-9798789900789

Edited by: Stephanie Segretto

For Parker Stanton

"Enter through the narrow gate. For wide is the gate and broad is the road that leads to destruction, and many enter through it. But small is the gate and narrow the road that leads to life, and only a few find it." Matthew 7:13-14

"Behold, I send you forth as sheep in the midst of wolves be ye therefore wise as serpents, and harmless as doves." Matthew 10:16

"The unrighteous shall not inherit the kingdom of God. Be not deceived: neither fornicators, nor idolaters, nor adulterers, nor effeminate, nor abusers of themselves with mankind, nor thieves, nor covetous, nor drunkards, nor revilers, nor extortioners, shall inherit the kingdom of God." 1 Corinthians 6:9-10.

DAY ONE

CHAPTER 1

"What do we have?"

Detective Parkerson asked the officer on the scene as he ducked under the yellow police tape surrounding the scene. It was an early, brisk autumn morning in Norman, Oklahoma. The sun was barely showing itself to the world as the morning dew glimmered off the grass. A light fog was setting the scene in a clearing within the woods of the park.

"Female, mid-twenties."

Detective "Park" Parkerson walked around the dead body, which was bound to a large X made by two four by fours nailed together in the center. The victim was naked with her arms and legs stretched out, each bound to the separate lumber ties with nylon rope. Her head was bent backward, eyes wide open, looking towards the sky. She was petite, about 5'5" tall, with long blond hair hanging in front of her eyes/face. Although her eyes were bloodshot, you could still see the bright blue irises shining through. Her skin was fair, with no tan lines visible. She had a small nose and a round face. She was both pretty and innocent-looking.

"How'd she die?" Park asked the coroner.

"Strangulation. Well, at least preliminarily. Until we get an autopsy, we can't be one hundred percent sure."

The coroner walked Park around the body to the head. The

makeshift X was leaning against two trees in the middle of the woods in Lake Thunderbird State Park. "See here," he pointed at the victim's neck. "Ligature strangulation, probably by the same nylon rope they used to tie her to this thing. You can see the ligature mark around her neck. Is she supposed to be crucified?"

"It looks like it," Park observed.

"Wasn't there a murder a few months back with the same X thing?"

"Yes, there was, Male, mid-twenties. Crux Decussata." Park answered.

"What's that mean?"

"X-shaped crucifixion or the St. Andrew's Cross."

Park remembered learning that during the investigation of a similar case 6 months ago.

He never found the killer, not one shred of evidence. That victim's name was Anthony Miller. He was 24, finishing his master's in education at the University of Oklahoma City. He was the epitome of a model human being. He lived with his parents, so he could help take care of his father; he went to church every Sunday and volunteered regularly. Nothing about him would point to someone wanting to murder him.

"Do you think these cases are related?"

"I would think so, or we are looking at a very weird coincidence. So, did she die on this X or was she put here after she was strangled?"

"After. If she were strangled while on this contraption, you would see ligature marks on her wrists and ankles showing struggle. You only see a slight indentation around her wrists and ankles, like they have not moved.

Plus, the way the indentations on her wrists and ankles are, indicate that she was dead at the time of the binding."

"Just like Mr. Miller. So, the killer or killers strangled her and then put her on this X."

Park walked around the X, staring at the grass. He crouched down and pulled a nail out of the grass and bagged it and handed it to the officer trailing him. "Looks like they put this thing together here. There are no drag marks or tire marks, so the killer or killers walked the body and the materials to this location. If this were done by one person, he or she would have had to take multiple trips. We need to look around for shoe prints. Also, where is the closest place for someone to park a truck or SUV?"

"There is a parking lot, about a half-mile from here, that we passed driving into here."

Jon pointed over his shoulder.

Park started walking slowly towards the parking lot, looking down for any signs of the killer or killers. After about 10 minutes of scouring for evidence and finding nothing, Park found the closest uniformed officer and asked, "Do we have any identification as to whom the victim is?"

"No, sir, there was nothing to identify her at the scene."

"Who found her, are they still here?"

"Yes. That older gentleman over there. His name is Merrill Thompson. He takes a walk through here every morning." The officer pointed to an area back towards the body.

"A little off path for a morning stroll. Thanks." Park walked over to Mr. Thompson.

"Hi. Mr. Thompson. I am Detective Parkerson. Can you tell me how you came upon the victim?

"I... I take walks here every morning. I walked through the woods and there she was. I pulled out my cellphone and called 911 immediately and waited here for someone to show up."

"What time was this?" Park asked.

"5:46 a.m."

"Wow, that's pretty early."

"I don't sleep well, and an early morning walk through the woods helps my joints wake up. Also, watching the sunrise comforts me, but not today." Mr. Thompson responded.

"Do you usually go off the path when you walk? This is a pretty secluded place."

"I just like to wander through the woods. I came upon this clearing in the woods a few weeks ago and thought it was peaceful. You know, a nice place off the beaten path to clear my head, pun intended." Mr. Thompson laughed.

"Did you see anyone else around here?"

"No. No one."

"Ok. Thank you. I need you to give a formal statement. Officer McMahon will take care of you. If we have any questions we will get in touch, leave your number and address. If you think of anything, please call me."

Park handed him his business card and walked back towards his car. As Park drove back to the station, his thoughts centered on Anthony Miller. The scene was the same, and he was also discovered early in the morning. Park surmised that to mean the killer must have placed the body in the middle of the night or pre-dawn. The Miller case still haunted Park. It was one of the few cases that stuck with him. The type of case that when his mind was silent, it would spontaneously erupt into his consciousness, ruining his peace. It gnawed at him, causing many sleepless nights. Only bourbon would allow him to move past it. He wasn't an alcoholic, but he did need the warmth to blanket his mind and body, so he could sleep during certain nights.

Park arrived at the station. He sat at his desk, logged into his computer, and pulled up the Anthony Miller case, and started to read his notes.

Anthony Miller was found bound by his wrists and ankles to an X-shaped contraption with nylon rope at Andrews Park. The X was leaning against the amphitheater's stage. He was strangled with a nylon rope. He was dead before being bound to the wood planks, according to the forensic investigator at the scene. A city employee found him when he was emptying the garbage cans at 6:15 a.m. There was no physical evidence at the scene. No leads.

"Hey Park." A voice bellowed behind him.

Park turned around to see Lieutenant Gregory standing there. "What's up?"

"We just got a call about a missing woman. She never showed up to work this morning and has not been home since last night around 5:30 p.m. Fits the description of your VIC. It's her mother who called, Mrs. Janet Williams."

"Ok. You got her address?"

Park stood up and walked towards him, already knowing the answer. He grabbed the piece of paper from the Lieutenant's hand and walked towards the station's door.

CHAPTER 2

Detective Jacob "Park" Parkerson started his career out on the force like everyone else. He was assigned to the night shift and drove around an SUV pulling over drunk drivers and dealing with domestic disputes. Occasionally, he ran into some violent crime. Oklahoma had numerous guns circulating and people believed it was still the old west. Park was a counselor most nights and learned a lot about human behavior. He was interested in learning more about why humans do the things they do and went back to school, part-time, and received a bachelor's degree in Psychology, then became a detective 10 years ago. He continued to volunteer for any trainings that dealt with reading people or understanding them. This, he realized, would be a lifelong and difficult journey.

Understanding people is different from understanding the individual. No matter how many times Park thought he knew someone, they would surprise him. Park learned that without knowing every experience, trauma, achievement, success, failure, and many other factors, you can't always predict someone's behavior. He was great a hypothesizing, but there was occasionally one thing, sometimes small, that he would miss that was the key to the whole case. Park wanted to know the why of it all, not just prove it happened. Park continued to go over the evidence and his notes long after the trial was over, so he could comprehend why someone would kill another human. Consequently, the Miller case still troubled him. Not only did he not solve the case, or give closure to the

Miller family, he still didn't understand why. This tormented him the most. Why would someone do this? Park watched documentaries on Netflix about serial killers regularly, and he was always perplexed on how the brain, with just the right amount of trauma or neglect, could justify the killing of another human being outside of self-defense.

Park was concentrating on the road and trying to prepare himself for the worst part of his job, telling someone that the person they love has died, violently, and then asking them questions. He pulled up in front of the house and parked the car. It was a blue split-level ranch with a 2-car garage. The front door was a bright yellow, making it pop out from the rest of the house. The landscaping was meticulous, with perfectly formed bushes and colorful flowers. There was a stone walkway from the street to the front porch. Park took a deep breath and walked towards the house. Park knocked on the door. The front door opened.

"Mrs. Williams?"

"Yes. How can I help you?"

Mrs. Williams was in her mid-forties. She had long blond hair pulled into a ponytail, wearing a long, flowered dress with white canvas sneakers. She had a white cardigan sweater covering the top of the dress, buttoned up to the top. Her eyes were brown, and she had freckles around her small nose. Mrs. Williams wore no makeup and had fair skin. She was a naturally beautiful woman.

"I'm Detective Parkerson." Park showed her his badge. "You called in a missing person report?"

"Yes, but the officer who took my call told me that she isn't considered missing yet. My Becky wasn't gone long enough and because she was an adult, I should wait until tomorrow. He took my information and her description anyway."

"Can I come in, Mrs. Williams?"

"Of course, of course, sorry, please have a seat in the living room. Call me Janet."

She gestured to the room to his right. Park walked into the living room and sat on a couch, as Mrs. Williams sat in a chair across from him. A coffee table separated them. An open bible was placed in the middle. Mrs. Williams placed a bookmark into it and closed it. Park, being an atheist, thought religion was nonsense, but he did understand its psychological appeal. He saw the chapter and verse she had the bible open to, Jeremiah 29:11.

"Ma'am, is your daughter still missing?" Park slumped back into the couch.

"Yes. Becky still lives with us, me and my husband, John. We communicate all the time. I have tried calling and texting her since last night around 9 p.m. She always responds quickly. Even though I don't like those smartphone things, she always has it next to her. This isn't like her. I'm worried. I've been praying all night. I just know something is wrong."

"So, when was the last time you talked to her?"

"Um... it was right before she was going out on a date, uh... around 5 p.m."

"On a date? With whom?" Park leaned forward.

"I don't know, she didn't tell me. She only told me that she met this guy, and she wanted us to meet him soon. She doesn't date much. Boys always flirted with her, but she wasn't the type of girl, boys pursued if you know what I mean."

Park nodded. "I do." Park moved to the edge of the couch. "Can I see her room?"

"Why? What… Is there something you aren't telling me?" Mrs. William's face turned white, and her eyes yearned for Park to answer her.

Park's stomach turned. He really wanted to get into Becky's bedroom, but he needed to get through this part first.

"Ma'am, a body was found matching the description of your daughter this morning in Lake Thunderbird State Park."

"No… No… Not my Becky." Mrs. Williams howled, sliding out of the chair and onto her knees, putting her face into her hands, and started to sob.

"Ma'am, we need you to come down to the station and identify the body. We need to make sure it is your daughter. Can you do that?"

Mrs. Williams was now praying in between sobs. Tears flowed down her face as she whispered words with her hands clasped together. "Ma'am?"

Mrs. Williams stopped praying and without lifting her eyes whispered, "Yes, I can do that. I will contact my husband at his office, and we will come down to the station. How did she die?"

"I'm sorry Ma'am until we can get an identification, I can't disclose that. I am sorry. What, does your husband do?"

"I understand. He's a lawyer. Mostly Family Law."

Mrs. Williams stood, gathered herself, and took a deep breath. She wiped her eyes with the cardigan sleeve and started walking towards the door.

"Ma'am, before I go, would it be OK to look in Becky's room?" Park knew he was pushing it, but he couldn't wait, he needed to investigate now.

"Of course." Mrs. Williams walked Park down a hallway to the last bedroom on the right.

"I'm going to go and put myself together. Let me know if you need anything."

"I will. Thank you."

Park stood in the middle of the room. The walls were painted a shade of lavender. On the walls were pictures of Becky with her parents, and some with her friends. She had a couple of posters of a band he never heard of. The entire bed set was white: a queen-sized bed with headboard made up with a white comforter and matching decorative pillows. Above the headboard was a rendition of The Creation of Adam, with a close-up of just the hands. Her room was a shrine to Christianity. There was a cross on the wall, dozens of books on Christianity, three versions of the Bible. Her whiteboard and corkboard were filled with bible verses and religious quotes. On the wall closest to the door was a poster of the poem, Footprints, depicting a beach with a single set of footprints in the sand.

Lying on her bed, was a purple Samsung laptop. Park opened it, finding it password protected. He closed it back up and decided he would revisit it later. He then walked over to Becky's desk, looking for any clue to where she was going or who she may have been with. Her desk was tidy and clean, with no events marked on her desk calendar. He superficially looked for journals but couldn't find any that were out in the open. Park had found, over his years as a detective, that young women usually wrote in a journal. However, with the advent of social media and apps, he was finding it more difficult to find physical ones.

"Did you find anything that could help you find... I mean..."

Park interrupted her, so she didn't have to say those words, "No. Do you know her password to her computer?"

"No. I'm sorry."

"That's ok. Can I take this with me?" Park was holding the laptop now.

"Yes. Mr. Parkerson, I mean Detective, I would like to go get my husband now."

"Yes. Of course. I will see you at the station later. Thank you, Mrs. Williams."

She nodded. She had already prepared herself with what she knew was the truth, her daughter was dead. Her face didn't hide her sadness or pain. Park knew from prior experience that there was nothing he could say that would help, so he just nodded and left the house.

CHAPTER 3

After Park returned to the station, he stopped by the IT department with Becky's laptop and asked them to access its contents. They told him that they would have it back to him by tomorrow morning. He leaned back in his chair, rubbed his face, and let out a big sigh. He was tired and foresaw that this investigation would take a toll on him, and he knew that he needed to mentally prepare for it.

Park logged onto his computer, opened Google, and typed "Rebecca Williams and Norman, Oklahoma" into the search engine. Jackpot. He was staring at a Facebook page, Instagram page, and several newspaper articles. The first stop was to everyone's favorite place to divulge their secrets, Facebook. Her page wasn't private, but it didn't really show much, except pictures of her friends and family, and the occasional religious meme. By all outward appearances, she lived a quiet, simple life based on her posts. Park closed Facebook and opened Instagram. He found the same issue; there was nothing that would help him. He then opened the local newspaper articles.

The first one was from, The Norman Transcript, dated May 29th, 2016. The headline read, "Rebecca Williams, Valedictorian, leads the graduating Norman High School Class of 2016." The article described Rebecca's 4.1 GPA and her involvement in student government, the debate team, chorus, band, and volleyball. It also mentioned that she volunteered once a week at a local homeless shelter. Her yearbook quote was, "To me, this isn't an ending, but a beginning. This journey has prepared me for the world ahead. I know now that I must use these skills that I have learned in order to spread Jesus's love and compassion." Rebecca was going to attend Oklahoma Christian University to study Psychology, intending to later become a Family Therapist. Why would anyone want to murder this person?

The next article from the same paper, dated May 20th, 2020, and was titled, "Local Homeless Shelter Celebrates Local College Graduate, Rebecca Williams." The article explained that Rebecca had been volunteering at the shelter since the age of 16 and continued to do so. It seemed that she had recently graduated from Oklahoma Christian University and had decided to work at the shelter while she attended graduate school at Oklahoma State University, pursuing her Marriage and Family Therapy degree.

The rest of the articles were the same, dating as far back as 2010 and up to 2020, all celebrating and highlighting Rebecca Williams and all her accomplishments. Based on the quick internet search, she was, on paper, an upstanding, modest young woman. She wasn't posting seminude, drinking, or partying pictures of herself. There weren't any self-serving humblebrag-type posts. She didn't have a TikTok where she was doing the most current filter or dance trend. She genuinely seemed dedicated and driven to help people.

Although Park was annoyed by Christianity and its followers, he admitted that Rebecca at least lived by what she preached, thus far. She didn't appear to be one of those hypocritical Christians, like so many that Park routinely encountered. He often found that the most public Christians he'd encountered are later arrested for murder, rape, theft, fraud, and public drunkenness. He knows of many other Christians too who partake in drug usage and extra-marital affairs. Rebecca didn't seem on paper to be one of these people.

"Park, they're here," his Administrative Assistant,

Rhonda, said from two desks away.

Park pushed himself up from his desk. He rubbed his eyes, straightened his tie, and ran his hands through his thinning hair.

"Thanks."

Park walked to the elevator and pushed the B button. As the doors opened, he was in the morgue. He turned right and saw Mr. and Mrs. Williams sitting in the waiting area. Mr. Williams was holding Mrs. Williams as she prayed.

"Mr. Williams?" Park asked.

Mr. Williams stood up and shook Park's hand. "Yes, call me John."

Park was always amazed at how people, even under the worst circumstances, still held on to social norms, mores, and manners.

"You can follow me. When you enter the room, they will lift the sheet off the body and show her face. I know this is difficult, but we need you to indicate if it is your daughter or not. We will let you stay in the room with her as long as you need if it is her. Do you understand?"

They both nodded. Park held the door open as the Williams's walked into the room. The technician lifted the sheet back as Park stayed by the door. Mrs. Williams fell onto her daughter, sobbing, yelling "Why!" to the universe or to her God. Mr. Williams just lifted his hand to his mouth and stumbled back towards the wall. Park moved towards him thinking he might fall, but Mr. Williams regained his balance long enough to crumple onto the floor weeping. Park never knew what to do in these situations. He knew his empty condolences were useless but expected. Park would have preferred to just rip the band-aid off and get to the job ahead, solving this crime and giving Becky justice.

"I'm so sorry for your loss. I'll give you some space, I'll wait for you outside." Park nodded at the technician and they both walked out of the room.

Park paced back and forth for about 5 minutes when the door opened and Mr. And Mrs. Williams walked out, his arm wrapped around his wife's deflated body, almost holding it up.

"What do we do now?" John Williams asked.

"Well, you will need to come with me and sign some paperwork. I need to ask you some questions if you are up to it."

"Yeah, sure, when can we take Becky home?"

Park was hit hard by that comment. He can usually keep his emotions in check, but something about this man asking to take his dead daughter home overwhelmed him. He held back tears, gathered himself, and said, "We can talk about that upstairs." Park led them to the elevator and back upstairs to a conference room.

"Can I get you some water or coffee?"

"No, we're fine." Mr. Williams answered for both.

Park placed a legal pad and a pen down on the table separating them.

"I hate to ask this question, but where were you between 10 p.m. and 4 a.m. last night?"

The coroner gave the time frame to Park before the Williamses arrived.

"Are you kidding me?" Mr. Williams boomed.

"Sir, I have to rule you out, it is procedure. You are a lawyer. You know that most murders are committed by someone the victim knew."

Mrs. Williams interjected, placing her hand on Mr. Williams's arm, calming him.

"We watched T.V. until around 10 p.m. and then we went to bed."

"Thank you."

He hated the redundancy of questioning people.

"Do you know anyone that would want to hurt your daughter?"

"No, no one, she was loved by everyone." Mrs. Williams finally spoke up.

"What about this guy she was dating?"

Mr. Williams swiveled his head quickly towards his wife, indicating that he didn't know his daughter was dating.

"Um..."

She squirmed, met her husband's eyes apologetically, and then swiveled her head back towards Park,

"...as I said before, she didn't tell me anything about him, just that she wanted us to meet him soon."

"You said to me that your daughter didn't date much, so how would she have met this guy?"

"I don't know, I mean, school, or work, or I don't know, maybe through friends."

"Does she work with any men that, um, that she would date?"

Mrs. Williams took a second to think.

"The only guy that she might date, or consider dating, would be Cameron. He's about her age, a little older. He's attractive and single. They seem to be friendly when I have seen them together."

"Why wouldn't she tell you about him if they were dating?"

"I don't know, I mean, her father and I..." she placed her hand on his. His eyes were staring at the table. "...we really didn't want her to date as she is finishing school. She wasn't allowed to date in high school or college. That was our rule as she lived in our house. She didn't seem to mind, she understood."

"So, you think she would hide dating this guy..." Park looked down to his pad. "... Cameron, because she thought you guys would be angry?"

"Maybe, but I wouldn't call it angry. More like disappointment. We wanted her to concentrate on her life before a man influenced her. Also, we didn't want her to be tempted to...well, we believe that sex is only for married people, so..."

Park interrupted.

"You didn't want her to be tempted to have sex before marriage. You are practicing Christians, I assume?"

"Yes, we are Seventh Day Adventists."

"Is your daughter, I mean was she active in your church?"

"Yes. Very. She is close to our Pastor and is involved in all aspects of our church."

"What is your Pastor's name?"

"Why? Do you think..."

Park interrupted again.

"I'm just trying to figure out her life and places and people who might know what happened, so I can bring you and your daughter justice."

"How did she die?" Mr. Williams whispered.

Park paused and leaned back in his chair.

"She was strangled and then tied to a large X and placed in the park."

Both of their faces turned white. Mr. Williams just stared, as Mrs. Williams sobbed into her hands.

"She was crucified." Mr. Williams said.

"Yes. St. Andrew's cross. She wasn't alive when she was placed on the cross, however. So, not technically crucified, sir."

Mr. Williams nodded.

"Why would someone do that to her? I don't understand...." Mrs. Williams paused and then remembered Park's question. "Morris. Pastor Morris."

"Thank you. We are going to do everything we can to figure it out."

Park saw the defeat and sorrow in their eyes and knew he couldn't continue.

"We can be done for now. You guys can go home. I'll be in touch."

Mr. Williams stood up and then interjected, staring straight into Park's eyes. "Isn't this just like the Anthony Miller murder? The one that you haven't solved yet? Shouldn't there be another detective assigned? You know, fresh eyes."

Park swallowed hard and broke eye contact, looking down at his hands. "Yes, this seems like it is the same M.O., but it is too early to determine if they are related. I can assure you, Mr. Williams, that I will do everything I can to bring justice to your daughter."

"Well, then, if you say so. But, if it is OK with you, I might have a little conversation with Lieutenant Gregory. He and I go way back. We grew up together here in Norman."

Park suppressed a response. He nodded and simply said, "Sir, whatever you need to do, I will support it, but I'm a good detective and I will do what I can to solve this case."

"John, leave the poor man alone and let him do his job. Take me home." She grabbed Mr. Williams by the arm and guided him to the door. Park opened the door and let the couple leave. They stopped to sign some papers and listened to how and when their daughter's body would be released before walking out into a different world than the one, they knew before walking into the station.

Park slumped down at his desk and Googled Seventh Day Adventist Norman, Oklahoma.

CHAPTER 4

On her phone screen, a message popped up, "So, whatcha doing?"

She contemplated a response and typed, "Nothing much, just lying in my bed." Three dots danced in front of her.

"I wish I was there."

She rolled her eyes and deleted him from her list of approved men. She then opened the message board to see who else was on. There he is, good ole Mark. She clicked on Mark's picture and started to type in the provided message window. "Hey, I enjoyed chatting with you the other night. I wish you didn't have to get off so soon." She attached a smiley emoji. Three dots danced again.

"Hey there, Jen! Sorry about the other night. What are you doing on this fine evening?"

"Nothing much, just lying in my bed."

She waited for what seemed like minutes, but a few seconds later he responded.

"That seems relaxing. So, tell me about your day."

She smiled. Maybe he is the one.

CHAPTER 5

After a couple of hours searching the internet for anything that would give him a lead and finding nothing, Park decided to head home.

"Calling it a night?"

Lieutenant Gregory asked, watching Park stand up and stretch his back.

"Yep. I need sleep,"

He meant bourbon.

"I'll be in early. I need to get a list of everyone Rebecca knew, and I need to look through that laptop. I will see what forensics turned up from her room."

"See ya tomorrow. Hey Park. Mr. Williams called me and asked if I could assign another Detective." Park was about to speak, but the Lieutenant held up his hands, silencing him. "Calm down, I told him you were my best, and I wasn't going to switch. Park," the Lieutenant made sure Park was paying attention, "you need to be careful with this one, Mr. Williams is a big deal, and their church has a lot of influence if you know what I mean. I know how you can get, but go where the case leads you, Ok?"

Park contemplated a response but knew no response was warranted or would matter. He knew he had the propensity to obsess over cases. In the past, if a case seemed to be solved, he would still try and fill in every missing piece of the puzzle even though the picture was evident. Park just nodded and left for the evening.

Park drove across town to his small two-bedroom house. It was his childhood home that he inherited after both his parents passed away five years ago. His father had died at 68 of a heart attack and his mother died at 66 of a stroke; both deaths were just seven months apart. Park wasn't close to them, but he was their only child, and he took care of them when he could. After their death, Park started to wonder if he was destined to die the same way. For a few months, he ate healthily and exercised. That was, however, short-lived. Being a detective was hard enough without the simple pleasures of life like bourbon, the occasional cigarette, and bacon cheeseburgers.

Park pulled his car into the driveway and got out of his car. He didn't live in the best neighborhood, but he didn't mind. He never felt he earned to leave the neighborhood he grew up in. As he walked towards his porch, he saw movement.

"Who's there?"

"Hey, Jake." A woman said sitting on the stairs.

"Jesus, Julie, I almost pulled my gun. What are you doing here?"

"You didn't return my calls or my texts."

"I've been busy," Park said, putting one foot on the first stair, twirling his keys.

"Busy. Right. Why are you calling me and then hanging up? I told you to leave me alone. It's been 6 months. You have to stop."

"I didn't call you."

"Jake... "

"Don't call me Jake, you know I hate that."

"Jacob, you do know that I can see your number when

you call, even from your work phone. I also saw you drive by a few nights ago."

Park was embarrassed but couldn't lie to her. She broke it off with him during the Anthony Miller case, aka, the other crucifixion. They'd been dating for about 6 months when she complained to him that he was turning into a cliché detective, putting his work before everything and everyone. Park's response was to work harder and become more withdrawn. After some time, she just stopped coming over and Park did nothing to convince her to come back. He knew who he was and that he wasn't right for her. About a week ago, Park was having a tough time sleeping and after trying Jack Daniel's as a sleep aid, he missed her. He wanted to talk to her, but he knew that he ultimately couldn't give her what she wanted nor did he want to use her, so he hung up. Unfortunately, this happened a few times.

One night after work, he just wanted to see her. He wanted to see her long brown hair, her tan skin, her beautiful brown eyes, and those long legs. So, he drove by and found her sitting on her porch with her 23-year-old daughter. Julie's eyes found his. Since she saw him, he gave her a quick wave, to not look like a stalker.

"I'm sorry. I... I just wanted to talk to you. I know I shouldn't."

"It's ok. I don't care if you want to talk, but I can't go down that road with you again unless things are going to be different, but I'm always here for you as a friend. Just stop hanging up."

"Ok. I'm sorry."

"Well, I'm here, what did you want?"

Julie patted the spot next to her, directing Park to sit down."

"I better not. I'm fine. I got another big case. It looks connected to the other one, you know the one."

She knew. Most nights, she would wake up alone in bed. When she found Park, he was sitting on the couch with the Anthony Miller case in his hands and a bourbon in the other. In the beginning, she would complain and drag him back to bed, but later, near the end of their relationship, she just turned over and went back to sleep.

"Ah, that one. Well, call me if you need to talk, but only to talk."

Park shifted his gaze to his feet and kicked the ground, trying to swallow the next question from leaving his lips, but it forced itself out.

"Are you seeing anyone?"

"That isn't any of your business."

Julie stood up, brushed off her bottom. She kissed Park on the cheek.

"But no, I'm not. Take care of yourself, Jacob."

Julie walked out to the sidewalk and down the street to her car.

Park watched her, shook his head, and went inside.

CHAPTER 6

"So, do you want to meet for coffee tomorrow?" Mark's message popped up on Jen's phone.

"Um… sure. Where and when?" Jen typed.

"You know the place on Alameda?"

"Yes."

"How about we meet after dinner? 7?"

"Sounds perfect, see you there."

Mark sent a smiley emoji, a thumbs-up emoji, and a coffee emoji.

Jen smiled. He's the one.

DAY TWO

CHAPTER 7

Park woke up early, as he has done for the last 6 months. 4 a.m. came every morning and slapped him awake. He liked waking up before the sun rose. To him, when the sun rose, it lifted a comforting blanket off the earth that exposed everyone to the harsh reality of the world. Before the sun rose, he would sit out on his porch, drink some black coffee, and go over the most current case he was working on, or the occasional case that haunted him. He would do this every day, even on his days off. Every second Park didn't solve a case, was a second that consumed him with a burning sensation, slowly killing him.

Park was certain that the Anthony Miller and Rebecca Williams murders were related and, regrettably, he would have to soon contact the FBI. He knew that they would send someone, and he would have to share information with them. He also knew that they would share information with him, but on their terms. It was not an equal and fair relationship. The last time Park worked with the FBI was during a murder investigation that leaked into a federal drug investigation. Park lost the jurisdiction battle on that one, but the murder was solved. Unfortunately, the killer got a reduced sentence because he cooperated with the Feds.

Park wrote on a legal pad everything that both cases had in common. Anthony and Rebecca were both practicing Christians, were in their mid-20s, seemed like perfect individuals, college graduates, and attractive. According to his friends, Anthony was seeing someone, but they hadn't met her nor did they know her name. They explained that Anthony was private and didn't talk about the girls he dated unless it was serious. Park tried to find out who this woman was, but there was nothing to indicate who she was. Anthony's computer was a dead end, and his phone was never recovered. This mystery woman was still a person of interest, but all signs pointed to a man or men doing this to Anthony, due to how he was displayed. A woman couldn't have done this to him, not alone.

Park couldn't let the one similarity go. Both victims were dating someone that their closest friends and family hadn't met or known much about. Rebecca's phone wasn't recovered either; this wasn't a coincidence. Park knew that her computer wouldn't give him anything, either, but he couldn't wait until the morning, to go get it from IT. He couldn't figure out why this little fact gnawed at him. What if Anthony and Rebecca ran around in the same circles? They had to know each other. Park had to re-visit the Miller case and start treating this like one case. The sun started to lift the comforting blanket of night off the earth. Park finished his coffee and went inside to get ready for the day.

CHAPTER 8

"Hey Park." Rhonda greeted Park like she did every morning. She was always there at 7 a.m. sharp, even though she didn't have to be there until 7:30.

"Hey Rhonda, how was your night?"

"Pretty good, Craig and I watched a good movie on Netflix."

"Great. I'll talk to ya later."

Park hated small talk. He knew that she wanted him to ask her about the movie, but he didn't care. He just wanted to get to work.

Park sat down at his desk and pulled out the Anthony Miller file. He poured through the notes, photos, and interviews to start making a list of the similarities that he started on his porch. He pulled out his interview with Anthony's parents and reread the whole thing, looking for previously missed clues.

Mid-20s, check. Volunteered, check. Graduate School, check. Park stopped and circled graduate school. Athletic, check. Wants to help people, check. Christian, like strict Christian, check. Park circled that one too. A small circle of friends. Check. I need to talk to Mr. And Mrs. Williams again and get a list of Rebecca's friends and acquaintances. Mystery Dating, check. Park stared at this one for a long time. He circled this one, multiple times. I need to talk to that Cameron guy and the Pastor.

Thinking of the pastor, Park rummaged through more of his notes on Anthony to see if both victims attended the same church or at least practiced the same religion. Park scoured through everything until he landed on a notebook with "Baptist" written next to the question about what Anthony was involved in. Park was disappointed that there wasn't a connection, but still had a gut feeling he was on the right path. He remembered visiting a church, talking to a Pastor Ross, and getting the same answers about Anthony. Park wrote down a summary of what he deduced.

Both victims were in their mid-20s, attractive, and athletic. They both attended graduate school after having extraordinarily successful high school and undergraduate careers. They both volunteered more than the average citizen. Their career paths both focused on helping and teaching people. They both lived at home with their parents that were still together. They were well-liked, respected, and had many friends. Furthermore, they both didn't partake in the social media faze. Christianity was the center of their lives. Lastly, they both were dating secretly.

Park circled the word "dating" again. He felt that was the road he would eventually be on. He still had some preliminary work to do before he could investigate that lead. The FBI was next on his list, and then hopefully the computer would be ready.

CHAPTER 9

"So, where are we at on the Williams case?" Lieutenant Gregory asked Park, sitting down at the chair next to his desk.

"Well, I'm fairly confident that the Williams case is related to the Miller case from 6 months ago. I was just about to call the FBI and see if they can help us."

"You are inviting them here? Do you think that is necessary?"

"Yes. I have a feeling this is bigger than just Norman, or at least it means we might have a serial killer on our hands."

"With just 2 victims? I don't know, Park. Let's wait and see what turns up. Give me something that directly relates the two cases, and then we can reach out to the FBI."

"You mean besides the two bodies being strangled and placed on a wooden cross?"

"You know what I mean. There is nothing to indicate that this isn't a copycat."

"Trust me. I found nothing in the Miller case, and I have a feeling I'm going down the same path here. Maybe the FBI has similar cases and can connect them to these." Park explained.

"Let's wait and see what turns up." Lieutenant Gregory stood up and walked back to his office.

Park didn't understand the reluctance. He understood that no local law enforcement department wanted the FBI involved, but in this case, they could only help. Frustrated, he stood up and walked down the hall to the IT department.

"Hey, is the laptop from yesterday ready?"

"Yep, you can access whatever you want," the IT technician walked over to a counter and picked up the laptop and walked it over to Park. "Here ya go, let me know if you need anything else."

Park never met a friendlier guy. It made him more nervous than relaxed. "Thank you."

Park walked back to his desk, sat down, and opened the laptop. It opened directly to Windows with no password granting access. Park didn't know what to do first. He just stared at the screen. He opened the computer's files and looked at what she saved. Mostly, she saved schoolwork. In her picture folder, all he saw was a bunch of group pictures of her friends at school and work. He printed some of them. One young woman popped up a lot in her pictures.

Park immediately went on Facebook and looked through Rebecca's pictures, finding the same woman. The tag on those photos indicated that she was Maria Burrows. Park wrote her name down on his legal pad. He opened Facebook Messenger and scrolled through her conversations. Nothing. Park couldn't believe that nothing was indicating where she went that night or any mention of the guy she was dating.

After about 3 hours of combing through Instagram, Snapchat, Twitter, TikTok, and her search history, Park had nothing, just like in Anthony Miller's case. I can put that on the similarity list. Park was frustrated. How can two victims both have nothing on any social media site that was less than perfect behavior? Park grabbed his legal pad with the similarities on it and wrote, *Are they being targeted because of who they are and how they act?* Park wondered if the fact they both appeared to be remarkable citizens was why someone was hunting them down. He contemplated that maybe the killer is their opposite, someone who didn't get all the breaks in life, lived their life immorally, a loner, and an outsider. Park needed to find out more information about Rebecca and who she was around. Park needed to see Mr. and Mrs. Williams again.

CHAPTER 10

Mrs. Williams opened the door with a similar outfit from yesterday.

"What can I do for you, Detective?"

"I'm sorry to bother you during this... well... um... Do you mind if I come in and ask you some more questions?"

"If it will help catch who did this, then you can ask me anything. When can we bury our daughter?" Mrs. Williams' eyes welled up.

"Soon, I'll check for you when I get back."

Mrs. Williams fully opened the door and gestured for Park to come in and sit on the same couch. Park settled on the couch as Mrs. Williams took her spot in the chair. Park noticed the same bible on the table opened to a different passage, John 11. She once again placed a bookmark in the book and closed it.

"What do you want to know?"

Park took out his legal pad and asked, "Can you give me a list of Rebecca's friends?"

"Well, she mostly spent time together with Maria, at least that is who I met...oh... and Cameron, who I told you about. Other than that, I don't know of anyone else. I know she has many people in her life, but only a few she calls, friend."

"What is Cameron's last name?"

"Anderson."

Park scribbled Cameron Anderson on his pad. "Can you tell me more about the Pastor?"

"Oh... Pastor Morris, we call him Pastor Jim. Why would you want to know about him?"

"Ma'am, I need to figure out what happened to your daughter, so knowing about her life will help me put the puzzle together. Pastor Morris could be a missing piece or just an edge piece, it's my job to investigate everyone and everything, no matter how insignificant."

"Ok. Well, Pastor Jim and his wife have been really close to our family. He and my husband are friends. John goes to his house often and they, you know, watch sports, talk about faith, and other guy stuff I presume."

"Did your daughter spend time a lot of time with him?"

"I don't know if you call it, a lot, but he helped her with a program she developed."

"What program was that?"

"Well, she met Maria when she was experiencing some issues in life. She went to the Pastor and pitched an idea that members of the church who have the means to help lost souls could get together and help them find the right path. You know, a second chance."

"Interesting. So, who were these members that helped?"

"Mostly lawyers, doctors, politicians, and other jobs with, well, power. John volunteered. He helped Cameron, that is how he met Becky." Park saw her eyes turn red and well up."

"So, this program was created by Rebecca with help from the Pastor because of Maria, and Cameron was one of these lost souls that got help?"

"Yes."

"What did Cameron do? How long ago?"

"I don't know. Only the volunteers know the details. I don't care either because in God's eyes we are all his children, and we all deserve the opportunity to repent for our sins."

"How long has this program been going on?"

"Hmm…maybe about two years, maybe three? That's all I know; I'm not involved with the details."

Park paused before continuing. "Mrs. Williams, your daughter seemed to be a remarkable woman, um… person. Is there anything you know of that would…" Park paused, trying to be sensitive. "…well… that um… would want to hurt her? Was there anyone she ever talked about that she didn't like or fought with?"

"No, never. Cameron and her snip at each other, but I think that is about unrequited love. She didn't see him as more than a friend, and he, well, wanted more."

"Thank you, Mrs. Williams. If you think of anything that would help, please contact me."

"I will. Detective?"

"Yes?"

"Are you going to catch him?"

"Ma'am, I will do everything I can do. I admire the strength you are showing, Mrs. Williams. I appreciate you allowing me to be so intrusive in this horrible situation."

"Well, Detective, I am broken, but my faith tells me she is in a better place. She was… is God's child, the epitome of what Christ wants us to be. My sadness will diminish over time. I will miss her, but my soul will celebrate the gift she was given." Mrs. Williams led Park to the door.

Park sat in his car thinking how someone can lose their child and still utter the word "celebrate." He shook his head and started contemplating his next move. He stared at his pad, set it aside, and then drove away.

CHAPTER 11

"1655 Briar Meadow Rd."

"Thanks." Park hung up the call.

Park parked his car in the street and walked up to the house. He knocked on the door and a young man answered the door.

"Can I help you? My parents aren't home right now."

"I'm looking for Cameron Anderson."

"Who's asking?"

"My name is Detective Parkerson." Park showed him his badge.

"I'm Cameron. Is this about Becky?" Terror escaped his face, as he tried to maintain his composure.

Noticing this, Park knew he was on the right path. "Yes. Can I come in?"

"Um... I'm just about to... um... I have to go to work."

"This will only take a few minutes. I'm sure the shelter will understand. Can I come in?"

Cameron recoiled after Park mentioned the shelter. "Sure." Cameron walked into the kitchen and stood behind the counter, gesturing for Park to sit at the stool on the opposite side.

Park sat down, flipped to a clean page on his legal pad,

and placed it on the counter.

"How do you know Rebecca Williams?"

"I work with her."

"How long?"

"Uh... a couple of years or so."

"How would you describe your relationship?"

"Relationship? What do you mean?" Cameron turned red.

"Yeah. Friends. Enemies, Acquaintances. Lovers?" Park watched Cameron turn even redder.

"Um... Friends, I guess. We only talk at work."

"So, you haven't been to her house?"

"Well, yeah, sometimes I go over there, and we listen to music and talk and stuff."

"So, you don't talk just at work then. Are you with her alone at her house?"

"Well, her mom is there usually. Mostly, her friend Maria is there too."

"Did you date Rebecca?"

"No. No. We are just friends."

"Was that your choice or hers?" Park looked up and made eye contact with Cameron. He wanted to see his reaction.

"Um... hers. I mean, she is... um... was remarkable. Any guy would want to be more." Cameron walked to the refrigerator, grabbed a bottle of water, and drank half the bottle. Park noticed sweat beading on his forehead, even though it wasn't hot in the house.

"Did this make you angry?"

"Angry? No. What are you saying?"

"I'm just trying to learn about Rebecca and who was in her life."

"We are, were, just friends. I accepted that."

"You didn't keep trying to, I don't know, change her mind about you?"

"I mean, I flirted with her, but she made it clear that we were just friends, and yes, that was frustrating, but I was ok with it."

"Ok. Was she dating someone else?"

Cameron paused longer than Park expected. "Not that I know of."

"Wouldn't she tell you if she was? I mean, your friends and all."

"Nope. She didn't say anything about dating someone."

"Well, her mother said she was on a date the night she died. You don't know anything about that?"

"As I said, she didn't tell me anything. I've got to go to work now."

"Where were you the night Rebecca went on her date?"

Cameron paused. "I was home. I have to go to work." Cameron walked past Park towards the front door. Park got up, grabbed his legal pad, and followed him. Cameron opened the door to let Park out.

"Well, Mr. Anderson, if you think of anything that could help, please call me. I will be contacting you soon when you have more time."

Park handed him his card and walked towards his car. Sitting in his car, he watched Cameron put his card in his pocket, close the door, get into a car, and drive away. Park could see that Cameron was now talking on his cell phone as he sped away.

CHAPTER 12

Park checked the time in his car, 3:30 pm. Park decided to head back to the station and check in. After sitting at his desk staring at his computer, he picked up the phone and called Pathways, the homeless shelter where Rebecca Williams and possible suspect Cameron Anderson worked.

"Pathways, how can I help you?"

"Could I speak to the Supervisor or Manager?"

"Hold on."

After about 30 seconds, "Hi, this is Ruby."

Park guessed Ruby was in her early fifties based on her voice; he was good at these things. "Hi Ruby, my name is Detective Jacob Parkerson, I'm investigating the death of Rebecca Williams..."

Ruby interrupted, "My God, I am so heartbroken, I just can't believe it. She was... was so beautiful and kind, why would... "

Park returned the favor and interrupted, "Mm-hmm, I was wondering if I could ask you some questions."

Ruby, now holding back tears, answered, "Of course."

"Does Cameron Anderson work there?"

"Yes, he's been here for a couple of years. Why? Is he...?"

"Ma'am, I'm just covering all my bases." Park knew exactly what would happen if he asked this question. No matter what he said, she now will be looking at Cameron differently and maybe even treat him differently. Park was hoping for the trifecta, in which she would start asking him questions. He wanted to kick the hornet's nest if you will. If Cameron was involved, he wanted him to squirm and make a mistake. This was all conjecture at this point, but after meeting Cameron, he, right now, is his only lead.

"Of course."

"Is he working right now?"

"No. He is off today."

"Hmm, does he work somewhere else?"

"Not that I know of. He works here full time. He works tomorrow from 7 a.m. until 3 p.m."

"Thank you. Could you tell me if Cameron and Rebecca were dating?"

Ruby laughed. "No. Cameron has a..." Park heard Ruby swallow. "... *had* a huge crush on her, but she made it clear she wasn't interested in him like that. They were friends, though."

"Did they ever fight?"

"Not that I have seen."

"Did Rebecca ever talk to you about a guy she was dating?"

"No, but Rebecca was all business and didn't talk about personal things at work that often."

"Thanks. Ruby, what is your last name?"

"Granderson, Ruby Granderson."

"Thank you, Ma'am. One more thing, could you tell me if Cameron was in any legal trouble in the past?

"Why yes, he was. I don't know what, but that's why he

worked here. He started here as just a volunteer. This was a condition for him to be part of the program."

"Program?" Park figured it was the same program that Mrs. Williams mentioned, but needed to hear Ruby's perception of it.

"Oh, yeah, um, the church I and Rebecca's family belong to, helps troubled souls find a new path." Park could see that the description was nicely scripted. She continued. "We, at the shelter, allowed some of these young people to volunteer here as part of their penance. It is such a wonderful program. Rebecca created it."

"I see. Thank you. I might ask you some more questions down the road if that would be ok with you?"

"Yes, of course."

"If you think of anything else, please contact me."

"I will."

Park hung up the phone. He knew he had to be patient to see if this stirred anything up or not. Park read many books, mostly ones that involved Detectives. He knew that those books always had a twist or two, but in real life Park usually knew who it was quick, and, in this case, Cameron fits the mold. Park didn't find this to be a typical case, he started thinking of all the David Baldacci novels he read. *They just might help.* Park scribbled a note next to Cameron's name on his legal pad, *Connection to Anthony Miller?*

Park jumped on Google again and typed in *Cameron Anderson + Norman, Oklahoma.* Cameron had accounts on Facebook, Snapchat, Instagram, TikTok, and Twitter. They were all private. There were multiple Cameron Andersons, so Park had to weed through the results. He was about to call it quits when he saw a police blotter from 3 years ago for the Cleveland County Sheriff's Department with a "Cameron Anderson" listed. He clicked on it.

Cameron Anderson

Town of Slaughterville

Possession of a Controlled Dangerous Substance

Drunk in Public

Petit Larceny

Park looked it up in the database and found the arrest. It was definitely him. His mugshot verified it. He looked even more awful than most mugshots. After digging some more, he found out that although Cameron was convicted, he didn't have to serve any jail time. He was instead placed on probation, had to pay fines, and do hundreds of hours of community service.

Park then called Cameron's probation officer and found out that Cameron was kicked out of school and moved back into his parents' home. He was doing community service at Pathways and because he did so well, they offered him a job. Also, Cameron started going to the same church that Rebecca and her family went to. According to Mr. Jorgenson, the probation officer, Cameron was a changed young man. He explained that everyone thought he was a good kid. He'd been inexplicably found at a gas station in the middle of Slaughterville with another man's wallet that was reported stolen, had a small amount of meth on him, and he was blackout drunk. A lawyer from a local church took on his case. According to Mr. Jorgenson, the lawyer, John Williams, decided to take on this case after reading about this kid's fall from grace and was known for his legal success.

Rebecca's Program, Park thought to himself.

CHAPTER 13

Park just stared at his legal pad. *I need a drink.*

"Hey." Lieutenant Gregory said while sitting down next to Park's desk.

"Hey."

"So, any leads?"

"Well, I do have a potential person of interest, Cameron Anderson. Looks like Cameron Anderson was a perfect kid and then poof..." Park made a gesture with his hand like a magician. "...he was a criminal...drugs, theft, and public drunkenness. Come to find out, Rebecca Williams' father, out of the kindness of his heart, took on his case. He pled down and got community service, where he served at Pathways homeless shelter. The same shelter he met Rebecca Williams. He was interested in her romantically, but she turned him down. So, he is, like I said, a person of interest."

"Have you connected him to Anthony Miller?"

"Not yet. I need to bring Cameron in."

"Go home, Park. I don't want you burnin' out as you did with the other case. It's been only 2 days, and you are already killing yourself."

"I'm fine."

"Go home."

"Ok."

Park left the building, got into his 2015 Toyota Camry, drove through a fast-food drive-through, and parked his car in front of Julie's house, hoping to get a glimpse of her. He wasn't ready to go home yet again to an empty house. Park sat in his car far enough away from her house to go unnoticed, but close enough for him to see her in all her beauty.

He was never good at relationships, as the cliché goes with cops. There was a type of woman who married cops, and Julie wasn't one of them. To make things work with Julie, Park would have to stop being the type of cop he was. If Park did that, though, he wouldn't be good at his job, and his job was everything to him. There was no such thing as "off the clock." He was always working the case. But Julie was special. His attraction was more than just physical; he was deeply attracted to her mind. She was generous, assertive, funny, brilliant, and most of all, compassionate. Time after time, when Park struggled most, she was there for him in the exact way Park needed her. She would give him space when he required space. She would hold his hand when he needed a connection and would make love to him when he needed the release. When Park needed to purge his emotional baggage, she would hold him.

Park couldn't reciprocate. She would give and give, and he would just take. He didn't know how to give in return. He lacked the skills needed to be there for someone, to truly be there for someone selflessly. No matter how much he wanted to, he just couldn't. There was no good explanation other than something preventing him from giving his whole self to someone else. This, and the Anthony Miller case, inevitably led to the demise of their relationship.

Park was finishing his fries, when he saw Julie walk out of her house with her daughter, Mia. Mia was 23 years old and was still living with Julie. Julie had tried everything to motivate her, but eventually, she gave up and just let her be. The last Park knew Mia was working at a local restaurant as a bartender after dropping out of college for the second time. That was six months ago.

As the two walked to the car parked in the driveway, they appeared to be yelling at each other. They both got into the car and slammed the doors in unison. Julie sped off in the opposite direction of where Park was. *I wonder what that was about.*

Park started his car and went home, alone.

CHAPTER 14

"So, Mark, tell me about yourself." Jen looked him up and down and liked what she saw. Even though she had been able to see his pictures and video chatted with him once, she was always surprised at how guys could look so different in person.

"Well, I work at the Ford dealership as a Car Salesman, but I want to use my business degree and find a corporate job in Oklahoma City someday. The thing is, I want to avoid being the typical white-collar executive, I want to start a business that helps people, that gives back. I mean, I want to make a good living, but it's about time we start creating businesses for the people and not just for profit. How about you?"

Jen was in awe. At first, his business degree threw her off. He seemed so altruistic in their conversations. His Christianity was what he primarily touted. The dating app she used was for Christians, so a business degree doesn't usually jibe with those beliefs. Mark is one of the good ones.

"Well, I am working as a server right now just to make ends meet, as I finish my degree in Psychology. I'm not sure what I want to do with my life. I didn't start college until I was already in my twenties. So, tell me about what you do for fun." Jen looked down and slowly looked up without lifting her head, meeting his eyes.

"I like to golf and play basketball with my friends. I am an avid reader and movie buff."

"What's your favorite movie?"

"I like the classics. My favorite movie is Casablanca."

"I've never seen that one. Maybe you and I could watch it some night?"

"That would be great."

"So, where do you go to church?" Jen asked.

"I'm a Baptist."

"That's wonderful."

"How about you?"

"Well, to be honest, I am struggling with my faith, so I haven't been to a church in a while."

"Oh."

"Is that a problem?"

"No. Not at all, I just figured you were a practicing Christian like me. Why are you on that app? If you don't mind me asking."

"Well, I guess I am searching for someone to help me get back on the right track."

"That makes sense. Well, if you want someone to talk to, I'm your man."

Jen smiled at him. Mark returned the smile. Jen thought to herself that he may be exactly what she was looking for. Mark reached out and touched her hand. "Would you like to get out of here? Go for a walk in the park?"

Jen wasn't sure if she should yet. She hesitated and then agreed. "Sure." Jen smiled.

"Great. Let's go. I love the park at dusk."

"Do you go there often?"

"Yes. I like to hike and take walks in all the parks around here. Lake Thunderbird is my favorite." Mark smiled.

"Great." Jen and Mark stood up, and he let her go ahead of him out the door.

"I'll drive." Mark unlocked his car with his remote.

CHAPTER 15

Park sat on his porch with his bourbon. Through his open windows, he could hear the music of John Prine. His thoughts were focused on Julie. She was the only thing that would get his mind off his cases. Part of him pined for her and wanted to try it again, but he knew she would just get hurt, and he loved her too much to do that to her again. While taking the last swig of his drink, his phone buzzed. Park picked it up off the table.

"Detective Parkerson."

"Good evening, Detective, this is Special Agent Sonia Brambilla from the Oklahoma City field office. Could we meet tomorrow to go over the details?"

"Details? What do you mean?" Park was hesitant to just agree to anything.

"Oh, Sorry. Ha! Your two murders involving the crucified young adults came to my attention, and I have some information I would like to share with you. I prefer not to discuss this over the phone. 9 a.m. tomorrow? Northside Diner? My treat."

Park was hesitant, especially after the Lieutenant's position, but he didn't call her, so he ultimately agreed. "Ok. See you tomorrow."

He walked into his house and poured himself another bourbon, three fingers this time. Returning to the porch, his thoughts returned to Anthony Miller and Rebecca Williams.

DAY THREE

CHAPTER 16

When Park arrived at the diner, Special Agent Brambilla was already sitting in a booth by the far wall. He knew immediately it was her. She was wearing a short-sleeved light blue blouse tucked into black dress pants; black leather boots finished her ensemble. Her hair was shoulder-length, jet black, and curly. She turned towards Park and smiled. She had dark tanned skin and beautiful big brown eyes. Park figured she was in her mid to late 30s.

"Hello, detective. I hope you're hungry. I'm starving."

Park sat across from her in the booth. On her left was a small notepad and her cell phone on top of a blue folder. "Do you mind showing me identification?"

"Yeah. Sure. Of course." Special Agent Brambilla lifted her identification.

"Thank you. So, what do you have?"

"Patience. Patience. No foreplay for you, huh? Let's eat and get to know each other before I let you see into my files. Ha!" She laughed at her joke and then winked at Park.

Park didn't know what to make of her, but he knew when he had to play along. "Fine." Park motioned for the server to come to the table. They both ordered breakfast.

"So, detective..."

"You can call me Park."

"So, Park, how long have you been on the force?"

"25 years. I started when I was 22 years old."

"When did you become a Detective?"

"10 years ago."

"Married? Kids?"

"No and No." He started getting annoyed at the examination, but he continued to play along.

"A looker like you didn't settle down. Yeah, me either."

"You know the cliché: job comes first."

"Are you busy as a homicide detective in Norman?"

"More than I should be."

"Crazy times, Cah-ray zee times. Am I right?"

"Yes, they are. How about you; when did you become an FBI agent?"

"I grew up in New York, and I always wanted to be an FBI agent, mostly because of *The X-Files*. I loved Gillian Anderson as Scully. I was 10 when that show came out. So, I went to college, and then I was recruited by the FBI. I now specialize in Violent Crime and dabble in Serial Killings."

"Married? Kids?" Park returned serve.

"Ha! No, and yes. He lives with his dad, he's 14. I see him one weekend a month. It's ok. I'm too busy, and he and his father are like best friends. We were never married, but we tried to stay together after Joshua was born for about 6 years and, well, casualties of the job and other stuff." Park nodded, showing her that he understood.

They sat in silence while they ate their breakfast. After the server cleared their table and they both ordered another cup of black coffee, Special Agent Brambilla grabbed her files and slid them over to Park.

"You've earned a peek into my files."

"Well, that was easy enough." Park retorted as he opened the file. He saw 3 photographs, 1 man and 2 women tied to a large X, naked, eyes open, staring up. "Fuck."

"Yep. So, with your two, that makes five. There is only one problem. The pictures of the two women were from about 30 years ago in Nashville, Tennessee, and the picture of the man was from about 10 years ago in Colorado Springs, Colorado."

"So, are we talking about the same person or persons doing this?"

"I don't know. This wasn't even on our radar until I got wind of your two cases. I like to find some obscure murders and see if anything pops up elsewhere. I searched for crucifixions in our databases. I got a bunch, but three were the same MO. Nashville caused some buzz 30 years ago, but after decades of no leads, they were just filed into the cold files database and never really thought of again. The man in Colorado didn't even get on the FBI's radar until yesterday when I was researching. Preliminarily, I see no connections."

"Is it a cult thing?"

"Could be, but we have no files on any cult that acts in this manner."

"Can I see the files on those murders? I would like to see if the victims fit into a profile I'm working on."

"I have them in my hotel room, wanna shoot over there and look through them?"

"Are you seducing me, Ms. Brambilla?" Park winked.

"Ha!" She laughed. "Well, let's just start with my files, and we'll see what else I'll let you look into."

"Ok. Are you ready?" He was starting to like her.

After paying the check, Park and Agent Brambilla headed to the Holiday Inn down the street.

Sitting at the round table in her room reviewing the 3 murder victims' files, the two remained silent as they read.

Park finished reading the files from the local departments and the FBI. All three victims seemed perfect: young and attractive Christians. Cameron, Park's only potential suspect, wouldn't have been born yet when the first murder happened. This didn't rule out his involvement in Anthony Miller's case or if he killed Rebecca or not, it just made things more complicated. Park needed to somehow connect these murders.

As if reading his mind, Special Agent Brambilla broke the silence. "We need to connect these murders."

"You read my mind."

"Tell me everything you have up to now."

Park explained that both his victims were dating a mysterious person and that they both were upstanding citizens. He explained how both victims were devout Christians, practiced what they preached. Park explained how Cameron seemed to hit rock bottom and Rebecca's family helped him get back on his feet. He also discussed Cameron trying to date Rebecca; how he was anxious and how he lied to Park about going to work.

"I still need to interview Rebecca's best friend and the Pastor, but I will also revisit Cameron."

"Sounds like a plan. Any forensics come back?"

"Forensics turned up nothing from the scene or from Rebecca's bedroom. We got a partial shoe print, but it is a heavily walked area, and it won't lead to anything. We found a nail, but it was clean. I have Rebecca Williams' laptop. I gave it a once-over, but I need to go through it again."

"Ok. Let's visit the friend."

CHAPTER 17

"Hey there." Jen typed on her smartphone.

"I had a wonderful time last night." Mark typed back.

"Me too. Whatcha doing tonight?"

"I'm watching a movie right now."

"Which movie?" Jen asked.

"*Misery*."

"Never saw it."

"You want to come over and watch it with me?"

Jen hesitated. She hovered her fingers over her phone. *Am I ready?* Jen said to herself. "Sure." Jen typed and felt anxiety creep into her brain. She wanted to avoid doing anything to ruin it.

"Great. I'll see you soon." Mark quickly responded. After Jen received Mark's address, she walked out her door.

CHAPTER 18

"Coming." A voice shouted from behind the door. The door swung open, and a young black woman opened the apartment door.

"Maria Burrows?" Park asked, even though he recognized her from the Facebook pictures.

"Yes...who are you?"

Park and Special Agent Brambilla both showed their IDs. "I'm Detective Parkerson and this is Special Agent Brambilla, can we come in and ask you some questions?"

"Is this about Rebecca?" Maria asked with a whisper as if she preferred not to say it too loud, making it more real.

"Yes, Ma'am, can we come in, please?"

"Yeah, sure." Maria opened the door all the way and motioned them to sit on the couch in the living room. Park and Sonia sat next to each other on the old leather couch, and Maria sat across from them on the matching love seat.

"I'm so sorry to be asking you these questions under these circumstances, but I need some information from you. What was your relationship with Rebecca?" Park asked.

"We were friends; best friends, I guess. I mean, we don't label it like that, but I mean that is what we are... *were*." Maria's eyes started to well up.

"You spent a lot of time with her?"

"Every day. If we didn't hang, then we would FaceTime or text."

"Who was she dating?" Park just wanted to rip the band-aid off.

"I don't know." She shrugged. "No one that I knew of."

"Her mother told me that she was on a date the night of her murder. Are you telling me that she didn't talk to you, her best friend, about it?"

"No. I mean, I knew something was up, I could tell she was hiding something. Some days she wouldn't respond to me as quickly as she usually does."

"Did she date a lot?"

"No, I honestly have never seen her go out on a date. We would go out in groups, and she would be flirting with some guys from school or church, but it was all innocent."

"Guys from school?" Sonia asked.

"Yeah, some guys from around here that go to school with us."

"Where would you guys go? Bars?" Sonia continued the questioning.

"No. Never. We aren't allowed. I mean, we don't do that."

"You don't do that? What do you mean? You are in your mid-twenties, what else do young adults do when they 'go out'" Sonia air quoted "go out."

"Our faith demands that we do not engage in those types of behaviors."

Park jumped in. "Seventh Day Adventist?"

"Yes. As I said, our faith prohibits us from drinking or going to bars."

"Do you only hang out with young people from your church who share the same faith?"

"Pretty much."

"Pretty much? Who doesn't?" Park sat more upright now.

"There are a few guys and girls from other churches, but we all are committed to our faith."

"I see," Park said condescendingly. "Where were you on the night of Rebecca's murder?"

"I was here watching TV by myself."

"She didn't text you or call you that night?"

"No, she did. She said she had something that she couldn't wait to tell me."

"What time was that?" Park eagerly asked.

"Around 7 p.m., I think."

"Did she text anything else?" Sonia took the baton.

"No. I responded to her asking her what it was that she wanted to tell me, but that was the last text I received." Maria showed them her texts.

"Thank you." Park shifted on the couch and was now sitting on the edge of the cushion. "What can you tell me about Cameron Anderson?" Maria's face changed just in the slightest. Park could sense Sonia catching it too and turned her head towards Park.

"I don't know, he was just a friend." Park noticed Maria start picking her thumbnail with her middle finger. He figured this was a nervous tick.

"Just a friend? *Your* friend?" Park needed to push a little. Again, Park felt Sonia was on the same page as him. He felt her adjust and reposition herself more offensively.

"I guess, but mostly Becky's friend. I mean, I liked him and all, but he just didn't pay much attention to me. He was more her friend than our friend if you know what I mean."

"Did they date?

"No. Becky didn't like him that way."

"Did Cameron like her in that way?"

"Yes. It was obvious. I would catch him all the time looking at her. Once I caught him peeking in her room when she was changing. I didn't say anything to either of them about that, I just chalked it up to boys being boys."

"So, Cameron wasn't part of your church? I mean wouldn't, being a Peeping Tom be against your faith?"

"He was part of our church, but not like the rest of us."

"What do you mean?" Sonia again tagging Park out.

"I mean, he only joined our church after he got into all that trouble." Sonia looked over to Park, indicating that she didn't know what that meant. Park nodded, signaling to her that he did.

"You mean when he was arrested for drug possession and other things?"

"Yeah."

"Didn't you also get the same help from the church? Did Mr. Williams help you too?"

"Yes. I got into some problems when I was an undergrad. Rebecca helped me, and some people from local churches saved my life. I am now part of their community. I'm going to grad school part-time with Rebecca and working my way through. Mr. Williams and other people have helped me."

"What other people?"

"I don't think, I'm at liberty to say. You should ask our Pastor."

"Pastor Morris?"

"Yes."

"So, Rebecca's father, out of the kindness of his heart, helped Cameron get out of jail time, then Cameron joins their church, and then Cameron befriended Rebecca and you. Is that how you became friends with Rebecca?"

"Yes."

"Thank you. Special Agent Brambilla, do you have any questions?"

"Yes. Maria, who do you think killed her?" Park glanced over at her with a confused look.

"Um. I don't know. Why would I know? I have no idea." Maria's face was contorted with confusion.

"So, when you heard she was murdered, no one came to mind?"

Maria paused. "No. No one." Maria looked down.

"Ok. Thank you." Sonia stood up. "We will be in touch."

"Yes. Thank you." Park stood up and they let themselves out.

They got into the car and started driving back to the hotel.

CHAPTER 19

"What was that question?"

Sonia laughed. "I like asking that question. Maria's body language and her response told me she thought of someone, maybe Cameron. Almost everybody considers someone to be the killer when a murder takes place."

"Yeah. You can tell she totally thought of someone when she paused, you could see it in her face." Park just smirked. He was impressed with Sonia. "I think Cameron is involved in some way, maybe he just knows something. Should we bring him in?"

"Yes. He knows something."

"Do you think Cameron was jealous and killed Rebecca because she was dating someone else?" Park wondered aloud.

"Well, that would be the simplest answer, but that doesn't explain the other four murders."

"What if he just copied the Anthony Miller murder to throw everyone off?"

Sonia pondered that. "That's an interesting theory. Well, we have more digging to do."

"I still need to talk to the Pastor, he is the last person who was close to Rebecca, who knew her well. Other than professors and other people at school, but my gut tells me this has nothing to do with her school."

"Well, let's call it a day. What's a good place to eat dinner around here?"

"Hmm...do you like Mexican food?"

"Yum. Love it!"

"There is a place on Porter. I can give you directions, or you can just plop it into Google Maps."

"Oh no, you are coming with me."

"I can't, I have to..."

"You have nothing to do. You are coming with me."

"Fine, but I need to go home first and change."

"You look fine to me." Sonia smiled at Park.

"Do you always hit on the locals?" Park slyly side-eyed her.

"Only the good-looking ones. Ha!" She snorted. Park couldn't contain his laughter. He liked her and her quirkiness.

They pulled into the restaurant and walked toward the entrance. As they were smiling at each other, flirtatiously, Park heard someone calling out to him. "Jake?" Park whipped around and saw Julie walking towards him with three other women.

Sonia and Park turned around and faced the group of women, with Julie leading the pack. Sonia leaned closer to Park and asked, "Who's that?" She elbowed him in the side.

Park whispered. "My ex."

"Oh, this is wonderful. Ha!"

"Jake!" Julie was now walking quickly towards him, about 20 feet away. Park was now settling in for an awkward moment. Park hated small talk. He especially hated sharing personal information with people. Now he was stuck talking to his ex-girlfriend in front of a colleague, who just happened to be a gorgeous woman, and in front of said ex-girlfriend's friends. Park let out a small sigh. Sonia heard it and chuckled softly. "Jake, what are you doing here?"

"Just getting a bite to eat."

"Hi. I'm Sonia." Sonia stuck her hand out towards Julie. Julie looked at it like it was foreign to her, but she grabbed it and shook it demurely.

"Hi. I'm... um... Julie."

"Hi, Julie."

"You never eat out, Jake. What's the occasion?"

Sonia again butted in. "I'm new to town and he, being the gentleman he is, offered to take me to dinner."

"Oh."

"She's working on a case with me. She is from the FBI." Park jumped in.

"OH. Well, that makes sense." Julie's face went from confusion to looking like she just figured out a riddle.

Sonia, enjoying the back and forth, replied with a smirk on her face, "Yes, we are working together, but it is difficult keeping it professional with this one, I mean look at those eyes, am I right? HA!" Sonia interlocked her arm through Park's and laid her head on his broad shoulder.

Julie's face went back to confusion. "Yeah, I bet it is." Park could sense how uncomfortable Julie was, and he was enjoying every moment.

"How do you know Park?" Sonia assertively cross-examined her.

"Oh. Um... Well, we used to date."

"OH MY, how awkward for all of us. Ha!" Sonia released

from Park and slapped him on the back. "Well, you can have him back after I'm through with him." She let out a pleasing passive-aggressive fake laugh. Julie returned with a fake laugh, as did her friends behind her. Park rolled his eyes. The situation went back to being uncomfortable.

"Well, we better go inside, we have a lot to go over," Park interjected.

"Yeah. We should get inside as well, 2 for 1 Margaritas." Julie waved her hand and smirked. Everyone politely laughed.

"Nice to meet you, Julie." Sonia turned around with Park, and she interlocked her arm within his again as they walked into the restaurant.

Park was relieved that they were seated at a booth nowhere in the eyeshot of Julie and her friends. Sonia looked over the menu, pursing her lips and moving her mouth back and forth as she decided what she wanted. "What's good here?"

"It's Mexican, it's pretty much the same thing in different tortillas. Meat, cheese, vegetables stuffed in some type of flour or corn shell. You can't go wrong."

"Ha! So true, I like my shell made with flour, large and flat. I'll go with the chicken burrito supreme with a side of rice and beans." She closed the menu and slid it to the edge of the table. "What's your pleasure?"

"I get the tacos. Beef, cheese, lettuce, and taco sauce."

"Wow... Exciting!" Sonia joked.

"I like what I like."

"So, Detective Park, what is your gut telling you?"

"About tacos? Well, they are going to taste delicious, and later my gut will expel them quickly out my ass." Park didn't usually joke, especially crudely, but Sonia just made him feel relaxed.

"HA!" Sonia chuckled and then snorted, which made her snort again. Park couldn't help but start laughing with her. She was infectious, and he even started to enjoy her saying "ha" when she thought something was funny. It was an endearing trait.

"No, what does your gut say about this case; what rock do you think we need to look under next?" Sonia was still wiping tears from her eyes from laughing.

"Hmm... I don't know. I've learned not to trust my gut over the years, too much emotion mixed up in there. That and tacos and bourbon."

Sonia smiled. "Bourbon man, huh?"

"Yeah. Cheap bourbon man."

"Well, before the night is over, we will toast to us solving this case with the cheapest bourbon we can find."

"I don't know, I didn't solve Anthony Miller's case and I prefer not to jinx it."

"Oh, bullshit. We will solve this. Now back to your gut, what are you thinking, where do we go next."

"Ok... Ok... we will toast. We need to bring Cameron into the station and ask him what he was doing that night, and then get his backstory. I would also like to talk to the Pastor of Rebecca's church and ask why they helped Cameron and Maria, and how well he knew Rebecca. Religion is obviously a huge factor in this."

"Alright. Well, I agree with you. I don't think Cameron killed Rebecca, even though I haven't even met him. I believe that all 5 cases are related. We need to find the connection. Cameron knows something, or he is involved in some way. We need to bring him in too, but we should talk to the Pastor tomorrow. The more information we have on Cameron and this situation, the more we can push Cameron."

The server took their order. Sonia ordered two margaritas, even though Park raised his hand in protest. She just rolled her eyes at him. Park felt her enchantment slowly seep into his skin and overwhelm his senses. Everything about her made him smile. He shook it off. The server returned with two large margaritas and placed them in front of Park and Sonia.

"Drink up Parky!" Sonia raised her glass and took an exceptionally long sip. "AHH. Delicious!" Park took a small sip and nodded.

"You are nothing like any FBI agent I have ever met. What's your story?"

"You haven't earned that yet, Park. I'm good at what I do, but I still like having fun. Do you like fun, Park? You don't seem very comfortable."

"Let's just say, fun never liked to hang out with me. I'm good at my job as well, and having fun just never fit into my method."

"Well, your record is very impressive; why have you stayed in Norman? Why not move up to Oklahoma City or somewhere bigger?"

"This suits me."

"Well, to each his own." Sonia picked up her drink and sipped it while she looked around the restaurant, taking in all the people. Park could see it in her eyes that she was analyzing them as she stared. Park liked to do this as well.

"The couple behind you at 10 o'clock will be divorced within 2 months." Park moved his head to indicate where to look. Sonia discreetly looked over her right shoulder as she slid to the end of the booth. She looked back to a couple scrolling through their phones as they shoved nachos in their mouths.

"HA! Good call. My turn." Sonia and Park traded their analysis of the customers until their food came. They ate and discussed music, movies, and the obligatory books they'd read.

After they finished their meals, Sonia looked at Park, steepled her hands, and said, "So, back to my place after we pick up some cheap bourbon? We should probably go over the Anthony Miller case as well as the three others with a fine-toothed comb."

"Um... Sure, that sounds good." Park was hesitant. He never could read a woman. He didn't know if she was trying to seduce him, or she was just offering to work on the case. Either way, he was uncomfortable. He liked to work alone. They both stood up and walked through the restaurant, Park following Sonia. He saw Julie and her friends in a large booth near the door. Sonia saw them too and reached back and grabbed Park's hand. She turned towards Julie, smiled, and mouthed, "Nice to meet you." Park looked down until they got out of the restaurant.

"What was that?" Park pulled his hand from hers.

"Just reminding your ex that you're a catch. You'll thank me one day." She elbowed him in the ribs and returned to the car. They drove to the liquor store and then to the hotel in silence. Sonia was singing along with the radio. Park kept sneaking peeks at her. He was infatuated.

CHAPTER 20

S3RP3NT5: "I think I have found the next passenger." The message appeared in the chat window.

SLVTNX808: "Good. How long until you know for certain."

S3RPENT5: "Not long. We had coffee and went for a walk. Watching a movie tonight."

SLVTNX808: "Keep us posted. I'll let them know."

SLVTNX808 signed off the Tor network.

CHAPTER 21

Park was sitting on the couch with Sonia in her hotel room. All the files were spread out in front of them. Park was just staring at the five pictures, three women and two men. They were all naked and tied to a large X with nylon rope. All five heads were leaning back, looking up with their eyes open. They all were strangled to death and then put on the cross. All five were attractive and in their mid-twenties. Four out of the five had ties to a Christian church, and they were all highly active. Only the first one didn't have any known connection to any church. Park reached out and pulled the file of the first woman from thirty years ago.

Gretchen Dorian was a college student at Vanderbilt University. There was no indication that Ms. Dorian was active in any local churches. She was from a small town, about an hour north of the University. Her parents indicated that they were Christian, and they were highly active in their church, their daughter wasn't. They also explained that they didn't talk to her much while she was at school and didn't know much about her life. Gretchen was an excellent student and was finishing her degree in Communications. All accounts pointed to her being an outstanding citizen who didn't get into any trouble. She had one close friend from her hometown that also reiterated that she lost touch with her since she went to school.

"It seems to me that the murders are linked to religion, specifically Christianity. Also, it seems that each of the victims was either dating a mystery person. What is the motive?" Park ruminated.

"Well, in our current victim, it could be unrequited love and jealousy, maybe it is the same for the rest. That doesn't explain the 30 years between the first and the last murder." Sonia countered.

"Unless Cameron knew about these murders, and he was a copycat. Is it possible that Cameron also knew Anthony Miller? Maybe Anthony Miller was dating someone Cameron liked and instead of killing the woman, he killed the suitor?" Park hypothesized.

"How would Cameron know about all the murders, if he killed Anthony Miller, he would have had to have known about the 3 other murders. How?" Sonia was staring at Park.

"Maybe since these are Christian murders, they are folklore in some churches, a story they tell their parishioners to scare them into submission." Park shrugged.

"You don't like religion so much, do you Park?"

"Not really. I understand it. I do understand the appeal, but I will never grasp the lifelong dedication to something so outrageous. I hope I'm not offending you." Park was now staring back at Sonia. Sonia scooched closer to Park and placed her hand on his thigh and smiled.

"Honey, you can't offend me. I'm not the religious type, either. I grew up in an extremely strict Catholic home, and I escaped when I went off to college to pursue my FBI aspirations. Furthermore, I don't talk to my parents or my extended family much. They don't approve of my life or my lifestyle." Sonia gazed into Park's eyes, hoping he would try and pry into that statement.

"Lifestyle? What are you into, Agent Brambilla? Should I be concerned about being in your company?" Park smirked.

"Let's just say I play for both teams." Park just stared at

her with confusion painted on his face. "What I mean to say is that I am both attracted to you as much as I'm attracted to your ex, Julie." Sonia raised her eyebrows, waiting for this revelation to sink into Park's brain.

"Oh." Park's face turned red.

"I always love people's reaction when I tell them I'm bisexual."

"I'm sorry, I didn't mean to offend you, it's just that, well, I... I don't really know what to say."

"What would you say if I told you I like pizza? That would be the appropriate reaction. Ha!" Sonia slapped his thigh and slid close to him so that they were sitting next to each other, touching. She laid her head back onto the couch. "It's ok. I hope you aren't one of those old school cops that believe..."

Park interrupted, knowing where she was going, "No I'm not one of those cops, even though I live in Oklahoma. I am a rare commodity. I have always believed that people should live the lives they want as long as they don't hurt other people. Also, I now know in my evolved state that people are born the way they are born, and even if it is a choice, who gives a fuck."

Sonia turned her head towards Park's and kissed him on the cheek. "Detective, you are a special guy."

"Well, on that note, we should call it a night. We need to bring Cameron in for questioning. I'll call him tomorrow." Park slapped his thighs and stood up.

"You don't have to leave," Sonia stated as she grabbed his hand.

"Yes, I do." Park grabbed her other hand and pulled her up. "I'll take a rain check after we solve this thing." Park hugged Sonia. He didn't remember the last person he hugged since Julie and even then, it didn't feel as warm and complete as his embrace with Sonia. Park released, only to have Sonia pull him back in.

"Not so fast," Sonia whispered. She held on for another 10 seconds and then released him. "I know we've only known each other for a day, but I like you, Park, you're a good man."

"Well, let me know what you think after you get to know me better."

Sonia kissed him on the cheek and walked him to the door. "Goodnight, Park."

"Goodnight, Sonia."

CHAPTER 22

"You've never seen *Misery* before?" Mark asked Jen as she covered her eyes during the scene in which James Caan was introduced to the sledgehammer.

"No, and I'm glad I didn't!" Jen buried her head into Mark's chest.

"Do you want me to turn it off?" Mark asked as he put his arm around her.

"No. I want to finish it." Jen took the opportunity to get close to Mark. She laid her head on his shoulder as they watched, wondering if he would make a move. During the rest of the movie, Mark was a perfect gentleman. "That was good. Thanks for inviting me over." Jen swung her legs over his and leaned in to kiss him. She released from his mouth and said, "That was nice."

"Yes, it was." He was staring into her eyes. His phone buzzed. "I have to respond to this. I'll be right back." He took his phone into his bedroom and shut the door.

Jen knew that Mark was who she had been looking for. She just needed him to show her what she needs to take it to the next level. After a few minutes, he returned to the living room. "Everything OK?"

"Yeah, just work. Nothing I can't handle. Now, where were we? Do you want something to eat, we can order in?" Mark sat next to Jen.

"Do you want to go out and get a drink? I know this great

club." Jen swung her body on top of him, and with her knees bent, she straddled him. She had her arms on his shoulders with her hands clasped behind his head, staring into his eyes.

"Do you mind if we just stay in? Clubs and Bars aren't my thing, I just want you all for me." He leaned in and kissed her.

DAY FOUR

CHAPTER 23

Park entered the station before anyone else, as usual. He sat down at his desk and pulled out Rebecca's computer. He wanted to look at her search history. Park started scrolling. Clothing, religious sites, school research, Pinterest, Facebook, Instagram, news articles, cooking sites, and YouTube videos were all he found among other irrelevant sites. He kept scrolling until one site popped out to him that was visited 6 months ago. A site that had an article titled, "Best Christian Dating Apps." "Bingo!" Park opened that article, and he now had the 10 apps that may give him the lead he was looking for. He knew that the laptop wouldn't help because she most likely downloaded the app to her phone, which was still missing. Park searched for the apps listed on her computer to no avail, only confirming that most young adults used their phones for everything. Park printed out the top ten list, wanting to share what he found with Sonia. As if she knew he was thinking of her, she sauntered into the bullpen and walked towards his desk with two coffees in a cup holder and a box of doughnuts.

"You must've read my mind!"

"Thinking dirty thoughts, I, see? Ha!" Sonia let out a guttural laugh. Park couldn't help but laugh aloud as well.

"No, ma'am, all pure thoughts."

"That's too bad. What are you working on? I assume you take your coffee black?" Sonia handed him a coffee.

"Yep black. I found something that might help." Park hands her the sheet of paper with the Christian dating sites as she sat down next to him. He then opened the box of doughnuts and grabbed a Boston cream, eating it while watching her scan the list.

"So, you think her mystery date came from one of these apps?"

"Yes, or at least **a** dating app. Have you ever had to subpoena an app before?"

"Yes. We have subpoenaed Snapchat many times. Many people use that for inappropriate relationships, since chats, pictures, and videos disappear." She made air quotes when she said disappear. "Nothing disappears."

"So could we subpoena these apps?"

"Yes. We would also need a search warrant to get more detailed information, but the subpoenas could indicate if she used any of those sites. After we have that confirmation, we then would use the search warrant to figure out whom she may have been talking to."

"Is that something your office would handle?"

"I will take care of it. I'll call my office."

Park looked up to see Lieutenant Gregory waving him into his office. Park excused himself from Sonia as she was on the phone. She held up her hand in recognition of him leaving. Park entered the Lieutenant's office and sat in the chair in front of his desk.

"What's up?" Park asked nonchalantly.

"So, I see the FBI is here. I thought I made it clear I didn't want them involved until you could link the two cases." He was furious as he spoke low but intimidatingly.

"She found me. I swear! When this murder was entered into the database, some bells went off in Oklahoma City. She has already changed the direction of this case. Come to find out, there were three other similar murders over the last 30 years."

"What? 30 years? *Here*? I don't remem..."

Park interrupted, "No; two in Tennessee 30 years ago and one in Colorado, 10 years ago."

"Jesus."

"Exactly. I mean, they all seem to have something to do with Religion. However, the person of interest I told you about, Cameron Anderson, we think he may have murdered both Anthony Miller and Rebecca Williams and made it look like the murders from 30 and 10 years ago."

"But how would he have known?"

"That's what we thought, our only guess would be that those murders may have made their rounds through churches as, I don't know, a warning or a fear tactic, like folklore or something."

"You really don't like religion, do you?" Lieutenant Gregory responded.

"Sorry, no offense, but in my experience, religion loves scaring the shit out of people."

"Fair enough." Lieutenant Gregory capitulated. "So, do you have anything yet?"

"Not really. We are chasing a long shot right now. I'll let you know if it works."

"Sounds good. Keep me in the loop. And Park, don't trust the FBI so easily. Don't make this bigger than it is."

"Will do, Boss." Park lazily saluted him and walked back to Sonia.

"All set, the subpoenas should be filed by the end of the day, and we should be able to get information by tomorrow, if they are cooperative, and they don't fight it." Sonia updated Park.

Park and Sonia reviewed all the files again on the five murders. Sonia went through the laptop and Park retrieved Anthony's laptop and went through it again. Park showed Sonia all his notes on Rebecca Williams and his list of similarities.

"Well, what we have is a victimology profile, this will help." Sonia smiled, touching Park's arm.

"You and your hoity-toity words, we just call that describing the dead around these parts," Park said in a terrible southern accent.

"Ha! Sorry, I'll dumb it down for you going forward."

"Much obliged, Ma'am." Park mimed tipping a cowboy hat.

"Let me see if I get what's happening here in Norman." Sonia stood up and started circling Park. "Two of your most upstanding citizens were strangled and then put on a crucifix, a St. Andrew's crucifix, naked with their eyes staring up towards the 'heavens.'" Sonia air quoted "heavens." "They were both attractive, intelligent, young people in their mid-20s. They volunteered and were going into careers that helped people. They both were strict Christians, and their faith was at the forefront of their daily lives. Likewise, they didn't drink, use drugs, gamble, or engage in any of the normal lewd behavior of the young and impressionable. They both didn't date much, however, at the time of their deaths, they both were secretly dating someone that no one knew about. Is that about, right?"

Park stood up and mockingly applauded her. Sonia took

a bow. "So how does Mr. Anderson fit into all of this?"

"Hmm... Well, let's forget about the other three murders for right now. Cameron either was the one who was dating both and killed them when they rejected him, or Cameron killed Rebecca because of unrequited love and killed Anthony because of who he was dating. What if Anthony was dating Rebecca?"

Park lifted his head and stared right into Sonia's beautiful, big brown eyes. "That is an interesting take. We need to call that boy in. Cameron may be dating men and women, that is something my old conservative brain didn't even consider."

"Well, us big-city folk are more evolved than you." "Ha!" They both laughed in unison.

"One of the other huge pieces, other than the mystery dates, is religion, more specifically Christianity."

"Great point. Why would someone fake crucify someone?"

"To send a message."

"To whom?" Sonia put her hand to her chin.

"To all of us? To other Christians? To sinners?" Park posited.

"So, you kill these two perfect humans, and you want the world to know it by using religious symbolism. That would make more sense if they were sinners than amazing Christians. Why would they send a message about being good?"

"What if the killer or killers hated religion, and they wanted to kill these perfect pompous self-righteous people, from their point of view, and use their own symbolism against them. They died for their religion's sins." Park stood up now and started walking around with Sonia as they analyzed the cases. Park didn't usually work with a partner. It didn't suit his style. But working with Sonia invigorated him, he felt like ideas were being built on top of each other, that their minds were wrapped up together working as one.

"Interesting take. So, here are our options for killers. Cameron, a jilted bisexual lover, or a religion-hating individual or individuals, who wants to send a message to believers."

"Why couldn't that be all one person? Cameron didn't grow up in that religion, he was recruited after the Church helped him out." Park turned towards Sonia and grabbed her shoulders. Sonia smiled.

"You may be on to something." Sonia lingered her stare. Park noticed he was still holding her by the shoulders. He quickly took his hands off her and sat back down.

"Ok, how 'bout we go talk to the Pastor? Then, we ask Cameron to come in for a visit." Park suggested.

"Sounds good. Let's go."

CHAPTER 24

Jen woke up in her bed smiling. After Mark kissed her, they sat together on the couch, and he held her as they watched *Casablanca*. She fell asleep on his chest. She woke up on the couch an hour later, and Mark had put a blanket over her. He was in his chair scrolling on his phone.

"Hey there. You passed out on me," he said with a comforting smile on his face.

"I did. Why didn't you lay with me?"

"I didn't think that was appropriate."

"Well, I better get going." Jen looked at him, waiting for an invitation to stay.

"Ok. Let me walk you out." Mark hugged her and then closed and locked the door behind him. Jen smiled. *Wow, he is a perfect gentleman.* Jen went home. He was the one, she just knew it. She wanted to move this on to the next level.

The next morning, Jen awoke feeling refreshed and energized. She grabbed her phone from the nightstand and typed, "Mornin' had a wonderful time, AGAIN!!!" She followed that with multiple kissy face emojis, then, "How about we go out to dinner this weekend?"

Jen usually allowed the man to dictate the pace. She liked it that way, but she felt this would get her to that next level faster. It seemed to her that Mark wasn't the assertive type, and she was too impatient for him to make the moves.

Jen just stared at her phone, willing a message to be returned. Jen moved on to scrolling through Instagram as she waited. After 30 minutes, she started to worry that she came on too strong. She felt anxiety spread from her brain to her breathing and her pulse. *Dammit, I screwed this up. Patience Jen. Patience.* She started to type a message of contrition when 3 dots appeared. Anxiety retreated, releasing its grip on her.

"That sounds perfect. Then afterward we can go back to my place and try another classic movie, how about *Citizen Kane*? How does that sound?"

Jen replied with a winky kissy face emoji.

"I'll pick you up at 6 pm, Saturday?" Mark confirmed.

She replied with a thumbs up and a heart. She then sent him a selfie of her lying in bed, with the covers doing their job. Only her head was visible. He didn't seem like a fella who would like a sexualized picture. He replied with a smiley face and with the words "BEAUTIFUL. LIKE AN ANGEL FROM HEAVEN."

CHAPTER 25

Park and Special Agent Brambilla parked their car in front of the Pastor's exceptionally large, 5-bedroom, 3-bathroom house with an attached 2-car garage. The lawn was well manicured and lovely. Park thought, *only in America.* Park stepped up onto the wraparound porch, furnished with the obligatory wicker chairs, a porch swing, and lovely flora. Sonia and Park gave each other a look, and then Park knocked on the door.

The door opens to a middle-aged, heavy-set woman with heavy make-up and hair-sprayed blonde hair, dressed in a blue and white pants suit. "How can I help you?"

"I'm Detective Parkerson and this is Special Agent Brambilla." They both showed the woman their respective badges. "We would like to speak to Pastor Morris."

"May I ask why?" Her face scrunched up, and she tilted her head to the right, moving her body completely in front of them.

"We would like to ask him some questions relating to the Rebecca Williams' murder."

"Oh, that poor dear. She was a lovely girl. So much promise. She's with Jesus now. I'm Dorothy, by the way, where are my manners?"

Park suppressed an eye roll. "Yes ma'am. Is Pastor Morris home?"

"Yes. Please have a seat on the porch and I will go get him." The woman closed the door. Park could hear her walking away, calling out *Jim!*

Park and Sonia sat in the two white wicker chairs to the right of the door, looking out into their huge front lawn. They sat in silence, enjoying the cool breeze, glancing at each other from time to time with a wry smile. The door opened and a tall, slender man with thinning gray hair came walking out. "May I help you? My wife Dorothy said you are here to talk about Rebecca. I'm not certain if I can help you very much…"

Park interrupted. "We just want to get a well-rounded picture of her life. Her mother told us that you and Rebecca had a close relationship."

"I don't know about that, but she did ask me for advice from time to time." Pastor Morris walked in front of them and rested himself on the porch railing.

Sonia jumped in. "Advice about what?"

"Oh, I don't know. This and that. You know, teenager stuff."

"No, I don't know. Enlightened us." Sonia quipped.

"Well, I remember her asking about dating boys when she was going off to college."

"Why would she ask you and not her parents?" Park retorted.

"She was asking, more from a religious interpretation point of view. She wondered if it was a sin if she dated and became intimate with a young man. Of course, we don't condone any premarital intercourse, but I told her that dating and some affections were fine. I also asked her to talk to her parents. Her father is pretty strict, beyond what his church tells him."

"What other things did she come to you about?"

"Let's see, when she was younger, she asked about hate

a lot. She asked me if she hated someone if she would still get into heaven. She was about 12 or 13 at the time. I figured it was some boy at school. Mostly, she would just try and understand sin and what it meant to be a Christian. She didn't come to me, since then, until she went off to college. Since then, she spoke to me often about community service projects and starting groups here at the church for young adults like herself. She was an extraordinary woman."

"When was the last time you saw Rebecca, Mr. Morris?" Park continued.

"Hmm, I would say it was last Saturday at our service."

"Saturday?" Sonia asked.

"Yes. We believe the Sabbath is on Saturday, as the Bible indicates." Park and Sonia both nodded. Park shifted himself in the uncomfortable wicker chair. His legs were falling asleep. He adjusted himself, so he was seated on the very edge of the chair.

"What can you tell me about Cameron Anderson?"

Pastor Morris looked nervous for a second but shifted back into pastor mode easily. Sonia subtly glanced at Park, indicating she saw his tell. Park just nodded in recognition.

"A troubled young man, but he seems to have found a new purpose to his life."

"What do you mean, Pastor?" Sonia now edging up in the chair asked.

"Well, you probably know of his crimes, but since then, he has been a pillar of society. He volunteers regularly at the church and in the community. He got a job at the local homeless shelter, and he sticks to how the bible tells us to live."

"So, he doesn't drink, do drugs, have sex, or any other normal young adult behavior?"

"No." The Pastor seemed a little annoyed at Sonia's tone and question.

Sonia continued. "What was the catalyst for this huge life change?"

"Well, we at the church like to help troubled youth and show them the right path to eternal happiness and salvation."

"Does that include using your parishioners to give these troubled youths free legal representation?"

"Yes. We have a group of men and women who donate their professional services to the church to help the community and the world become a better place. Services like legal, but also healthcare, insurance, accounting, tutoring, counseling and so on."

"How did you know about Mr. Anderson in order to want to help him? According to Maria Burrows, he didn't belong to your congregation." Park interjected, furrowing his eyebrows.

"Well, we have many connections. I believe we have someone in the Sheriff's department to let us know if a troubled youth or young adult needs help. Having multiple lawyers in the program doesn't hurt."

"You believe, or, you *do* have someone in the Sheriff's department," Park questioned curtly.

"We have."

Sonia stood up and walked to the Pastor's right and leaned on the same railing. "So, your church gets information from other professionals when someone might need help. You then send in one of your members to help them free of charge. Correct?"

"Yes. That's right. This program was created by Rebecca. She convinced her father to be the first volunteer, and the rest was easy."

"Do your rehabilitation projects always become church members?"

"Usually. We believe the only way to live a moral and decent life is through Jesus Christ and the Word of God. So of course, we would encourage lost souls to improve their lives. We are not the only parish to be involved, we have members from other denominations, all Christian though."

Park struggled not to roll his eyes. "Cameron is now part of your church?"

The Pastor smiled. "Actually, Cameron's parents, and he, were always part of our church. His parents, not so much anymore, but Cameron is fully involved. During his dark times, that is what we call them, he started slipping away from us."

Sonia stood up and crossed her arms, standing in front of the Pastor, "Well, I guess he is lucky he was arrested, or he may have fully separated himself from you and your church."

"Are you implying we are happy he struggled? Well, I wouldn't call it happiness, but I would call it relief. God intervened and put him back on the proper path."

"Well, I guess 'God' works in mysterious ways." Sonia air quoted the word, God.

Park stood up as he was sensing the tone shifting to more of an antagonistic one. Park needed to change the subject. "You said that Cameron's family was always part of your church, what was Cameron like before he got in trouble, or how did you say it, 'dark times?'"

"Cameron seemed like a well-rounded and upstanding member."

"So, what happened?"

"I'm not quite sure, but according to what the rumors were, Cameron was struggling with following our doctrine. He had urges, you could say."

"Urges?" Sonia jumped in.

"He met someone and, well, he wanted to give in to his immoral and primal desires."

"How long before he was arrested, did he leave the church?"

"Not that long, I would say about 2 months."

Park looked at Sonia at the same time Sonia looked at Park. Park cleared his throat and turned his gaze back towards the Pastor. "How many others have you 'saved?'" He air quoted saved.

"About a dozen."

"Can you get me a list?"

"I doubt that's appropriate. How will that help you find Rebecca's killers?"

"Sir, let us do our job. Any information might help."

"Well, I don't think I can break confidentiality. You will have to get a subpoena."

"Ok. We can do that, Mr. Morris."

"Are we done? I have to get to the church."

"Yes, we are done. Pastor, we may need to visit you again." Sonia pledged.

"Of course, whatever I can do to help, I'll do."

Park and Sonia returned to the car and drove away in silence.

CHAPTER 26

SLVTNX808: "The FBI is involved." was typed and sent securely.

SLVTNX222: "So. They don't know anything, and they won't."

SLVTNX808: "How can you be so confident? I told you the crucifixions were too much!"

SLVTNX222: "We must send a message about what we are doing. Relax."

SLVTNX808: "What are you going to do?"

SLVTNX222: "I'll handle it."

SLVTNX808: "If the FBI is involved, they probably know about the others, because of your stupid crucifixions."

SLVTNX222: "Let them know, I want them to. I want the entire world to know."

SLVTNX808: "Do you think they will link the others?"

SLVTNX222: "No, but again who cares if they do, it won't lead back to us, we made sure of that."

SLVTNX808: "Well, I hope you know what you are doing. Colorado wasn't sanctioned, so how are we sure you didn't make a mistake? I'll let you know when I know more about their progress."

SLVTNX222: "Good. Now stop worrying. Colorado was a judgment call, and they didn't and won't find anything."

SLVTNX808: "The next passenger is about ready. Are we going to do the crucifixion thing again, with the FBI snooping around? Isn't that risky?"

SLVTNX222: "I DON'T FUCKING CARE ABOUT THE FBI. WE MUST DO WHAT WE ARE MEANT TO DO!"

SLVTNX808: "Ok. Ok. No need to use all caps."

SLVTNX222: "LOL. Sorry. I will prepare for the new passenger."

CHAPTER 27

"Can't wait until tomorrow night." Jen typed along with the predictable emojis. She just stared at the screen, waiting for the 3 dots to appear. After about 30 seconds, a message popped up from Mark.

"Me either. I have something special to give to you."

"Oh? Do tell."

"And ruin the surprise? You will have to wait."

She inserted a frowny face and then typed, "Well, I may have a surprise for you as well." She then inserted a winky face.

"See you tomorrow."

"CU"

CHAPTER 28

Park and Sonia remained silent back to the station. Both were trying to fit the oddly shaped piece the Pastor handed them into the larger puzzle. A few times they would trade glances at each other, both with a serious inquisitive face, not knowing what to say. After getting back to the station, Park sat down in his chair and Sonia sat in the chair adjacent.

"So, what do you think?" Park asked.

"I don't know, he struck me as..." She paused to conjure up the most appropriate word. "...creepy. Maybe it's my bias against religion. I don't know."

"I felt it too, he seemed like he was hiding something. Do you think he is involved?"

"Not sure. My gut says he knows something about what happened. I mean she was murdered and then displayed in a deeply religious matter, it stands to reason that the leader of the church, a very strict religious dogmatic church, would know something. Maybe we should have asked him about the significance of the cross."

"I know some about what that cross means, but that would've been a good question for him. Next time. I'm sure there will be."

"Tell me about what you know about the cross. I didn't have a chance to do any research before I drove down here." Sonia inquired.

"Well, the X-shaped cross known as *Crux Decussata* or

the St. Andrew's Cross, is the type of cross that St. Andrew was crucified on. It is said he refused to be crucified on the same cross Jesus was. He was also bound, not nailed, just like our victims."

"Why do you think our killers are putting the victims on this cross?"

"I don't know. St. Andrew was one of the 12 disciples and died a martyr, so are they saying that our victims are martyrs or a disciple of Jesus? Or are *they* the disciple and the victims are just punished? I don't know."

"This is starting to sound a little more culty. I might have to contact our cult expert."

"That's not a bad idea. Would you like to attend church with me tomorrow?"

Sonia smiled. "I would love to. What's your plan?"

"I just want to listen and observe. Maybe their behavior will show us who we need to talk to next."

"Do you want to call Cameron in today?"

"Let's wait until Monday. I want to see what we get from the church, and then I may have additional information to go on when we interrogate him."

"Good plan. The dating sites' information probably won't get here until Monday as well. I'm getting hungry, want to go get some dinner and maybe unwind?" Sonia asked.

"Yes, that sounds lovely. I'm going to go home and freshen up, and I'll pick you up at your hotel, let's say..." Park glanced at his wrist out of habit, he hasn't worn a watch in years. He shook his head and laughed. He looked at his phone. "... 6 p.m.? That gives us a couple of hours."

"It's a date." Sonia winked. They both exited the station.

A couple of hours later, Park knocked on Sonia's hotel room door. She answered, dressed in jeans and a light sweater, with her hair pulled back. Park's eyes instinctively glanced up and down, taking in her curves and beauty. As his eyes returned from their journey, they met hers. She smiled and said, "Like what you see?"

"I'm sorry. I just... well... you look so different."

"Honey, I will never mind a handsome man like yourself checking out my goods. I mean, I don't spend 15 hours a week running, so no one would notice. HA!"

Park laughed. "Ok. Well, you look beautiful."

Sonia returned the favor and looked Park up and down. "I see you went with the jeans and T-shirt with the sports jacket look. Nice choice. Do you shop at Detectives R Us?" She walked past Park and slapped him on the butt. "HA!" Park just smiled, shook his head, and followed her.

Park took her to an Italian restaurant where they engaged in small talk and then predictably onto the case. "I think this case is bigger than we think," Park said as Sonia sipped her Cabernet Sauvignon and snacked on the provided breadsticks, waiting for their food to arrive.

"Why do you think that? Bigger than five cases spanning 30 years?"

"Yes. We are only looking at crucifixions. What if they don't always use that method, what if they started that way but stopped. What if they resurrected the practice, no pun intended?" Sonia let out a big, "HA!" "If it is a cult, or something like that, doing this, do you think they just paused for 20 years and then for another 10 years, that makes no sense? Unless it isn't a cult, and it is just one person. I don't know. I'm rambling." Park hated feeling lost like this and looked down at his glass of wine with a defeated demeanor.

"I love your mind, Park. I really do. You are on to something. First thing Monday morning, I will cross-reference murders by the victims, not the method." Sonia reached across the table, grabbed Park's hand, and smiled.

Park didn't pull away. He just met her eyes and smiled. The server interrupted their moment with their Chicken Parmesan and Lasagna. They released from each other and ate their food, occasionally meeting each other's eyes and smiling. Park felt himself falling for her even though he just met her a couple of days ago. He doesn't usually react like this to women, but he liked it. It felt like new energy was flowing through him. He felt invincible; 10 years younger.

They finished dinner and decided to go to a bar before turning in for the night. Park took them to a bourbon bar he frequented from time to time when the confines of his living room didn't thrill him enough. They both sauntered up to the bar and sat in the high-back leather stools.

"Pick your poison." Park gestured to the bourbon bottles sitting on glass shelves in front of large mirrors covering the whole wall behind the bar. As the shelves went higher, so did the price of the bourbon. There were five shelves. Park explained this to Sonia.

"I've been to a bar before, Park. Let's start at level 1."

Park chose a shelf 1 bourbon, and they sipped it together. "Well, I'm not confident if we need to go to any other level, after I drink this one, I wouldn't care what kind of bourbon I'm drinking."

"Ha! So, True. This one is rather good." Sonia agreed, Park agreed with a nod and another sip.

"Ok. Park, tell me about your love life. Why haven't you found Mrs. Park? What happened to you and Julie?"

"Wow. Jumping right in, huh? Well, I guess I'm not cut out for the long-term relationship thing. I am a stereotypical detective. I put work first. Not only that, but I can't think of anything or anyone except the victim when I'm working a case. Julie was great. She was very understanding at first, but over time she just couldn't feel alone anymore. It was my fault. We remain friends and I still care about her, but I want to avoid hurting her. So, I am destined to die alone." Park raised his glass, tilted it towards her, and sipped.

"No Park. You need to find a woman who understands your passion. Someone who can appreciate your mind and give you your space to use your talents. Julie may have been great, but she obviously didn't get you. I have the same problem sharing my life with someone. Most men don't like independent women, and the women I date are usually very needy and clingy. We are a rare breed that requires the right partner. I've noticed that most FBI agents, other law enforcement officers, and detectives typically are more successful marrying someone in the same field or at least an adjacent field. You will find someone, Park. You check all the boxes." Sonia smiled at him, tilted her glass towards him, and took a sip. As her eyes went from her drink to looking ahead. Park surprised her by kissing her. She leaned into the kiss and reached her hand around the back of his head and pulled him in. Park released, took his glass, and gulped down the last sips of bourbon.

"Sorry. I just had to see something." Park, facing the bar, turned his head towards Sonia to await her reaction.

"Sorry? For that? You may do...that... as many times as you want! HA! What did you have to see? Did you see it?" Sonia made a curious face at him.

"I wanted to see if the feelings I had inside translated to external feelings...er...reactions. Well, they did, even with the bourbon." Park had a wry smile on his face.

"Oh, well, I can also say the same thing. You want to get out of here?"

"Yes. Yes, I do." Park threw two twenties on the bar. Sonia swallowed the last of her bourbon and slammed the glass down on the bar.

"I'm getting laid. HA!" Sonia declared. Park just laughed and shook his head, grabbing her hand and leading her to his car.

Park drove her back to his place. The drive felt like an eternity. They held hands and just smiled contently staring through the windshield, eager to arrive at their destination. Park pulled into the driveway, and they exited the car. They walked up to the porch, arm in arm.

A loud thump came from inside the house. They released from each other and looked at each other with a confused look. Park grabbed his holstered Smith & Wesson hidden under his sport coat. Sonia lifted her jeans and grabbed a Glock 42 from around her ankle. Park and Sonia moved like they were partners of 20 years. Park went to one side of the door, as Sonia moved to the other. He motioned with his head towards the pried open front door. Another loud noise came from within the house. Park made eye contact with Sonia and mouthed, "On three." She nodded. He then mouthed. "One. Two. Three." Park pushed the door open quietly and with his gun in both hands moved into the house, moving the gun systematically back and forth as he moved slowly forward. Sonia followed suit and stayed low, moving back and forth opposite of Park. As he swung right, she swung left and vice versa. Park could now hear a rustling noise coming from his office. He pointed towards the hallway. Sonia nodded. They both crept forward with their guns pointing towards the bedroom on the right, where the noise was emanating. Park was now in front of the dark bedroom. He placed his back to the wall next to the half-open door. Sonia positioned herself in the opposite side bedroom on one knee. Park nodded and mouthed. "One. Two. Three." He spun and kicked the door open, immediately dropping to one knee into the room and yelling, "Freeze." In the dark room, only illuminated by an outside streetlight, Park saw a figure standing over his desk to the right. The startled figure fell backward and hit the far wall with a thud. The figure scrambled to his feet and ran towards the door, straight towards Park. Park recognized the figure. He recognized the man. Park, not wanting to fire his weapon, went to tackle him. As he went to wrap his arms around the man's waist, Park was elbowed in the face, dropping him to the ground. Sonia appeared in the doorway, just as the man plowed into her. She wrapped her arms around his legs as they both fell into the hallway. The man kicked Sonia in the stomach. She tried to stand up to grab him again, but he kicked her in the head. Reaching for her gun that had fallen next to her, she rolled onto her stomach, ready to fire, but he was gone.

After recovering from their blows and searching the rest of the house and finding no signs of the intruder, they sat down on Park's couch. "Are you ok, Sonia?" Park handed her an ice pack. She placed it on her head and Park grabbed her hand.

"I'm fine. Just embarrassed that he got away. I guess bourbon doesn't do well with my fighting instincts. How are you?"

"My cheek is sore, but I should be fine. Well, you were just introduced to Cameron Anderson."

CHAPTER 29

A loud pounding from the front door awoke him. He shook his head, rubbed his face, and put on his slippers, opened his night table drawer, took out his pistol, disengaged the safety, and carried it with him down the stairs. The pounding continued. The man walked towards the front door, putting his arm with his gun behind his back. He peered through the front door window. *Jesus Christ.* The man threw open the door.

"What are you doing here, get inside before someone sees you." The man pulled Cameron Anderson through the door and into the foyer. "Why would you show up at my house?"

"I... I... I didn't know what to do." Cameron was shaking and had tears in his eyes.

"What did you do?"

"I did what you asked, I broke into the detective's house and looked for anything he had on the murder... "

"AND?" The man was getting impatient, exposing his gun from behind his back. Cameron's eyes widened as he noticed the Glock.

"What is that for?" Cameron pointed at the gun. "Are you going to kill me?" Cameron started to back up into the hallway.

"Calm down. I didn't know it was you! It's late and I grabbed it for protection. But, if you don't tell me why you are here, I may just kill you."

"Ok. Well, he came home while I was still there. I did what you said, I made sure he wasn't home, and then I started searching his house. Then they walked in."

"*They*? Who else was there?"

"A woman, she had a gun. I barely made it out of there, they didn't shoot at me. I elbowed him in the face and kicked her in the face. It was close."

"Did they see you? Do they know who you are?"

"I don't know, it was dark, but I was pretty close to the Detective when I hit him."

"Ok. Ok. Did you find anything?"

"I found a notepad with a list of similar things between Rebecca and Anthony."

"Anything else?"

"Not really, he has some of his notes from Anthony Miller's case on his desk, but I didn't see anything."

"Ok! Excellent job. Did you plant the cameras?"

"Yes, on in his living room and one in his office."

"Great. Nice job Cameron."

"He wasn't supposed to be home. I watched him enter the bar, he must have only stayed for 15 or 20 minutes. What if he saw me? What do I do?"

"Go home. I'll take care of the rest. You be ready. We have our next passenger."

"So soon after Rebecca?

"This is our moment, we must continue to do God's work and if the opportunity arises, we must act, no matter what. It is rare to find our passengers so close together."

"Ok."

"Cameron, you did good. Next time, just call me, don't show up here again. You're lucky I was the only one that woke up."

"I'm sorry. I was scared."

Cameron left the house and went home.

The man walked into his downstairs office and turned on the computer. After it booted up, and he signed in, he opened the secure messaging system and waited for his prompt.

SLVTNX808: "We have a problem."

CHAPTER 30

Park drove Sonia back to her hotel room. They sat next to each other on her bed.

"Well, I guess we will have to take a rain check on me getting laid. Ha!"

Park put his arm around her and squeezed her. She put her head on Park's shoulder. "I guess we will. Are you sure you don't want to go to the hospital to make sure you don't have a concussion?"

"I'm fine, Parky. You go home, we have a church date in the morning." She lifted her head off his shoulder and kissed his cheek. Park stood up, kneeled in front of her, and kissed her on her lips. Her soft, full lips pressed against his, sending warmth throughout his body. He stood up.

"You get some rest. I will see you in the morning. Make sure you are dressed in your Sunday's best, or should I say Saturday's best."

"Oh, I will be in my sexiest church outfit I can find."

Park smiled and left her room.

He was back in his car and promptly drove to Cameron Anderson's home and parked his car across the street. Cameron's house was only illuminated by a streetlamp, half a block away, and a front porch light. Park just stared at the house, looking for any type of movement. *He must be home by now. There were no lights on in his house. It's late, but not that late. Either his parents aren't home, or they go to bed early on a Friday night.* Park lifted his hand to his face where Cameron elbowed him. He gingerly touched the spot right below his left eye. He winced in pain when he pressed too hard. *I hope I don't get a black eye. That won't look good for church.* Park's eyes started to get heavy. As he was about to start his car, he noticed a car slowly idling down the street with its headlights off. Park squinted his eyes trying to make out who it was. Cameron Anderson, sitting in the driver's seat, appeared in the luminescence of the streetlamp like a spotlighted actor, center stage. *Where the hell has he been?* Park waited until Cameron went inside and then started his car and drove home.

Park pulled into his driveway, exhausted and in pain. He closed his front door and propped one of his dining room chairs under the front door handle, keeping it closed. The damage to the door made it impossible to lock it. Park walked into the kitchen, poured bourbon into a glass, and swallowed it, and then repeated. He grabbed a frozen bag of peas, that he would never eat, out of the freezer, and pressed it on his swollen face as he walked into his office to inspect the damage. The first thud he'd heard with Sonia was Cameron busting open the locked office door with his body or his foot. The second thud he'd heard was Cameron knocking over a small table next to his desk, that had a potted Peace Lily that Julie bought him. Park tried to put the plant back in its pot, but to no avail. This made Park a little sad. It felt like a piece of Julie was gone. Park then shifted his attention to his desk to accommodate for the rustling noise he heard. The pile of papers was strewn about on his desk, with his notepad placed on top. He looked down on what was written on it and realized that Cameron now knew what Park was putting together about Anthony and Rebecca, Christianity, Master's Degree, and dating. Park thought to himself that if Cameron was just getting home when Park saw him, then he went to see someone. *Cameron isn't working alone.*

DAY FIVE

CHAPTER 31

"Good morning, Park," Sonia said as she stood in front of the hotel room door.

"How's your head?"

"I'll live, I just popped four ibuprofens. Let me look at your face." Sonia put her hands on each side of Park's face as she inspected the left side. "Hmm... that could've been worse. Only a little redness."

"The magic of frozen peas and bourbon." Park winked at Sonia.

"Are you ready for some church!"

"Always. You ready?"

Driving to the church, Sonia turns to Park and asked, "So what are we going to do with Cameron?"

"Well, now we don't have to ask him to come in, we can just arrest him. We can use his pending charges as leverage. He'll talk if he doesn't want to go to jail again. We'll bring him in first thing Monday morning."

"Sounds like a plan."

Park and Sonia pulled into the packed parking lot of the Church. Park purposefully arrived late so that he could sneak in the back and not be noticed. As they walked in the front door, they entered a lobby area. They could hear Pastor Morris giving his sermon through the doors to their left. Park opened the closest door and he and Sonia walked into the chapel area.

The room was large, with 20 rows of pews, divided by the main aisle and two walkways. Four rows of pews were in all. The chapel had a seafoam-colored rug, and the wood walls were decorated with the typical chapel tapestries in red. The front of the chapel, where Pastor Morris spoke, had a pulpit, on top of a stage, and a choir sitting behind it. He was surrounded by a rustic brick-stone wall, with a stained-glass window in the upper middle.

They sat in the back pew on the left side of the chapel. There were easily 200 or more people there. Park looked around, surveying the attendants. It was difficult, however, to make out anyone he knew from the back of their heads. Pastor Morris was discussing how real men handle real problems. He was reading from the Book of Job. Sonia turned towards Park, leaned in closer to him, and whispered, "What do you think they would say about a loudmouthed, independent, horny bisexual FBI agent?" Park had to suppress a laugh by covering his mouth with both hands.

"Stop it." Park elbowed Sonia like they were siblings in church with their parents.

Sonia and Park didn't pay attention to what the Pastor was talking about, they cared more about who was in attendance and how they interacted with each other. Park felt like there had to be a connection somewhere inside this congregation.

"Park. Isn't that your Lieutenant?"

Park looked at where Sonia motioned her head and from behind it looked like Lieutenant Gregory with his wife and his two daughters, Kathryn, and Madeline. They were both attending The University of Oklahoma at Headington College. "Yes, it is. I didn't know he went to church; he never talks about it." Park whispered. "Why didn't Lieutenant Gregory tell me he went to church at the same place I was investigating?"

"I guess he is a private man."

"I guess." Park wasn't sure that was it. He would have to talk to him on Monday.

Park and Sonia listened to the sermon until it was finished. They stood up and moved to the back corner of the room to be as inconspicuous as they could. They both were fixated on Lieutenant Gregory and watched him get up and walk over to the Williamses. He shook Mr. Williams's hand and then hugged Mrs. Williams. At the end of the sermon, the Pastor informed everyone about their loss and informed the congregation that the funeral will be held next Tuesday morning. The Williamses were getting a stream of fellow Adventists giving them condolences, hugs, handshakes, and the obligatory, "If there is anything I can do." Mr. Williams had wrapped his arm around Mrs. Williams like he was protecting her from the onslaught of well-wishers, almost holding her up as her grief pulled on her. There were moments where Park could see something peak out of her, like the sun through heavy clouds. In the moments between the calvary of sorrowful friends, it seemed to Park that she was content, almost joyful in her expression. Mr. Williams put on his best stoic face. He went through the motions of nodding sadly and thanking all that was kind. Park chalked this up to Mr. Williams acting as all men do in times like these, "Be strong. Keep your head up." This religion was big on traditional gender roles taught in the Bible. Men are men and women are servants of those men. Men were the protectors and the authority. As Park scanned the room, he could see this play out repeatedly. Men standing in front of women, women with their heads down and hands clasped in front of them. They all wore the mandatory uniform of a southern evangelical wife. Almost every woman wore some sort of dress that went below the knees and a blouse. Most had hats covering their well-styled hair, and they didn't wear any flashy jewelry except for wedding rings. Another symbol of ownership.

"I don't see Cameron," Sonia observed.

"I don't blame him. I wouldn't want to be out in public right now."

"You think he knows you can identify him?"

"Maybe, but would you take the chance?"

"Will he run?"

"I doubt it. He doesn't seem like a person who would survive exceptionally long."

Out of the corner of his eye, he saw Maria Burrows talking to the Williamses. She was talking to Mr. Williams. It felt cold. She went to embrace Mrs. Williams when she turned away from her. Maria looked embarrassed. She took the hint and left the church.

"I'm on it," Sonia said as she followed Maria out of the church. Park needed to speak to the Williamses again but thought he should wait until they're home.

Sonia briskly followed Maria into the parking lot. "Maria! Ms. Burrows!" Sonia, hoping to make her stop. Maria turned around.

"You're the FBI agent. Ms. Bram... Ms... Brab."

"Just call me Sonia. Can I ask you what you and the Williamses were talking about?"

"I was just giving my condolences."

"But you seemed curt, almost cold to Mr. Williams. Why?"

"I don't know. He wasn't the friendliest of Dads. I didn't like how he controlled Rebecca. I mean, I know what our religion says, but it is the 21st century. Shouldn't we allow women to be more than, wives? All Becky did was be perfect for her father. She used to tell me that when she was a little girl, all he talked about was sin and being a sinner. I just think he is a little overbearing. I don't blame him for her death, but maybe if he wasn't so hard on her, she would've been more open about the guy she was with, and she would be alive."

"I see."

"I know he's grieving. Becky's death was a knife in his heart, but it is still hard to look at him."

"Why did Mrs. Williams dismiss you like that?"

"I don't know. I'm really hurt by that. Maybe, she blames me or something. Possibly, she thinks I know something that could have saved her. I really don't know."

"Do you?"

"Do I what?"

"Know something?" Sonia said with a tilted head and a curious look.

Maria snipped back a reply. "NO. What are you implying?"

"Just doing my job. Where is your family?" Sonia asked.

"I don't have one. They died when I was in high school. Car accident. I didn't join this church until I met Becky."

"How did you meet her? Well, I um... got into some trouble in college and Becky helped me out."

"What kind of trouble?" Sonia asked as she saw Park approaching them. He stood next to her and joined the conversation.

"I met this guy, online, who went to the same school as me. We went out a few times, and he was great. He kept trying to sleep with me, but I said no, and he was fine with it. I was a virgin. My faith... let's just say I wasn't ready. But he kept trying, and I finally gave in. I never even had a drink before I met this guy. Well, after we had sex, he changed. He was distant. I thought he was ghosting me. Then, one night, he texted me to meet him at a party. So, I did. I don't remember what happened after I showed up. I ended waking up in a guy's room, I don't remember meeting. I was... um, naked and laying on his bed. I ran out of there. I never knew who the guy was or where I was. Later, I was emailed pictures of myself. Pictures of me having sex and without my clothes on. They also took pictures of me doing coke and stuff. I have no recollection of it. I don't remember even drinking that night. I took the email as some sort of blackmail."

"How did Becky come into the picture?"

"She saw me crying outside on a bench and sat down next to me. Well, long story short, we became best friends, and she helped me. She brought me into this church, and it changed my life, even if I don't agree with all of it. These are good people. Those pictures never found the light of day."

"Can I go now?"

"Yes. We'll be in touch if we need you." Park joined them as Maria finished telling her story.

Maria nodded slowly and entered her car. Park and Sonia moved out of the way as she drove away.

"Hmm," Sonia said as she lifted her hand to her chin.

"What?" Park asked.

"I just wonder if this program, Rebecca's program, is related to why she was murdered."

"How?"

"I don't know Park. What if they helped the wrong person or didn't help the wrong person, and they are punishing them?"

"But how does that relate to Anthony Miller or the other three similar murders?"

"We aren't any closer to solving this, huh? Drive me back to my place, I want to go over the files again. I also want to call my office and see if we can cross-reference the victims with other victims, regardless of method."

"Do you want me to stay with you?"

"I think I need to be alone for this one, my head still hurts, and I just want to take it easy."

"Sounds good. I could use a day myself. I am going to look over Anthony Miller's case again, maybe look at his computer."

Park dropped Sonia off at the front door of the Hotel. "I'll call you later, Park." Sonia blew him a kiss. He smiled and drove away.

Clouds overtook the bright, sunny sky as Park drove back to the station to retrieve the Miller file and computer from evidence. Small pockets of sunshine pierced through the clouds like a divine being shining his spotlight on us. Light rain fell onto the windshield as Park pulled into the parking lot of the station. As he entered the bullpen, he noticed Lieutenant Gregory, still in his suit, sitting at Park's desk going through his files.

"Can I help you, Boss?" Park said curtly.

The lieutenant lifted his eyes and met Park's. He didn't even look startled or guilty. "Hey, Park. Just seeing what you have been up to. What are you doing here on a Saturday?"

"Coming to get some files and stuff, so I can work the case from home with some Saturday bourbon and the blues.

Why are you looking through the Williams file?" Park didn't like his vibe. He seemed too calm.

"Mr. Williams asked me to see how your progress is coming. He wants to know who killed his daughter. I told him I would let him know."

"Oh. Why didn't you just call me?"

"I was on my way home and figured I'd just stop by and see for myself."

"On your way home from where in a suit nonetheless?" Park wanted to see if he lied.

"From Church. The Williamses are part of the congregation with me."

Park didn't expect him to be so forthright. "Oh, why didn't you say anything?"

"I like to keep my personal life separate, especially my faith. I would've told you if it became pertinent to the case. So, how's the case coming along?"

"Well..." Park didn't know how much to divulge now that he knew he might tell John Williams. "...we have a lead. Cameron Anderson. We will be bringing him in on Monday." Park left out the breaking and entering and the assault on a detective and a federal agent.

"Cameron, huh? I know him from the church. He is close to the Williamses. They helped him turn his life around. So, you think he did this?"

"It seems he was involved somehow. We have no evidence yet, but we will know more by Monday when we bring him in."

"Good. Good. Ok, then. I'm going home. I'll see you Monday."

"Ok Boss." Park watched him leave. Park, for the first time in their 10 years working together, didn't trust Lieutenant Gregory.

CHAPTER 32

Sonia sat on the couch staring at the picture of the five victims. *What is the connection?* She strained to find anything that would connect the locations of Nashville, Tennessee; Colorado Springs, Colorado; and Norman, Oklahoma. In her career, she has solved as many cases as she didn't. Her experience and education reminded her that serial killers tended to be male, white, and with some Psychotic disorder that stemmed from trauma in their childhood. The evening sunlight pierced through the hotel window, illuminating the files on the coffee table. One word danced off the file of Mary Bronson, the first victim. Vanderbilt University. Sonia straightened up, grabbed the file, and read.

Mary Bronson attended Vanderbilt University. She was finishing her graduate degree in Religion.

Sonia grabbed the second victim's file and read.

Gretchen Dorian attended Vanderbilt University. She was in her first year of the Social Work program.

Sonia grabbed the third victim's file and read.

Christopher Reed attended Nazarene Bible College to become a Pastor.

Sonia took out a pad and wrote down *College/Graduate School. Every victim attended Graduate school, except for Christopher, who was trying to become a pastor. Every victim was enrolled in a program that was either a religious or altruistic program.*

She didn't understand. Her brain swirled, trying to figure out why every victim was attending some type of college or university. Sonia went to bed, hoping some rest would allow her brain to put some pieces together. Morning Sun blanketed the room. Sonia rubbed her eyes, sat up in bed, and an idea popped in her head. "Fuck! It's not school!" Sonia yelled. She leaped out of bed in just her underwear, trying to locate her phone. Throwing the covers back, tossing clothing and used towels didn't locate her phone. She sat on the couch retracing her steps and instantly, she moved the files on the table and her phone revealed itself. She picked it up. *I forgot to charge it!* Sonia ran into the bedroom and plugged the phone in. After the lightning bolt appeared in the middle of the battery icon, she pulled a pair of jeans on from a pile and threw a bra and T-shirt on. She returned to her bed and sat down. Picking up her phone, she saw Five percent under the battery icon. She powered up her phone. It was only 6:30 a.m., but she couldn't wait. She pushed the phone icon and dialed the phone.

"Hello?"

"Park, can you come over? I think I have something."

"That will have to wait. There is another body."

CHAPTER 33

After dinner, Jen and Mark went for another walk through a park, a small park called Oakhurst. The soft amber glow of the setting sun made it feel like a scene in a romantic movie, where the guy shows his passionate side. They have only been on three dates, but Jen knew from the first message, he was the one. Tonight, would be the final test for her. She was going to make her move and see if the relationship turns intimate. Until now, they had only kissed and held hands. She wanted to see if he was ready. She kept thinking to herself, will he accept her offer, or will she be rejected?

After walking around the paved path in silence, hand in hand, for about forty-five minutes, Mark sat down on a swing and patted the swing next to him for Jen to sit. She did. The warm breeze blew through her hair. The night air felt cleansing as the sun started to merge into the horizon and the streetlamps turned on.

"I like you, Jen. A lot."

Jen smiled. "I like you, too."

"Do you want to go back to my place and watch Citizen Kane with me?"

"I would love to." *This is it. It's now or never.*

They walked back the few blocks to Mark's apartment. Jen was wearing a jean skirt that hugged her figure, with a white top that just touched the top of the skirt. She kicked off her flip-flops and bent her legs to the side, sitting on the couch sidesaddle. He returned from the kitchen with a bowl of popcorn and two glasses of diet soda.

"Are we ready?" Mark asked, clapping his hands and rubbing them together with excitement.

"Wow, you really like this movie, huh?"

"I do!" He sat next to Jen and turned on the movie. Just as the movie started, Jen decided to make a move, since Mark didn't. She slid her hand from his thigh into his crotch and gently squeezed. He turned towards her and was about to speak until she pushed her mouth onto his and started kissing him. He resisted at first, but then gave in to her and kissed her back. She moved on top of him, pulled off her shirt, exposing her breasts. Mark's pupils dilated as his eyes surveyed her bare chest. She started to unbutton his jeans and pull down his zipper when he suddenly picked her up and moved her from his lap. He stood up and fixed his pants.

"I can't. I just can't, Jen. Please put your shirt back on."

"Why? Don't you think I'm attractive?"

"Of course, I do, but as a devout Christian, we can't take this any further, I can't allow it. Even having impure thoughts about you is wrong."

"Come on, Mark. It's natural. We don't have to go all the way."

"No!" Mark barked. "I need a second." He went into his bedroom and closed the door.

Jen never heard him get upset before. She took out her phone and texted. Mark came out of his room. "Are you leaving? Who are you texting?"

"No, I... I was just texting my friend, you know girls, we check in on each other while we are on dates."

"Listen. I'm sorry, but if you prefer not to date a twenty-five-year-old virgin, I get it."

"No. I'm ok with it. You are exactly what I'm looking for. I'm sorry."

Mark smiled. "I'm sorry I overreacted, but it isn't easy fighting against evil urges. You are so pretty. It feels like I am being tested by Satan himself right now. Many women have rejected me because of my faith, but that just makes me stronger."

"Maybe you are being tested by Satan." Jen made an evil face, used her fingers as horns, and laughed an evil laugh.

Mark gave Jen a crooked smile. "Ok. I think it's time I give you, my surprise." He walked back into his bedroom. Jen could hear him rustle around in a drawer. As Mark walked back into the living room, someone was knocking on the door. "I wonder who that could be?" He set a bag onto the counter and walked to the door and opened it.

"Hey, Mark." A man stood in the doorway. Before Mark could say a word, from behind him, a nylon rope wrapped around his neck, squeezing the air out of him. His hands ripped at the rope, trying to get any air he could. The man at the door grabbed his hands, as Jen twisted the rope, tightening it and pulling Mark backward into the living room. Jen guided him to the couch, where he landed with a thud. She was now behind the couch as Mark was clawing at the rope. The other man was now sitting on him, holding his hands and legs in place as Jen, behind the couch, was pulling with all her might. Mark thrashed around, his eyes wide open, as his face turned blue. The man could feel wetness through his pants, as Mark urinated. A gagging, gurgling sound was the only indication he was still alive. Jen twisted the rope one more time while she pulled down with all her might. Finally, Mark gave one last sound, and his lifeless body went limp.

"Damn, that was hard. Why are you here? Where's Cameron?"

"Cameron is M.I.A. He was supposed to be here, but he never confirmed, so I was sent."

"Well, I guess you'll do. This one was hard."

"Yeah, but that's what happens when you have the rope." The man said.

"Was Rebecca difficult?"

"Nah, she was easy. Cameron pussied out there too. Let's get this over with. I got everything we need in the car. I will go get the bag, so we can put him in it. You wipe down the place."

"Will do. Hurry."

Jen found some bleach underneath the kitchen sink. She mixed the bleach and some water into an almost empty spray bottle. She grabbed a hand towel and started to wipe down all the areas she had ever been to. After she erased any DNA or fingerprints from the apartment, she then ransacked his room for anything that would lead to her. Jen always liked choosing someone who lived alone because it is much easier when you need to cover your tracks. She took his laptop and a notebook where he had written Jen's name down with her phone number and address. As she went to get a garbage bag from the kitchen, she saw the bag on the counter. She opened it, and it was a collector's edition of the movie, "Misery." *I chose the right one.* She grabbed the garbage bag and threw in the laptop, the notebook, the bleach, the sprayer, the towel, and *Misery*.

The man returned with a large duffle bag. Before placing Mark's dead body into the bag, they stripped him naked and placed his clothing along with his smartphone into the garbage bag. Jen scrubbed Mark's lifeless body with bleach, and then the man picked him up and laid his still warm body on top of the bag. They then systematically shoved his body one part at a time into the bag and after pushing the two-hundred-pound man into the last possible space, like overstuffed luggage, they zipped the bag.

"I'll drag this down the back stairs, you go into the hallway and see if anyone is out there. Don't forget to wipe down his car. Has anyone seen your face? Do we have others we need to take care of?"

"Nobody saw me. Even if they did, do you know how many 28-year-old, hot blonde, five-foot-five girls are around here? I'm a dime a dozen."

"Ok. So, where are we going?"

"Oakhurst."

DAY SIX

CHAPTER 34

Park was already in the middle of the scene when Sonia arrived. He was surrounded by the usual figures. She stopped to watch him work. The naked male body was bound to a large X, leaning on a swing set. The head, like the others, was bent back with the eyes open and staring at the heavens. Even though Sonia was still 30 feet away from the unidentified victim, she could see the ligature marks on his neck. Park was now walking around the victim looking at anything and everything, searching for evidence. She liked how he moved. His mind was on full display to her as he navigated the scene. She could almost hear what he was thinking as he studied the body and the surrounding area. Moving towards him now, she made her presence known, "Hey Park."

"Hey. Well, can we officially call this a serial killing now?"

"I guess we can. We still have to find a connection. Did you find anything? Who's the VIC?"

"Just like Anthony and Rebecca, we have nothing at the scene. No fingerprints, no fibers, no blood, or other fluids. No shoe prints, tire marks, or drag marks. I'm sure after the autopsy, they won't find anything except death by strangulation from a nylon rope. We haven't ID'd the VIC yet. I'm sure we will get another missing person's report soon."

"Who found the body?"

"A jogger. A woman, she was pretty shaken up. We are clearing her now."

"Is there anything I can do?"

"Not right now, unless you want to have a look before they take the body down."

"Sure." Sonia ducked under the yellow tape as Park lifted it for her. As she passed him, she laid her hand on his back. The body looked like a statue; the skin looked like stone. The victim's muscles looked chiseled from marble as he lay on top of the wood structure. As Sonia approached, she looked at the brown and red ligature necklace around the victim's neck. She made a note that the ligature marks weren't raised upward, indicating that the strangulation wasn't from above the victim. The assailant was directly behind as they choked the life from the man on the cross. Sonia walked towards the bound hands. Using her pen, she lifted the nylon rope to look at the wrists. As the pictures from the other crime scenes indicated, there were no signs of struggle, the victim was placed on the cross postmortem. With her gloved hand, she lifted the wrist, as much as she could, off the board to inspect it further. "Bingo!" She exclaimed.

"What?"

"Look." Sonia pointed at a red half oval on the inner wrist as she held it up. "A thumb made this."

"Shit! How did we miss this?" Park shook his head.

"Easy enough, someone would have found it during the autopsy. Looks like we are looking for at least two suspects. One that strangled him, the other was holding him down, so he couldn't use his hands. Get a picture of the thumb mark."

"I've always suspected that at least two people had to have committed these murders. Isn't it possible that the same person made that mark and also strangled him?"

"Sure. But, where the print is, indicates someone was

trying to hold his arms down at the wrists."

"So, we should probably bring Cameron in today, huh?" Park said with a smirk.

"Yes, we should."

CHAPTER 35

For the third time in a week, Park was at Cameron Anderson's house. This time with Sonia. They walked onto the front porch and Park knocked with his fist, Thump-Thump-Thump. "Police. We are here to speak to Cameron Anderson." Within 10 seconds, the door flew open. A middle-aged woman with graying brown hair answered the door in a housecoat that you would see in a 70s sitcom.

"Can I help you?" The woman asked.

"Is Cameron here?" Park sharply asked.

"No, I haven't seen him since yesterday morning."

"And you are?" Sonia jumped in.

"I'm his mother, Doreen. Doreen Anderson."

"Are you here alone, Ms. Anderson?"

"No, my husband is in the kitchen. What is this about?"

"We have an arrest warrant for your son, ma'am. We need to find him."

"I... I don't know where he is, he is usually home. I'm worried. What did he do now?"

"Breaking and Entering, assaulting a police officer, and assaulting a federal agent." Park motioned his head towards Sonia, indicating to Ms. Anderson, that she was the federal agent who was assaulted."

"Oh, dear. I really don't know where he is. He's been acting strange since Becky's murder."

"Ma'am, can we come in and talk to you?" Park was already moving into the house.

"Of course." She moved to the side as Sonia and Park made their way into the living room.

"Will you have your husband join us, Ms. Anderson?" Park sat down on the couch and Sonia followed suit.

Ms. Anderson raised her voice, "Honey, could you come here please?"

Mr. Anderson walked into the living room. Cameron was the perfect likeness to him. Both Cameron and his father were of average height, with thin, lanky bodies and short-cropped blonde hair. Mr. Anderson wore glasses and had a beard.

"Mr. Anderson?" Park stood up.

"Call me Michael." He reached his hand out and Park shook it firmly. They all sat down. Mr. and Mrs. Anderson sat on the love seat opposite the couch.

"Mr. and Mrs. Anderson, your son broke into my house two nights ago and then assaulted us as he ran away. If I didn't recognize him, I would've shot him." Park explained.

"Oh my." Mrs. Anderson lifted her hand to her opened mouth.

"That fucking kid." Mr. Anderson exclaimed, shaking his head.

Sonia continued. "Do you know why he would do that?"

"No. I mean, we don't know. Cameron hasn't been around a lot lately." Mrs. Anderson answered. Mr. Anderson nodded and then continued to shake his head.

"You said he's been acting strange lately, can you explain

what you mean?" Park interjected.

Mrs. Anderson closed her eyes and took a slow breath in and then out. "Cameron was a great kid. Top of his class in high school. He was extremely popular and always had dates. He was a good boy. He always went to church with us, and he took his faith seriously. And then…"

Mr. Anderson took over. "And then… college. He was doing great. He attended Oklahoma State University and lived with us as he commuted. His senior year, he got a place in Stillwater with some guys. He wanted to be a teacher. He planned to get his master's degree right after he graduated. Then… everything changed."

"How so?" Park asked.

"Well, he got arrested in Slaughterville a few months before he was going to graduate."

"What was he doing in Slaughterville, over an hour away from Stillwater?" Sonia wondered aloud.

"We don't know. He never did drugs. He never got in trouble." Mrs. Anderson's voice started to crack as tears filled her eyes.

"What can you tell us about the guys he was staying with?"

"Not much, Detective. We only met them once when we helped him move it. There were three of them, all attending Oklahoma State. They seemed like normal College kids."

"Was Cameron dating?" Park glanced at Sonia.

"I don't know. He didn't talk about anyone with us, but that is normal, I'm sure. Like I said before, he always had dates, but he never went steady, or what do the kids call it nowadays…?"

"He never had a girlfriend." Park finished.

"Not that we knew of, he never talked about it with us."

"Tell us about Cameron's relationship with the Williamses."

"Well, Mr. Williams helped Cameron stay out of jail, and then he befriended his daughter Becky. They worked together and hung out all the time. I think Cameron liked Becky. Why wouldn't he? But she never showed him any interest. I could tell that bothered him. He was frustrated. It was like he needed to date her, and he was failing. That is how it looked to me, it wasn't the usual unrequited love response, it was more like he failed a research project. It was weird. He kept saying to me, 'she has to like me. She has to.' He never gave up."

"Do you think it was strange that Mr. Williams helped your son without even knowing him?"

Mr. And Mrs. Anderson looked at each other. Mr. Anderson indicated he would take this one. "Not really. I mean, at first, we were thankful and surprised. After meeting with the Pastor, he explained how his church helps young people in trouble. It sounded like what churches do. He explained that many of the congregation have dedicated their professional talents to helping people. Another lawyer helped him as well. I don't remember his name. We never met him. Cameron just referred to him as the lawyer. He met with him from time to time."

"What do you think of the Pastor? Do you trust him?" Park asked.

"Hmm..." Mr. Anderson looked at his wife, as to indicate he needed to tag out on this one. Mrs. Anderson responded. "Yes. We trusted him, I guess. We didn't know him that well, but he seems like a nice man. I mean, he saved our son from going to prison."

"Did Cameron ever, um…" Park was stuck on how to ask this question.

"Do you think Cameron could have killed Rebecca?" Sonia took over.

"What? NO!" Mr. Anderson barked.

"Not our Cameron." Now Mrs. Anderson put one hand on her chest and the other over her mouth. "Why do you think…"

"Ma'am, we are just covering all the bases. Cameron had a motive, and he was caught breaking into my house, seeking knowledge about this investigation. Where was Cameron between 9 p.m. and 4 a.m. the night of Rebecca Williams' murder."

"He was…" Mrs. Anderson stopped.

"Ma'am." Sonia leaned in.

"Well, he was here when we went to bed at 10 p.m. that night." Mrs. Anderson looked at Mr. Anderson before continuing.

"Mrs. Anderson?" Sonia insisted she continues.

"I heard the front door close around midnight. It was softly closed, but I was up, going to the bathroom. I could hear the latch click." Mrs. Anderson had a concerned look on her face. She could not make eye contact with Sonia any longer. Mr. Anderson started to shake his head again.

"Where is your son? Do you know where he could be?" Park stood up.

"I… I… don't… maybe the church or the Williamses. He was close to Becky's parents and started to attend their church with them. He was deeply involved in his faith again. We don't go to Church anymore. Some of those people take it way too seriously. After his arrest, Cameron was seduced, I don't know if that is the right word, but he was seduced by that church. He read the Bible every day. He also read books about faith a lot."

"Can we see his room?" Sonia now stood while asking.

"Of course." Mrs. Anderson stood up. Mr. Anderson just sank into the love seat like he was trying to hide in it. Mrs. Anderson walked Sonia and Park upstairs and into Cameron's room. "Look around as long as you want, whatever will help you find Cameron." Mrs. Anderson left the room.

Park and Sonia were standing in the middle of a young man's room. The decor, decorations, and the overall feel, however, screamed teenager. There were posters on the wall of sports stars. On his dresser sat multiple trophies showing Cameron's athleticism. Next to his bed was a religious shrine. He had a King James Bible and other religious texts on the top shelf of a bookshelf. On the bottom shelf were self-help books and a smattering of fiction books. Cameron was a Stephen King fan. There was no computer to be found in his room. Sonia was rummaging through his desk, looking for anything tying him to any of the murders. Pushing around clothes in the dresser, Park was attempting to uncover some hidden item that Park didn't want his parents to find but found nothing of the sort.

Did you find anything?"

"Nope, other than this book that he was reading. He was flagging pages and underlining passages." Sonia handed him the paperback. It was titled, "Perfect Ascension" by Reverend Daniel Nelson. Park rippled through the pages, seeing all the pages where Cameron underlined sentences. On many of the pages was written, *I am the serpent,* in the margins.

"Did you find anything?" Mrs. Anderson said, standing in the doorway, startling Park.

"No, we didn't find anything that would help us locate your son," Park answered, putting the book back on the desk.

"We will be getting out of your hair." Park paused and turned to face Mrs. Anderson, gently saying, "You must contact us if you hear from your son. If you want him to be safe, we need to find him. He might be caught up in something dangerous."

"Dangerous? Like what?" Mrs. Anderson covered her mouth.

Park regretted those words immediately. "What I mean, Mrs. Anderson, is that with Cameron's history and with the recent murders, we want him to be found by us and not by someone who would harm him. Ok?"

"Yes, Detective."

"Thank you." Park and Sonia exited the house and drove back to her hotel room. They entered the room and they both sat down on the couch next to each other and let out a big sigh in unison. They laughed an exhausted laugh together.

"Park, I'm going to drive back to Oklahoma City tonight. I need to check in. I'll be in touch in a couple of days. I have to relax a bit and get my head around this."

"Ok. I think I'm going to go home and take a night off, myself. Talk to you soon." Park turned to walk towards the door when Sonia grabbed his hand. He turned around and she pulled him into her. She kissed him and then buried her head in his chest as she hugged him.

"Be safe, Park. I have a bad feeling about this one."

"I will. I do too." He left the hotel, entered his car, and drove home.

CHAPTER 36

S3RP3NT5: Now what?

    SLVTNX808: We won't need you for a while.

    S3RPENT5: When will I be done? Not that I mind helping.

    SLVTNX808: Soon, Jen, soon.

    S3RPENT5: What happened to Cameron?

    SLVTNX808: It's being taken care of.

    S3RPENT5: Ok.

    SLVTINX808 signed off the secure network.

CHAPTER 37

Sitting in his recliner, swirling a bourbon, neat, Park stared at the blank TV. He wasn't in the mood to laugh or follow a story. The news just depressed him, and he wasn't desiring a documentary. He stared at himself in the reflection on the TV. He wondered if the Park on the TV screen had things figured out, since he most certainly didn't. Park swigged down the rest of the bourbon in the rocks glass, stood up, and walked to his office where, just days ago, Cameron greeted him by running him over. He grabbed the Anthony Miller file and brought it out into the living room. *What did I miss?* Park thought to himself as he spread out the papers across his coffee table.

Ever since Park was a young boy, he liked order. His parents had him tested for Autism when their frustration was too much. They struggled with him always getting upset when things weren't in their right place, or a schedule wasn't followed. The specialist told them that he was fine, that he was just an incredibly special kid who had his quirks. *Quirks*. Park hated that word. Every time he would do something his father got frustrated with, he would hear, "You and your fuckin' quirks." What worsened it, was when his mother would defend him with, "Oh, calm down, it's just his quirks." With order came calmness. Park tried to explain this over the years to all his romantic partners, family and friends that tried to fix him. Order made the world turn. Order made things easier.

When he was about fifteen, a schoolmate of his, Trent London, not someone he knew well, was found dead in the woods. Trent was odd. He mostly stayed to himself. Before his death, Park noticed that Trent was becoming even more withdrawn. This concerned Park, but he said and did nothing about it. Guilt crept in. He couldn't stop obsessing over one question, swirling around his adolescent mind, *Could he have stopped him from dying?*

Park continually read newspapers and looked up information about the death online. He had to know why. He had to finish the puzzle. The death was never solved. The coroner ruled the death a homicide. Trent had died from a blunt force trauma to the back of the head. The police never found a weapon or any evidence identifying the killers.

Close to thirty years later, that death still haunts Park. As a detective looking back, he deduced that a classmate did it, making that person Park's age today. Someone, that Park probably knew, that was more than likely living in Norman, killed that kid and got away with it. Becoming a detective was the only thing that balanced the universe for Park. He was in control when he was solving crimes. Solving crimes brought Equilibrium to the universe, or at least, he thought. He closed cases at a 95 percent success rate. The 5 percent haunted him. Trent London's death from 30 years ago whispers to him in his quiet moments, as Anthony Miller screams at him.

Picking up the photos, statements, evidence, and other documents from the table, Park was trying to give it another angle, knowing what he knows now. He picked up the transcript from Anthony's parents' interview. He read it line by line.

Detective Parkerson: "When was the last time you saw Anthony?"

Mrs. Miller: "As I told you when you were at the house, we talked on the phone around noon the day before he was found."

Detective Parkerson: "What did you talk about?"

Mrs. Miller: "I asked him how school was going, if he was eating healthy, if he met anyone, you know mom stuff."

Detective Parkerson: "Did he seem any different?"

Mrs. Miller: "No, he seemed <pause> happy."

Detective Parkerson: "Was he dating?"

Mrs. Miller: "He didn't answer when I asked that question. He just said 'Mom' in the way children do when they don't want us to pry. He did finally say that it was early, but he did meet someone. I think he said he met her online. I wasn't sure about the online thing, but I was happy for him, but I changed the subject to…you know…small talk."

Detective Parkerson: "Did he give you a name?"

Mrs. Miller: "No."

Detective Parkerson: "Did you know of any girls who liked him?"

Mrs. Miller: "There were always girls that liked him, but he never really dated much. He was dedicated to school, to sports, to the church. There was one older girl who hung around him a lot in high school and a little after. Her name was Patricia Sullivan, but I don't think he had not seen her for years. I don't even know if she lives here anymore. She didn't have a good family life. I think he felt sorry for her."

Detective Parkerson: "How about friends? What can you tell me about his friends?"

Mrs. Miller: "I don't know. He had a few from high school that he still spent time together with when they were home from college. He made a couple of friends in college that I have met. There is John, I don't remember his last name"

Mr. Miller: There was this other kid, some kid name Cam. He wasn't in grad school with him, but they met somehow. Anthony would talk about him. I think he felt sorry for him, too.*

Park lifted his widening eyes from the transcript. *Cameron?* He turned white and lifted the glass to his lips to feel the burn of bourbon, and to his disappointment, the bourbon was gone. He scurried to the kitchen, grabbed the bourbon bottle, and returned to the couch. Lifting the bottle of bourbon to his lips, he felt the wonderful burn with his lips, then pass his tongue, land in the back of his throat, and as he swallowed hard, slowly trickle down his esophagus into his stomach. Feeling calmer, he returned to the transcript.

Detective Parkerson: "Were these kids' trouble, I mean were they into anything that could put Anthony at risk?"

Mrs. Miller: "Not that I know of."

Mr. Miller: "Didn't that Cam kid get arrested or something years back? I remember Anthony telling us about that."

Detective Parkerson: "Arrested for what?"

Mr. Miller: "I think drugs, but he seemed like he got his life together since. I don't think he had anything to do with this. I don't even remember the last time he saw him."

Park shook his head and lifted the bottle to his mouth again. *Why didn't I investigate Cameron then?* Park always followed or checked into all leads, even small ones. He knew that he made a mistake. He lifted the bottle again, but this time, swallowed 3 huge gulps. He wiped his mouth with his sleeve. "Fuck, Park." He yelled at the empty house and to himself. He continued to read. The words started to blur.

Detective Parkerson: "Are there any other people in his life?"

Mr. Miller: "Just my brother. He keeps trying to get us involved in his church. That just isn't our thing. He gets mad at us all the time and preaches to us. Anthony, however, was close to him and used to go to church with him every week and even attended some church groups or something. It seemed to help Anthony, so we didn't object."

Mrs. Miller: "Yeah, his brother is a freak about his religion, I never liked him. He was always good to Anthony. Treated him like his own son."

Detective Parkerson: "What's his name?"

Mr. Miller: "Oh, I don't think you need to bother him. He would never hurt Anthony. He loved him."

Detective Parkerson: "Ma'am, I have to follow every lead, puzzle pieces. Some may be small, some large, some don't fit."

Park stared up at the ceiling and shook his head. *Follow every lead, my ass.* Park put down the transcript and laid his head back on the couch. He felt weird. The bourbon started to push his eyelids closed as the ceiling started to spin. He fought the urge to sleep, but the bourbon won.

Park slowly opened his eyes. His vision was blurry. He felt peculiar. Pain was shooting through his skull. His wrists and ankles throbbed, and he could feel his shoulders strain. Blinking his eyes, the room spun around him. Wood was underneath his arms and legs. He was tied to something, leaning against his office wall. The room started to come into focus. It all made sense to him all at once, he was tied naked to a St. Andrew's cross. *Am I dead?* His brain went into detective mode. *I'm not dead, but I'm on a cross.* He looked around and couldn't see anything. Slowly, he got his breathing under control, so he could try and hear if anyone was still in the house.

"Hello?" Park yelled. "You're fucking with a detective. Cameron, is that you? Hello?!"

After about two minutes of straining to hear anything, Park deduced that he was alone. He tried to pull his hands and feet free to no avail.

"Park!" A voice yelled from the front door.

"In here!" Park returned. A few seconds later, a large figure came into view. "Lieutenant?" Lieutenant started to loosen the rope around his wrists. After his wrists were freed, Park bent down and loosened the ropes around his left ankle, as Lieutenant Gregory loosened the rope on his right. After Park was free and off the cross, he scuttled into his bedroom and threw on some clothes, and returned to his office, where Lieutenant Gregory was inspecting the cross.

"We need to call this in, Park."

"I am not convinced that is a good idea. This was a warning. I'm not sure what will happen if we do. Let's see if they left anything for us to find. This means I am making them uncomfortable."

"Your call. What do you mean *them*? How are you making *them* uncomfortable?"

"I don't know. It feels like more than one person. I didn't think we were close to solving this yet. I feel like I'm just scratching the surface, but obviously, someone thinks I am."

"What have you found?"

"Well, I was reviewing Anthony Miller's..." Park stopped. He trained his eyes on the lieutenants. "Why are you here, Lieutenant?"

"Um... I... Well, to be honest with you, I wanted to find out what you and the FBI agent have found. This case, well, the Williamses are close to me, and I felt like I could help get them the answers they crave."

"Why not just talk to me at the station?"

"I guess I wanted us to just chat as men. I wanted to hear your gut feelings, not just what you have. You are so close to the chest when it comes to cases. I was hoping coming to your home and having drinks with you would open you up more."

"I'm not comfortable telling you anything at this point."

"Why not?"

"Well, you just said it, you are close to this case. You attend the same church as our lead suspect and the victim's family. Also, what I have learned is that that parish is very close-knit. My gut is the killer or killers are in that congregation or connected somehow."

"Ok." The Lieutenant accepted his answer. "What happened, how did you end up...well, crucified?"

"I don't know, I was in the living room..." Park blinked hard and then darted into the living room. The lieutenant followed. "FUCK! It's gone!"

"What?"

"The Miller file! I left it on the coffee table." Park looked down at the barren table. He looked around the living room for the bottle of bourbon he was drowning his regret with, but it wasn't anywhere. He scanned the rooms and noticed the empty bottle sitting in the middle of the kitchen counter. Park hurriedly moved towards the kitchen. The bottle was sitting on a typed note. Park lifted it and started to read.

Detective,

You do not understand what you are getting yourself into. Stop digging up old wounds. Next time won't be a warning, and you will not be the target. You should be thankful. You have been given a gift and can redeem yourself according to God before it is too late. Maybe we should save your FBI girlfriend, or maybe you would respond to someone you care about dying for your sins.

<u>The fearful, and unbelieving, and the abominable, and murderers, and whoremongers, and sorcerers, and idolaters, and</u>

all liars, shall have their part in the lake which burneth with fire and brimstone: which is the second death. -- Revelation 21:8

The Serpent

Park turned white. He was frozen with indecision. *Serpent? Where have I seen that before?*

"Park, what is it? What does it say?"

"I... I need to go. I will update you at the station tomorrow morning. Right now, I need to go."

"Park, what did it say?"

"I don't feel comfortable telling you anything right now, I hope you understand."

The Lieutenant lifted his hand, holding up one finger about to protest, but he understood and left Park's house without a word.

Park threw on a jacket and a pair of sneakers and sprinted towards his car. He jumped in the driver's seat, slammed the door, and sped away.

CHAPTER 38

SLVTNX222: "So you sent a message to the Detective, I see."

SLVTNX808: "I told you I would handle it. Jen and I took care of it. She's good. The cameras Cameron placed around his place paid off."

SLVTNX222: "Why didn't you tell me?"

SLVTNX808: "I didn't want you to be involved. Plausible deniability."

SLVTNX222: "I could've helped."

SLVTNX808: "We've got plenty of help. Well, we need some new blood, now that Cameron is M.I.A."

SLVTNX222: "What are we going to do about him? He could ruin everything."

SLVTNX808: "He knows what will happen to him and his family if he says a word. I'll find him and do what I must."

SLVTNX222: "He isn't thinking straight, ever since Becky."

SLVTNX808: "I guess he actually fell for her. It wasn't just an act. He knew what was going on. I'll take care of him."

SLVTNX222: "Should we take a break for a while with all the attention?"

SLVTNX808: "We knew that we would get attention. We want attention. That is why I insisted on continuing with the crucifixions. We are doing this to save the world. We can't do that if they can't connect the dots."

SLVTNX222: "Let me know if there is something you need from me."

SLVTNX808: "You have done enough for now."

SLVTNX222: "Ok."

SLVTNX808: "I'll need you to find a replacement for Cameron, soon."

DAY SEVEN

CHAPTER 39

Park pounded on Julie's door. *Answer the door. Come on.* The door swung open,

"Park? What are you doing? What's wrong?" Julie's face looked panicked.

"Where's Mia?"

"She's in her room with a friend."

"Ok."

"Park, you're scaring me. What is it?"

Park walked past her into her living room and sat down on her couch like he used to do after a long day. Julie's conditioned response to Park returned as she walked to the kitchen, pulled out a bottle of bourbon, poured it into a glass three fingers high, and walked it back to him. He lifted it immediately to his mouth and swallowed it all.

"Park. Start talking." Julie sat down next to him on the couch but was facing him.

"The case I'm working on...well...let's just say that I must be getting too close for comfort because they threatened to hurt you and Mia if I didn't stop. I was worried they may...well, never mind. You are OK. I'm going to make sure it stays that way."

"Jesus Park! I'm **still** suffering from your job. Now my daughter is too? Fuck! What do we do?"

"I have a car parked outside your house." Park gestured with his head towards the street. "You will have a car out there until the threat is gone. Is there somewhere you can go for a week or two?"

"Jesus, Park. I... I just can't leave right now. Are you saying I should?"

"It would be the safest, but I don't know how serious the threat is or who…"

"I'm scared." Julie walked towards him and put her head in Park's chest. He put his arms around her, and he could smell her shampoo that he loved. It felt so natural holding her, like the last few months without her didn't happen.

"What's going on, Mom?" Mia asked as she entered the living room. "What was the pounding? Why is he holding you?'

"Hey, Mia." Park retorted.

"Hey."

"Park just…well…he came over to make sure we were OK. We might be in danger, due to a case he is working on."

"Fuck, Mom! I knew he was a mistake."

"Mia!"

"It's ok, Julie. She's scared. I should get going. Are you sure you can't leave town for a few days?"

"I will see what I can do."

"I'm not going anywhere, Mom! You can't make me! I'm an adult. I have plans!"

"Mia, we will talk about this later."

A young woman with blonde hair came walking around the corner from the hallway and stood next to Mia. She quietly spoke. "Is everything OK? Should I leave?"

"We're fine. My Mom's ex-boyfriend is just a piece of shit."

"Mia! You apologize right now!"

"Julie, it's ok."

Julie turned towards Park and grabbed his hands. "Are we going to be OK?"

"Yes. I will make sure of it. I need to go. I'll call you later." Park hugged her. She let him. Park stood up and faced the young woman. "Hi, I'm the piece of shit."

The woman smiled, held out her hand, and said, "Hi, piece of shit, I'm Jen."

CHAPTER 39

Park returned home and noticed that his house had been cleaned up. The door was repaired and the cross was removed. He figured that Lieutenant Gregory did this for him. He still wasn't sure about his connection to all of this, but for now, he was thankful for him. The lack of control was eating away at him. His worst nightmare was happening all around him. For the first time as a detective, he didn't know what to do. The rest of the day, Park mostly paced around his house, trying to piece together this mystery. When evening crept in, Park could feel his anxiety rise. Sweat started to drip from his forehead, his breath started to feel labored, and he needed to sit down. *Am I having a Panic Attack?* He was scared. He missed Sonia and dialed her number. The instant she answered, he felt control spread through him again.

"Hey Parky, what's up?"

"Hi. I just needed to hear your voice."

"Aww. Miss me much? I haven't been gone that long. HA!"

"We have a lot to talk about."

"Yes, we do."

"When will you be coming back down here?"

"Well, I see your door has been fixed."

Park stood up, walked to the door, and opened it to see Sonia Brambilla standing in front of him wearing a pair of tight jeans, a sweatshirt, and a ball cap. She looked beautiful.

"Hey there, sexy." Before she could even finish her sentence, Park threw his arms around her and started to cry. She was startled, but as soon as she understood what was happening, she wrapped one arm around his back and placed her other hand on the back of his head. "Shh, Shh, Shh." That is all she knew what to say. They stayed in that position for minutes in the doorway. Sonia broke the silence. "How about we continue this on the couch, your neighbors are going to talk." He broke the embrace and walked over to the couch, wiping his eyes with his sleeves.

"I'm sorry. I don't…"

"You stop that Park. You needed a cry. That is what makes you such a great detective and an even better man." Sonia sat on one end of the couch and patted her lap. "Lay your head down and tell me what happened."

Park was scared for the first time in his life. He became a detective so that he wasn't scared so that the world made sense to him. Order has left him now. He felt like he was in the middle of a lake, treading water, not knowing where the shore was. Sonia was his lifeboat. He laid down on the couch with his head on her lap while she stroked his hair. He told her about what happened.

"Jesus," Sonia exclaimed. "What was in the Miller files that they wanted so badly? Were you rattling the wrong tree?"

"I don't know. I noticed that Anthony Miller had a friend named Cam. Shortly after that, I passed out and woke up on a cross."

"Were you that drunk?"

"I don't…no…no, I wasn't." Park felt uneasy. He stood up. "Was I drugged?"

Sonia started to whisper, "Park, do you think you're bugged?"

This never crossed his mind, but Cameron was alone in his house for who knows how long before they caught him in his office. He started looking for bugs in all the places they usually hide. Nothing. Park put his hands on his hips and let out a long sigh of frustration. His eyes caught something on the wall behind one of the fake plants Julie bought him, to liven up the place, as she put it. He moved it to unveil a small wireless battery-powered camera. He ripped it off the wall and turned it off. "Well, they now know I know." Park deduced.

Sonia walked over to where the camera was and crouched down to see what the camera saw. "Well, it looks like they had an unobstructed view of the coffee table. Depending on how good the camera is, they could have even read some words, or at least make out what you were reading. Do you think Cameron drugged your bourbon?"

"Fuck! Park walked over to the bourbon bottle still sitting on top of the note. He lifted the bottle, with a napkin, and sniffed it. He didn't know why he did that, being that he wasn't an expert on narcotics. Lifting the bottle to see if drug residue was at the bottom of the bottle, again, he didn't know what he was looking for. He was just emulating what he has seen on detective shows on TV.

"What ya doin' Park?" Sonia asked with a wry grin on her face.

"I don't know." Park laughed.

"We need your forensics department to run some tests on it and check for fingerprints."

Park returned the bottle in the same place it was. Order. He picked up the note and handed it to Sonia to read. After she read it, she handed it back to Park. "Fuck me."

He placed it in the exact spot it was and replaced the bottle in the exact place it was set. Order.

"You said your Lieutenant showed up? Isn't that odd?" She continued.

"Yeah. I'm not sure what his role is. He may be closer to this than I want him to be. For right now, he is officially out of the loop. Why are you back so soon? I wasn't expecting you for another day or two."

"I missed my Parky. Ha! I did miss you, but I got some information and I needed to share it with you ASAP."

"What do you got?"

"Well first, the other night I realized that Colleges and Universities weren't necessarily a connection, but they were more of an easy method of choosing their victims. College campuses, and their students, were easy targets, and they would have easier access to them. Not to mention, those who were attending graduate school, are the best of the best."

"So, what you are saying is, It's not just because they attend College, but those who do usually fit their criteria better, easily narrowing down their search? So, we are dealing with a killer or killers who are efficient and smart."

"Something like that. I also looked into other murders that fit the same MO and I didn't get any hits, but I did get this." Sonia placed a packet of information on his coffee table.

Park smiled. He was smiling because he felt safe with her, and he needed to feel safe right now.

CHAPTER 40

Cameron sat in the middle of the woods. His tent was up, and a small fire kept him warm. As a child, Cameron used to hike into these woods with his dad. Sitting on the ground, he stared at his phone, wondering what to do. Home, the Police, and the Church weren't options. He felt hopeless and needed to see how much trouble he was in before he decided what to do next. Every minute he stayed away; his parents would become increasingly in danger. They would kill them. Cameron dialed the number of someone who might help him, or at least tell him what to do.

"Hello?" The voice said over the phone.

"Detective?"

"Who is... Cameron, is that you?"

CHAPTER 41

Park sat on the couch looking over the information she procured from her field office. Rebecca Williams joined two Christian dating sites, "Saved 2gether" and "Cross my Heart." Sonia was also able to get the information on the men she communicated with. Rebecca talked to five different men, but only one of the men was communicating with her on the site around the time she was murdered. No communications were made on the day of her murder. Sonia pulled out another paper and put it in front of Park. It was the mystery man's profile. No picture. The name registered was Thomas Scaggs, and he lived in Oklahoma City. Sonia already attempted to lookup an address, and it didn't exist. Whoever this man was, he was able to circumvent some security features of the site.

"We're not going to find anything here, Park."

"Yeah, it looks like whoever was on these sites, covered their tracks, including IP addresses."

"What have you learned about the new murder, was he identified yet?"

"No, not yet. Early forensics show nothing. As predicted." Park started to pace.

"What is it, Park?"

"I don't know. Something is gnawing at me, but I can't figure it out."

"What were you looking at before you were drugged?"

"I was reading the transcript of the interview with the Millers. I saw Cam's name and... I don't remember, I need to look at it again. There was something else, I don't know..."

"Ok. Well, we can't do that tonight. Did you have any backups of the file or was what they took, everything?"

"No, I have some of it on my computer, and they keep a copy of the transcripts and the tapes we record interviews on. I just have to put it all back together again."

Park collapsed onto the sofa next to Sonia and laid his head in her lap. She played with his hair. "I hope Julie will be OK."

"She will be, Park."

"Well, I guess I just keep hurting her, even when we aren't together." Park closed his eyes. His thoughts swirled in his head. Large Xs appeared. Lieutenant Gregory flashed in front of his face, as did the Pastor. Cameron's sweaty face stared at him, but so did Anthony Miller and Rebecca Williams. Their cloudy white eyes followed his mind's eye. His eyes popped opened, and he sat up.

"What is it?"

"Nothing... I... just can't get them out of my head."

"Well, let's just do something else. Do you want to play cards, put some music on, and drink some wine?

"Really? You want to play cards at a time like this?"

"Yes. I play a mean WAR and Slap jack! HA!"

Park was smiling again. "Ok. I have some wine above the refrigerator, glasses are in the cupboard to the left. I'll put some tunes on. How 'bout we play some gin?"

From the kitchen, Sonia answered, "You'll have to teach

me."

"You've never played Gin?"

"Nope." She walked back to the living room with two glasses half-filled with a cheap pinot noir. She sat down as Park dealt the cards and explained the rules. "Where's the music?"

"Shit. I forgot." Park put down his hand and turned on the Bluetooth speaker with a remote. He pushed the Pandora app button and clicked on a playlist. Jason Mraz serenaded them as they sipped their wine and played cards.

"GIN!" Sonia yelled. They were on their second bottle, this time a Cab.

"You learn quick," Park responded with a smirk on his face. "I think I was conned"

"HA!"

Sonia started singing to the song playing through the speaker, "I'm a joker. I'm a smoker. I'm a midnight..."

"You like Steve Miller?"

"Sure. I like everything!"

"My dad loved the Steve Miller band, he would sing "Fly like an Eagle" all the time. He knew everything about that band. He would brag that he saw them live over a dozen times. When he was in New York City, in 1969, he saw them on Halloween, he would tell me about it over and over again." Park's face turned white. His eyes widened. He slowly turned his head towards Sonia.

"Park, you look like you have seen a ghost."

"Where's the dating app papers?"

"Why?"

"I just... I need to see them again."

Sonia stood up to retrieve them from her bag when Park's phone rang, startling them both. He picked it up. The screen said unknown caller on it. He pushed the green phone Icon.

"Hello?" Park answered.

"Detective?" A scared voice responded.

"Who is... Cameron, is that you?"

Sonia's head whipped around towards Park. Their eyes met. She could see the concern in his eyes.

CHAPTER 42

"Cameron, where are you?"

"I need to talk to you. I need to confess." Cameron's voice was quiet, raspy.

"Ok, Cameron. Tell me where you are, and I'll come to you."

"I'm not safe. I don't know what to do."

Sonia was sitting next to Park on the couch listening, putting her head next to Park's.

"Ok. Can you come to me? Is there somewhere we can meet?"

"I don't know." Cameron's voice seemed distant, Park heard him yell out, "Who's there?"

"Cameron, is someone there?"

"I have to go. I'll call you back."

"No. Stay on the...." The call went silent. Park tried to call back the number on his screen, but it just rang and rang. He stopped trying after five attempts.

"Jesus Christ! We need to find him. Any ideas where he would be?"

Sonia just stared at him, thinking, getting into Cameron's head. "Well, he isn't home, not safe. He might go to the church, but if your hunch is right, the people he is running from might show up there if they are looking for him. Did you hear anything in the background? Cars? Trains? Leaves crunching under his feet?"

"It was quiet. I could hear crickets. Maybe crunching leaves at the end. His breathing indicated that he may have been running."

"Ok. Maybe he was in the woods hiding out. Maybe his parents know of a place he would hide in the woods. But if he was spooked, then he is probably going somewhere safe. The Williamses!! He must be going there. If you can't go home, where would the next best place be? To the guy who saved you before!" Sonia slapped Park's arm.

"Ok. Let's give it a shot."

Sonia drove and parked her car a half block down from the Williams' house. They didn't see any lights on or any movement. They just stared, barely blinking, at the house. After thirty minutes, Sonia turned to Park and said, "We should call the Andersons and ask them where Cameron would hide in the woods, maybe he found a safe place to hide, and we can drive towards there, maybe he is en route."

"Should we knock on the door or call the Williamses? He may have contacted them?"

"Well, maybe if his parents don't know anything. Let's not piss them off if we don't have to."

Park called the Andersons.

"Hello?" A sleepy Mrs. Anderson answered.

"Mrs. Anderson, this is Detective Parkerson, is there a place where your son would hide out in the woods?"

"Why? Is he OK? What happened?"

"Ma'am, he's fine. Well...he called me, but then we got cut off. I just want to help him. Do you know of any place? Is there a place in the woods? Maybe where he has camped before?"

"I... I don't... Well, there was a place his father took him camping when he was a kid, just a place not too far in the woods, near the Christian Retreat Center off 84th Ave. I think it's about a mile south of the Center. There is a clearing where families sometimes would camp instead of staying in a cabin. Detective?"

"Yes?"

"Please bring him home."

"I'll do what I can, ma'am. I will let you know if we find him."

"Thank you, Detective."

Park ended the call. He knew she wouldn't go back to sleep. She will be pacing until he called her back. Breaking sad news or making people worry was collateral damage from investigating murders and other serious crimes. This is what wore Park down. Detectives are not happy people. They are drawn to crime: to solve crime, no matter the consequences on their psyche. Even when he solved a crime, and he would get the obligatory "thank you," and sometimes a hug, it came with an aura of sadness and despair that would cling to him. He absorbed these feelings and carried them with him. When you immerse yourself into a family's emotions, they become yours too. Each murder he solved can be recalled; every detail, at any moment, just by feeling those emotions. Her pacing was felt in his head, every footstep was a throbbing in his temples.

"I know where he might be."

Sonia didn't have a siren or lights to throw on the roof of her car like they do in the movies or on TV, but she drove as she did. She swerved around cars into the oncoming lane. Lucky for them, it was late, and few drivers inhabited the roads. Red lights were green, and the car would grip the pavement as it swung around corners. Park just sat there, like it was a Sunday drive. He was chewing on his fingers. He wasn't praying, since he was an atheist, but he was summoning the universe to intervene and help Cameron. Park had a bad feeling.

They got out of the car, which was still coughing and wheezing from the exertion. Park and Sonia pointed flashlights at the woods south of the main hall. They entered the woods and found a path made over the years by many hikers. They wanted to call out, but they didn't know who else was there. Slowly moving, trying not to make any sound, they systematically moved their flashlights from side to side. Up ahead, they saw a smoldering fire, with just a few embers glowing from underneath the wood. A tent was visible to the right. Park heard groaning and squeaking from his left. Before he could get his flashlight around to point at the area from where the noise came, his brain already fired its neurons into the auditory section of his memory, and a vision of someone hanging by a rope flashed in his head. This vision was replaced by Cameron hanging from a tree branch with a nylon rope around his neck, slightly swinging, his toes barely brushing the dead leaves. Park dropped to his knees and immediately thought of Mrs. Anderson pacing in her house.

"Park, what is it?" Sonia turned towards him and saw what made him drop. "Fuck."

CHAPTER 43

I killed Becky. I loved her. I couldn't live with the guilt any longer. I am sorry. I pretended to be someone else online and got her to meet me at the park. She freaked out when she found out it was me, so I choked her to death and made it look like the Anthony Miller murder. Tell the Williamses I am sorry, they treated me like a son. Tell my parents, I love them. Goodbye.

Cam

After Park reread the note found in jutting out of Cam's jeans pocket, he handed it over to Sonia. She read it and stared at him, scanning his face as if trying to read his thoughts.

"Park? What do you think of this?"

"My gut tells me this is bullshit, but this was my one and only suspect, so why wouldn't I believe it."

Red and blue lights filled the night air as the sounds of sirens echoed around them. They could hear the hurried footsteps through the woods as the paramedics, police officers, and the other regulars on a crime scene showed up. Park just stood near Cam, looking up at him. Sonia next to him, shoulders touching, not saying a word. A low masculine voice pierced the silence behind them.

"Detective?"

Park turned around to see Lieutenant Gregory standing there.

"Yes sir."

"What am I looking at?"

"Cameron Anderson appears to have died by suicide. Here is the note we found sticking out of his pocket."

Lieutenant Gregory read the note twice and gave it to a uniformed police officer. "Bag this." He turned back to Sonia and Park, "Well, I guess this wraps this case up."

"Lieutenant, I... I...um, don't think it does. I think he was killed."

"Ok. I'm all ears."

"Well, he called me right before, well, this. He didn't sound like he was going to kill himself. He told me he wanted to confess."

"It looks like he did."

"No. I mean, in person. He heard something when he was talking to me. He thought someone was there, and then he hung up the phone."

"Then we would find footprints or some evidence of someone here with him."

"This is a high traffic area for hikers and campers, I don't think we will find anything."

"Park, just because this doesn't give you answers about Anthony Miller, doesn't mean this case isn't closed. Cameron Anderson killed Rebecca Williams."

"Sir, with all due respect, I don't think we can close this case yet."

"Do you have any other suspects?"

"No."

"Any leads?"

"Not really. Not yet."

"Hmm... Well, if forensics finds anything indicating that this was a homicide, then you can continue investigating the Rebecca Williams case. Until then, you won't do anything. Understand?"

"Copy that." Park just watched as Cameron was photographed, taken down off the tree, and placed on a gurney. He watched as investigators searched the grounds while uniformed officers placed yellow tape around the area. A few journalists showed up as other officers pushed them back down the trail. Park could hear questions being shouted.

"Who is it?"

"Is this the work of the Crucifier?"

Park winced at that nickname. It doesn't matter what the definition of a serial killer is, the media will let you know when there is one by creating a nickname.

Sonia, still silently standing next to Park, leaned in and said, "I would have called him the Nylon Nuisance. Ha!" Park grinned. "There it is. Come on, let's go back to your place and work this out. Tomorrow we will probably get an I.D. on the newest victim." Park nodded, and they walked back to Sonia's car, ignoring the questions yelled at them from the ever-growing crowd of journalists.

Park sat in the passenger seat and turned to Sonia. "We need to make a stop first." Without him saying where Sonia drove towards the Andersons.

CHAPTER 44

After telling the Andersons about their son, they returned to Park's house and surrendered to the couch together. Exhausted, they laid their heads on the back, staring up at the old popcorn ceiling. Sonia's head slipped down onto Park's shoulder. He turned to look at her and saw her eyes fight gravity. "It's getting late." He spoke. She popped up.

"Yeah, I should get going. I haven't even checked into my hotel yet."

Park swallowed hard, not knowing if he should ask her to stay. He saw her stand up and yawn as she stretched her arms towards the popcorn. He smiled at her and blurted out, "You can stay if you want."

"Are you sure?"

Park nodded. "I can make up the couch for you."

"Oh. Um. Sure, that sounds perfect. I need to go out to my car and get my bag."

Park went to the closet and pulled out sheets, a pillow, and a comforter. They both made up the couch together. "I'll see you in the morning. We have a big day ahead of us."

"See ya Park. You, ok?"

"Yeah, I'm fine. Goodnight." Park crawled into bed, making sure he put on shorts and a T-shirt. He didn't think sleeping in the buff tonight like he usually does, would be a good idea.

After about an hour of tossing and turning, Park looked

for bourbon next to his bed but forgot he finished that bottle a few nights ago. He wanted to go into the kitchen and get more but didn't want to disrupt Sonia. He let out a big sigh and stared at the ceiling. His eyes closed as exhaustion started to pull him down into sleep. Just as he was drifting into slumber, Cameron's face appeared. His eyes popped open, and a rush of adrenaline filled his arteries. "Fuck!" Park punched the bed. He needed bourbon. He lifted himself and started to spin his legs off the bed when he saw Sonia standing two feet away from him, wearing only an oversized men's T-shirt. The light from the hallway allowed Park to see her beautiful curves, silhouetted underneath.

"Thought you could use this." She held up a bottle of bourbon and two glasses. She gestured for Park to scooch over, so she could sit with him. She sat down on the edge of the bed and poured the bourbon in the glasses, handing him one. She lifted it towards him, and they both swallowed the bourbon. She took the glass from him and placed it on his nightstand with hers. She stood up, faced him, and pulled off her T-shirt. Even in the dark, he could see the care she took for her body. Naked, just standing there, she wanted him to see her toned sculpted body with curves in all the right places. He gazed upon her for almost half a minute as a piece of art. Enjoying the masterpiece in front of him, he was, at the same time, analyzing it and trying to find the more in-depth meaning. Wanting to feel the beauty he was absorbing, he grabbed her hand and pulled her into him. She crawled on top, straddling him. He could feel the heat emanating off her inner thighs and netherworld. She maneuvered herself down the length of his body, gently pulling off his shorts and underwear. Park felt her soft lips kiss his ankle, then his shin, both his knees and then felt her teeth lightly bite his inner thigh. As her mouth moved north, Park laid his head back and allowed himself to feel her mouth envelop him. After a few minutes, he pulled her up and put his mouth on hers. Flipping her over, it was then his turn to explore her body. After the electricity that shot through Sonia's body dissipated, she pulled Park up and took him inside her.

DAY EIGHT

CHAPTER 45

The next morning, Park awoke and swung his arm over to Sonia's side of the bed, only to find that he was alone. He placed his hand in the center of her spot and felt the residual warmth from her body. Taking in a deep breath, he inhaled her scent. He sat up as a different smell wafted into the room. The tantalizing aroma of bacon filled the house, along with the beautiful sound of Sonia humming. He stood up, dressed, and sauntered into the kitchen. She was standing in front of the stove dressed in only the T-shirt from last night, her hair pulled into a messy bun with a scrunchy. Two plates with glasses of orange juice were on the counter. She was dancing, with no accompanying music, other than the song she was singing, "I'm a joker, I'm a smoker, I'm a midnight la la..." She would replace the forgotten words with "la. "This made Park smile. He came up behind her and wrapped his arms around her. She turned around and placed her hands around his neck, as he kept his arms around her waist.

"How'd you sleep?"

"Great, I don't remember the last time I slept that well," Park smirked.

"That's what happens when you get laid. HA!" She kissed him. She then turned her attention towards the eggs and bacon on the stove. She started to sing and dance again as Park walked over and took a sip of orange juice.

"I'm a smoker, I'm a joker, I'm a midnight la la..."

Park's eyes grew wide as he remembered his realization

from last night before Cameron called.

"Sonia!"

"What is it!"

"I need to see the dating site data again. Where is it?" Park looked panicked.

"It's over there in the blue folder, what is it?"

"The song you are singing. The unidentified man is someone I've previously interviewed."

Sonia turned off the stove, wiped her hands, and walked into the living room with Park.

"I don't understand."

"Steve Miller Band. The name of the guy on the dating site. His name was..." Park was looking through the pages of data, trying to find the page.

"Thomas Scaggs" Sonia interjected.

Park put down the folder. "YES! Scaggs is the lead guitarist's last name in the Steve Miller Band."

"Ok? But how..."

Park interrupted. "Miller! His last name is Miller."

"So, you think it is a made-up name, but with hidden meaning? Who's Thomas Miller?"

"Not Thomas. If I said Tom and," Park paused. "What name would you think of?"

"Jerry."

"Jerry Miller. Gerald Miller. Anthony Miller's uncle!"

Sonia just stared at Park. "Don't you think that is a stretch, Park? I mean, are you sure you aren't trying to fit the wrong puzzle piece?"

"No, I'm sure. Whoever is killing these people is arrogant; they think they are smarter than we are. Who knows? Maybe he wants everyone to know he's behind it all."

"So, what do we do now?"

"We eat the wonderful breakfast you made, then I'm going to take you into the bedroom, and after that, we are going to go interview Mr. Scaggs, AKA Jerry Fucking Miller!"

"HA! Can we change the order of that, just a little?"

Park walked over to her, picked her up, and walked into the bedroom. Breakfast can wait.

CHAPTER 46

As Park and Sonia entered the station, Lieutenant Gregory was there to meet them.

"Let's talk in my office."

Park and Sonia shrugged and followed him, taking the two chairs opposite his desk.

"So, are we clear about Rebecca William's case?"

"You mean that for right now we are going on the assumption that Cameron is the killer?"

"Yes."

"Well, I mean, if that's what you are telling me to do."

"With all due respect, Lieutenant, with the three crucifixion murders and the alleged suicide of Cameron Anderson, this would easily fall into FBI jurisdiction. I'm not even considering the other three murders from years ago." Sonia stood, presenting herself in a way Lieutenant Gregory would be reminded of her status. "As of right now, this is your case, but we can't stop until we can pin all three on Cameron."

The Lieutenant steepled his hands and stared at Sonia. "Let me be frank. We are getting a lot of pressure from the church community to put this to bed. They believe the longer this lingers, the worse it will be for their public image."

Park let out a laugh and then held his hand up apologetically. The Lieutenant continued.

"As I was saying, I want this case to be solved as well, but right now, Cameron checks all the boxes, let's not prolong this any longer than we have to. I understand that we have two other cases that need to be solved, but Rebecca William's case, well, let's just say, is paused for now. If we can't find any evidence of foul play, then I will expect you to move on."

Sonia and Park visibly squirmed in their seats as Park rebutted, "Ok. But if the other two cases lead us back to Rebecca Williams, then we will reopen the case. I wouldn't go and tell the Williamses just yet that Cameron was the killer."

"I'll give you 72 hours to come up with more evidence before I tell the public."

"You are being obtuse. There is no way Cameron was working alone, if he did it at all!" Park protested.

"What's more likely, that there is a conspiracy involving multiple people in Ms. Williams's death, or she was killed by the person who broke into your house, was your main suspect, and confessed in a suicide note? Ever heard of Occam's Razor, Park?"

"Yes."

"Well, then, you should agree that when you have two competing theories, the simpler one is the better."

"Actually, Lieutenant," Sonia interjected. "The saying is, *Pluralitas non est ponenda sine necessitate,* or *Entities should not be multiplied unnecessarily.*"

The Lieutenant was visibly annoyed, to Park's pleasure. "Well, you know what I mean. Park, you tend to overthink these things. You are welcome to continue to investigate the other murders, but tread lightly around the Williamses."

Park and Sonia simply nodded in agreement and left his office. They started to put together the Miller file from all the pieces again. Sonia went through Park's computer and printed out anything related to Anthony Miller. Park went to the records room and pulled the transcripts from his interviews. He sat down and skimmed through it.

"Here. Here it is." Park pointed at the transcript where Mr. Miller brings up his brother.

Sonia reads the transcript and responds, "Did you ever interview him? They seem to think he is a non-threat."

"Yes. Hold on." Park flips through the papers on his desk. "Ah, here it is." They both start to read it.

Detective Parkerson: "Thank you for coming down to speak with me. You are Anthony Miller's uncle, correct?"

Gerald Miller: "Yes, I'm his father's brother."

Detective Parkerson: "Tell me about your relationship with Anthony."

Gerald Miller: "We were close. I didn't have any kids of my own, so I treated him like a son."

Detective Parkerson: "When you say close, how often did you see him? What did you do?"

Gerald Miller: "Close. You know, like an uncle and a nephew. Nothing creepy. We would see each other a couple of times a week. I'd pick him up, and we would go to my church. They would have bible study or group for teens that I would take him to."

Detective Parkerson: "And he wanted to go with you?"

Gerald Miller: "Yes. He needed guidance. He started to be tempted, as teenagers do, so I helped him stay the course."

Detective Parkerson: "What religion?"

Gerald Miller: "Baptist."

Detective Parkerson: "Before he died, did he talk to you

about dating?"

Gerald Miller: "Dating? Um... no... not really. Occasionally, he would ask me questions about girls. When he got into his twenties, he didn't talk much about the women he was dating. Not even sure he was."

Detective Parkerson: "Where were you the night he died?"

Gerald Miller: "Am I a suspect?"

Detective Parkerson: "Sir, we look at everyone. Where were you?"

Gerald Miller: "I was in my home, by myself. I was researching on my computer."

Detective Parkerson: "Research for what?"

Gerald Miller: "I'm a lawyer, I was working on a defense."

Detective Parkerson: "Would you be willing to send me evidence of your computer usage?"

Gerald Miller: "Of course, I'm sure I can print out dates and times of my searches and downloads."

Detective Parkerson: "Ok, Mr. Miller. That's all I have for now. Is there anything else we should know?"

Gerald Miller: "No. He was a great kid...er...young man. Whatever I can do to help."

<end>

"What do we know about Mr. Miller?" Sonia asked.

"I do remember him walking in the station. He carried a certain amount of gravitas with him and owned the room. Although he was north of fifty, he looked like he was in his mid-thirties. He was born and raised here in Norman, Oklahoma, and is a lawyer in town."

"Ok, let's show a picture of this guy to Maria Burrows.

Maybe she saw him around Rebecca, or even online."

"Good idea." Park agreed.

CHAPTER 47

Two men sat silently in wooden chairs in the middle of the barren room. The room was dark, with the only light coming from two candles sitting on a wooden altar. They waited. A door behind the altar creaked open. The sound of wooden-soled shoes was heard reverberating through the room. Clip. Clop. Clip. Clop. An older man entered the room, grabbed a chair behind the altar, and placed it in front of the two men. The older man ran his hand through his gray hair and then raised his arms above his head, gesturing for the other men to rise to their feet. They obeyed. He then turned his hands, palm side down, and lowered them to his waist. The men kneeled and bowed their heads, hands clasped together. They did this in unison, as they have done dozens of times before.

The old man spoke in a deep, raspy voice. "You are the Serpent."

"I am the serpent." The men echoed.

"You are the sheep."

"I am the sheep."

"We walk in the midst of wolves."

"We are the path." They answered.

The old man sat. The other men followed.

The old man broke the silence. "I don't like what's happening. The detective and the FBI agent seem to be getting too close. The last ascension was too close to the girl. What happened with Cameron?"

"He was weak." The middle-aged man on the right bellowed.

"I know. That is why he failed and became a serpent. You were supposed to guide him and make him strong."

The other man interjected. "He was in love with the girl."

"How did he lose his way?"

"We should have pulled him out." The man on the right answered.

"Why didn't you?"

"I... I thought he would... the night he showed up at his door... we should've... I thought Cameron would have completed his task. He kept telling us he had her. When we saw him failing, we stepped in. The dating app came in handy."

"That was reckless. You also got involved with Jennifer's passenger." He pointed to the man on the right.

"She needed help and Cameron was a no show. We thought that would be for the best."

"You should've waited until we got a new serpent. If you are exposed, it will damage everything. We are the path. We are the way to God's kingdom. We will not allow this world to poison any more of God's purest children."

"Yes, sir." Both men said in concert.

"You know what you have to do. You can't rely on me anymore. Build your army. Who do you have in the works?"

"Well, I assigned her to watch the detective's ex-girlfriend's daughter, in case we needed the leverage." The man on the right answered.

"That seems risky, but it is your call." The older man

responded.

"Jennifer knows what she is doing. I trust her. She may come in handy if the Detective gets any closer."

The man on the left interjected, "He was told to stop looking for Rebecca's murderer, that it is a closed case. But..."

"But? Why is there a but?"

"But he has reopened Mr. Miller's case."

"He didn't find anything the first time; what could he possibly have now? Just to be safe, why not make Cameron responsible for all the murders? Let's give the Detective closure. Can I trust you both to make that happen?"

Again, in unison, "Yes, sir."

The man on the left spoke up timidly. "The FBI agent has been talking about other murders that may be related. What are we going to do about that?"

Agitation overtook the older man's face. He brought his right hand up to it and rubbed his face from his temples down to the chin. He spoke in a low, disconcerting voice. "This is why I hated the crucifixion displays. Now we may be exposed. It wouldn't take much digging if they get any leads or a name. We will not be so careless in the future. You two need to come up with a contingency plan if this blows up in our faces. We have too much work to do, to have it end now. Do not contact me until all of it is done. I'm leaving, I will be moving on. You know what I could do to both of you if you screw this up."

The old man stood up, as did the two men. After returning the chair behind the altar, the old man opened the creaky door and clip-clopped through it. As the sound of his shoes disappeared, the two men stared at each other.

"I will find a way to frame him for all three."

They nodded at each other, walked out of the cabin, entered their cars, and drove away in opposite directions.

CHAPTER 48

"Hello detective...special agent, how can I help you?" Maria Burrows opened her door and let them in. They sat on her couch as she sat across from them. "So, I hear Cameron killed Becky."

"Well, all signs point to that, but we aren't here about that." Park removed the picture of Gerald Miller from the folder and held it up to Maria. "Do you know this man, or have you seen him around... Rebecca?"

Maria took the picture and stared at it. "Um... No, I don't know who this is."

"Are you certain?" Park pushed.

"I'm certain. Who is it?"

"His name is Gerald Miller. We think he may have known Rebecca."

"I never saw him with Rebecca. I'm sorry."

"Thank you for seeing us." Sonia stood up abruptly. Park was surprised by the suddenness but followed suit.

"Why did we leave so soon, we could've pressed her more?" Park asked during their drive back to his house.

"She's lying. Waste of time. If she knows him, she will contact him, and it may create some movement."

CHAPTER 49

Maria stared at her phone. She couldn't sleep. Her heart pounded. She pushed the button. The phone rang.

"Maria? What is it?"

"They showed me a picture of you."

"Who?"

"The Detective."

"Why? I mean, how?"

"I don't know. They said they think you knew Rebecca. Why would they say that?"

"I don't know. Don't worry about it. They are on a wild goose chase."

"I'm scared. Can I come over tonight?"

"That's not a good idea."

"I'm tired of sneaking around with you. Why can't…?"

"Maria, you know why. People…well…they just wouldn't understand."

"Understand what? That I'm black or is it that I'm half your age? Which one?"

"Listen, I need you to do something for me. I promise after you do this, we can talk. Ok?"

"Yes. Anything. What do you want me to do?"

Maria got her instructions. "Can I come over? Please?"

"Not tonight. I have to go. I promise I'll call you soon." Gerald Miller hung up the phone.

CHAPTER 50

"I don't know what to do," Park whispered as Sonia's head was resting on his chest.

"We work the case," Sonia answered.

"Thanks, Captain Obvious. I mean, I feel like we are close, but at the same time, so far away from the truth. Do you think I'm trying to make this bigger than it is?"

"I don't know Park, but I don't think Cameron is responsible for all three, and obviously, he didn't kill in Nashville or Colorado."

"So, how do you think we proceed?"

"Well, I would visit Cameron's parents again, maybe talk to the Williamses. There has to be something we are missing about him."

"I'd lose my job if I talked to either of them."

"Well, I can. I can take this investigation anywhere I want. If I must, I can take over this case and make it an FBI investigation. I just need to link these murders with the others. That shouldn't be too hard due to the way the bodies were displayed, but due to the time gap, it may take more. Let's game plan tomorrow. Now go to sleep."

"I don't know if I can." Park looked around for his bottle of bourbon.

"You don't need a drink. I'll take care of you." Sonia moved her way down Park's body.

DAY NINE

CHAPTER 51

Park and Sonia arrived at the station. The Lieutenant called them during their breakfast with news that their last victim had been identified. Local dealership owner, Roger Trammel, came in to file a missing person's report after his employee didn't show up to work for the second day in a row. Based on the physical description he gave, he was shown the body. Mr. Trammel identified the victim as Mark O'Brien. The details given in Mr. Trammel's ensuing interview didn't surprise Park or Sonia. He had worked at a car dealership in Norman, Oklahoma. He was a devout Christian, had no family, volunteered regularly, and he was dating. According to Mr. Trammel, Mark explained his date as "wonderful" and only described her as a "beautiful blonde." Mr. Trammel didn't know anything else that would help in identifying the woman. Mark, like the other victims, was a private person and didn't talk to anyone about his personal life other than in vague details.

"Well, we are off to Mr. O'Brien's apartment," Park said, standing up, looking in the direction of his Lieutenant.

"Park, remember Cameron is our main suspect, try and find anything that will tie him to this case."

"I will work the case like I always do; I will let the evidence guide me to the suspects, not the other way around."

"You know what I mean, Jacob." The Lieutenant snapped.

Park knew to keep his mouth shut. The Lieutenant only called him Jacob when Park crossed the line. He nodded and walked out of the station as Sonia followed.

As they drove towards the apartment, Sonia broke the silence, "Ha!"

Park chuckled. "What was that for?"

"The tension is palpable. Always makes me uncomfortable."

"I have a bad feeling about the Lieutenant." He met Sonia's eyes. Sonia saw the Detective in him through his stare, churning the angles, deciphering the clues.

"Yeah. I don't like the vibe I'm feeling. Ever since you told me that he showed up at your house while you were...well...you know."

"We're missing something."

The rest of the drive was silent. Sonia held his hand.

They parked in front of the apartment complex. The manager was waiting for them at the front entrance.

"What can you tell us about Mr. O'Brian?" Park asked.

"Not much. He paid his rent on time, sometimes early. He kept to himself. No complaints from his neighbors. That is about it. I don't live here, so I don't really know my tenants."

Park and Sonia put on gloves and entered the apartment and looked around. The one-bedroom apartment wasn't that big, but it was very modern and nice.

The manager, recognizing she was no longer needed, slipped away, closing the door softly behind her.

"What are we looking for?" Sonia asked as they both snapped on latex gloves.

"Well, I would start with a cell phone, computer, anything that can help us identify this mystery date. I'm not optimistic about finding anything if this is anything like the others."

"Well, let's stay positive."

Sonia walked around the apartment, opening cabinets and drawers, lifting couch cushions, and crouching down on the floor looking under furniture. Park went straight into the bedroom that was adjacent to the living room. As he predicted, a black rectangle surrounded by dust was all that remained on the desk, where a laptop usually rested. The cords were still plugged into the wall and the laptop case was propped up against the desk on the floor. Park picked up the case and slid his hands into the pockets, finding nothing. He opened the drawers only to find old receipts, multiple phone chargers, and some other random items. Park walked over to the bed and sat and looked around. The room was plain: nothing on the walls, no decorations at all. Next to the bed was a nightstand with the obligatory lamp on it. He opened the drawer and found a King James Bible. Park silently chuckled, thinking how Mark's bedroom felt like a motel room. After looking through his dresser drawers and under his bed, Park returned to sitting on the bed and let out a sigh. He didn't expect to find anything, but it still frustrated him. His mind raced, trying to connect Mark to Rebecca to Anthony. *What was the connection?*

"You find anything?" Sonia asked as she walked into the bedroom.

"No. You?"

"Not really. It looks like this place was wiped down pretty good. It smells like bleach. The killer or killers were here."

"Yeah, I noticed that smell too."

Sonia picked up the laptop bag. "I had one of these bags, I bought it at Target." She'd pronounced it as Tar-Jay. "Did you check the hidden pocket?"

"What?"

"Yeah, this model has a hidden pocket within the front pocket where you can put stuff you don't want someone to find. I liked it for hotel rooms. I put my flash drives in there so if someone were to be nosy, they wouldn't find them."

Sonia unzipped the front pocket and then pulled back the material to display another small zipper to a hidden smaller pocket. She slid two fingers into the pocket and pulled out a flash drive. "And BINGO was his Name-O! HA!"

"Holy Shit!!" Park leaped to his feet and hugged Sonia.

"Easy, Champ, it probably just has porn on it. It may not have anything useful."

"I know, but it is the first real break in a long time. Let's get this back to the station. At least we have some porn to watch if that's all it has."

"HA! How about we take this to my hotel room? I'm not trusting your station right now."

"Good idea. I'll get some uniforms to get over here and canvass the neighbors." Park's phone buzzed. He took it out of his pocket and pushed the green button underneath the name on the caller ID, "Lieutenant Gregory."

"Yes. We'll head over there now."

"Who was that Park?"

"The Lieutenant. The Andersons found a journal of Cameron's. They say it has some pertinent information in it."

"Hmm."

"My sentiment exactly. Well, I guess we have a pit stop before we watch some porn."

CHAPTER 52

They entered the home of Mr. and Mrs. Anderson once again. Mrs. Anderson walked them up to Cameron's room. Laying on Cameron's bed was a manila folder.

Park picked the folder up, opening it to reveal printed-out Word documents of Cameron's thoughts. Sonia was next to Park reading them, shaking her head. The documents tied Cameron to all three murders. He admitted to copying the murders from Nashville. He had heard about them in church groups. Furthermore, he admitted to knowing Anthony Miller and killing him in a rage of jealousy. He then killed Rebecca because he told her he loved her, and she rebuked him. He then killed Mark O'Brian, claiming Mark was the new man that Rebecca was dating, and he was again jealous. The journal described Cameron as paranoid, delusional, and unhinged. He confesses to drugs again.

Park and Sonia looked at each other.

"Mrs. Anderson, where did you find this?"

"It was behind his bookcase, over there." She pointed to the two-shelved bookcase. "I was starting to pack his books up when I noticed it."

"Why haven't you noticed it before?"

"I don't know. I mean, I guess I just didn't notice it."

These are printed, where are his computer and printer?" Sonia chimed in.

"I... I don't know where his laptop is. The only printer in the house is in our bedroom."

"We are going to need to see it," Park stated. She walked them into her bedroom. He sat down at a desk and turned on the computer. He opened the event viewer and scrolled through the print history. No documents were printed in the last 2 weeks. The last time Cameron used it was over 3 months ago. "Well, this journal wasn't printed here. Mrs. Anderson, has anyone been in Cameron's room since his death?"

Mrs. Anderson's eyes were wet, her nose red. Her lips trembled as she spoke. "Yes. Maria came by. She asked if she could have a book of his. I let her go up to his room and get it. She was only up there for a few minutes."

"Did she have a purse or a satchel or something with her?"

"She just had her purse"

Sonia and Park looked at each other again.

"What book?" Park blurted out.

"Um... I'm not certain. It was the book that Cameron read a lot. I saw it peeking out of her purse. I don't remember the name. Something with the word *perfect* in it. I'm sorry. I didn't engage in conversations with Cameron when it came to religion; we didn't see eye to eye."

"That's ok ma'am. You gave us enough information. Thank you. We will be leaving now. Please call us if you find anything else, or if someone else stops by."

"Do you think Maria was up to something?"

"Not sure, ma'am, just looking at all the pieces," Park responded.

"Detective?"

"Yes ma'am?"

"Do you believe that Cameron killed all those people?"

Park considered how to answer this, knowing if he says the wrong thing, it could cause more harm to her and, his career. Park started to speak.

"No. I don't think he did." Sonia jumped in.

Park's head whipped around to meet Sonia's eyes. She met his eyes and just smiled with her eyes and nodded slightly; she was showing sympathy for the woman standing in front of them who was struggling to imagine a world where her dead son was a serial killer.

Mrs. Anderson walked towards Sonia and embraced her, letting all of her weight collapse onto her. Sonia wrapped her arms around the broken woman and held her up and whispered, "We are going to clear your son."

Mrs. Anderson whispered, "Thank you," and released Sonia.

CHAPTER 53

Back at Sonia's hotel, they sat on the couch in silence, holding hands. After about 5 minutes, Park sat up and turned towards Sonia.

"So here is what I have so far. Cameron, Jerry Miller, and Maria Burrows are involved in one or all of these murders in some way. My lieutenant is acting weird. The Pastor is creepy, and there may be another man and woman walking around who have dated our victims."

"Pretty much covers it. You just forgot about the murders from 30 years ago in Nashville and the one in Colorado a decade ago."

"Ok. So, tomorrow we need to visit Mr. Jerry Miller. We also need to visit Ms. Burrows again and take a little different approach. We both think she lied about not knowing Jerry Miller, and she also had that odd interaction with Mr. and Mrs. Williams."

"That's right. So, what's your theory, Park?"

"Hmm... Ok, so Cameron befriends Anthony Miller and Rebecca Williams. Jerry Miller is Anthony's uncle and Maria Burrows is Rebecca's best friend. How are they connected to Mark O'Brian?" He paused, stroking his chin. "Let's say Maria was Anthony's mystery date." Park stood up and started pacing back and forth in front of Sonia. Her eyes followed him. "Cameron set them up. Jerry Miller was Rebecca's mystery date, also set up by Cameron? Or was she set up by Maria? We'll come back to that. Maria and Jerry like to date people and then murder them, and Cameron helped."

Sonia chimed in. "But, that leaves Mr. O'Brian. Not to mention Nashville and Colorado."

"Fuck. Ok. Jerry may be old enough to be involved in Nashville and Colorado, so is he the connection?"

"Yes! Ha! All we have to do is look up his prior addresses. We could see where he went to school. 30 years ago, would put him at 23 years old. He would have been in law school."

"Nashville has a few law schools in that area. Ok, so for some reason, Jerry fucking Miller dates women, then kills them, and then binds them to a cross. Why?"

"He's a religious nut? Maybe these women rejected him? He's jealous? Maybe, he lusts for them, and he blames them?"

"Interesting. So, Jerry dates these women, and then when he becomes sexually aroused by them, he kills them?"

"Maybe." Sonia is standing now, and they are circling the coffee table.

"Then explain the guy from Colorado, Anthony, and Mark?"

"Jerry is bisexual. It seems to be all the rage nowadays." Park laughed. Sonia punched him in the arm. "Ow. You pack a wallop. I was only half-joking. Perhaps he *is* bisexual. But what is Maria's role, and why involve Cameron? In his interview, when referencing his relationship with Anthony, he said *not in a creepy way*. So, what if he was sexually abusing Anthony?"

"Are you implying that if someone is bisexual, they are also sexual deviants or abusers?"

Park couldn't tell if she was joking or not, but he understood the implication. "I didn't mean to imply that; I have seen too many relatives with close relationships turn out to be abusers."

"I know, Park. Just being a Devil's Advocate."

Park slumped back onto the couch and let out a big sigh. Sonia fell next to him and put her head on his shoulder.

"Well, let's go to bed. We have a long day ahead of us. Maybe we can get some answers tomorrow."

DAY TEN

CHAPTER 54

Park and Sonia parked a block away from Jerry Miller's house just before noon. "Let's watch the house for a few hours."

"Sounds like a plan."

After almost two hours, the front door opens. A young man, with short, curly blond hair, stepped out, heading north on the sidewalk. Thin and of average height, he was wearing tight skinny jeans and a green army jacket.

"Who the fuck was that?" Sonia blurted out.

"I don't know." They both look at each other.

"Was that a walk of shame? You may have been right about Mr. Miller."

"Should we follow him?" Park asked.

"What for? We need to go and talk to Mr. Miller."

They both started to reach for the handles when the front door opened again and out stepped Jerry Miller, dressed in a suit and an overcoat. Park and Sonia slouched back in their seats. Mr. Miller got into his car in the driveway and sped away.

"Should we follow HIM?" Park asked again.

"No, I have a better idea."

Sonia opened the door and before Park could say a word, she was scurrying across the street and around the back of the house. Park followed suit. He looked around to ensure no one was watching before he raced towards her. As he was about to go around the house, the front door opened just enough for Sonia to peek her head out. "This way!"

Park looks around again before slipping into Jerry Miller's house.

"What are you doing? We won't be able to use anything we find." Park looked at Sonia with a confused face, holding his hands out towards her.

"Relax, Park. We need a break in this case. We can't wait around for a search warrant, which we don't have enough to get right now anyway. Let's just look around quickly and see if anything stands out that will help us." Sonia grabs his hands, calming him.

"Fine. 10 minutes tops."

Sonia headed upstairs as Park stayed downstairs. He looked around the living room, opening any drawer he found. Next, he went into the kitchen. On the counter, Park spotted a pad of paper. It was evident that multiple sheets were ripped from it. Park found a pencil in a drawer and lightly shaded the top paper on the pad, revealing the imprints from the last message written. The word *cabin* and the time *7 pm* revealed itself to park. He tore the page off and shoved it in his pocket, then put the pencil away.

Park finished looking around downstairs. Other than some hygiene items, he didn't find anything of relevance. He was about to head upstairs when Sonia called down to him.

"Park, come here, quick!"

Park raced up the stairs and into a room that looked like an office. The walls were bookshelves, filled with law books on one side and religious books on the other. Some mainstream fiction books were sprinkled in.

"What'd ya find?"

Sonia held out a book.

"Perfect Ascension" by Reverend Daniel Nelson

"Ok? What about it?"

Sonia just gave Park a look, a look he knew well. Julie used to give it to him when he should have known something when he didn't. "What?"

"Do you recognize it?"

He took it and looked at it. "This was the book in Cameron's room, the one Maria took."

Park leafed through it and recognized the pages that were underlined. It was the same book that was in Cameron's room.

"Holy Shit! This ties Cameron to Jerry Fuckin' Miller."

"Hold on sport. This also ties Maria to Jerry Fuckin' Miller!"

"What is it about this book?" He asked.

"Well, let's buy a copy and find out," Sonia suggested.

"We don't have time, plus I'm a slow reader. It took me 6 months to finish *"You" by Caroline Kepnes*. It wasn't even that long of a book.

"The show on *Netflix?* It was a book?"

"The book was better. We need to visit Reverend Daniel Nelson. What does the bio say in the book?"

Sonia opened the front cover and read the author's biography. Her face lost all color as her eyes widened. She passed the book to Park to read.

He took the book from her and read the first paragraph.

Reverend Daniel Nelson received his Bachelor of Arts degree in Religious Studies from Vanderbilt University in Nashville, Tennessee, and his Master's in Theology from Colorado Christian University. He has made his home in Colorado Springs, Colorado for the last 20 years.

Park slowly lifted his head to meet Sonia's eyes. She was just slowly nodding and then smiled. "I'll book the tickets."

CHAPTER 55

"They were at your house."

"Who?"

"Who do you think?" Maria Burrows responded curtly.

Gerald Miller didn't speak for 10 seconds. It felt like minutes to Maria.

"Jerry?"

"How... Why? What were they doing? How do you know?"

"I wanted to see you so I..."

"Maria, I have told you, you can't just come over whenever you'd like!"

"Oh, stop it, Jerry. I know about your cute little boyfriend. I won't say anything. I can share."

"Maria..."

"Listen, I saw the Detective and the woman FBI agent enter your house around 2 pm. I was a couple of blocks away when I saw him run across the street, and she popped her head out your front door. She must've gotten in around back."

"Fuck. Did they take anything?"

"No. I didn't see anything in their hands. Was there anything there?"

"No, I mean... I don't think so. Why were they there,

what did they find? You put the

journal in Cameron's room, right?"

"Yes, like I told you when I returned your book to you."

"Why are they still hunting? Fuck. Thank you, Maria."

"What are you going to do?"

"Well, we have a contingency plan just for this occasion. I need to call Jen. Oh, and

Maria…"

Maria interrupted. "I won't say anything, what you do, or **who** you do, is your business."

Gerald ended the call, then made another call.

"Hey Jenn, are you still hanging with Mia?"

DAY ELEVEN

CHAPTER 56

The next morning, they landed in Colorado Springs. Sonia was driving the rental car to Reverend Nelson's office at the Nazarene Bible College. Park was leafing through Reverend Nelson's book that he purchased before their trip.

"Reverend Nelson claims that a Christian cannot be a true Christian without being tested. Without being tested, no true follower of Christ can claim worthy of ascension."

"Interesting, but don't humans get tested every day?"

"He talks about true tests, conducted on Christians, by true believers. If not tested against one's weakness, no ascension is possible. He posits that Christ died because he wouldn't denounce God as his father even when threatened with death. A true, devout Christian should be tested, like Christ, especially in this modern world of sin."

"So, how does that relate to our murders?" Sonia questioned.

"I'm not certain, yet."

Park continued to flip through the book, skimming through chapters. Park saw a familiar word, stopped flipping and leaned closer into the book to read. His eyes darted back and forth as he absorbed the words. Sonia could see he'd furrowed his brow and as his eyes concentrated hard on the words he was reading.

"What ya find, Sport?"

Park held up one finger towards her without looking up. After about another 2 or 3 minutes, he lifted his head and just stared out the windshield.

"What?" Sonia was getting impatient.

"There is a whole chapter on St. Andrew and *Crux Decussata*. Reverend Nelson states that a true believer, a true disciple of Jesus, should die like St. Andrew. He explains that no matter how society tries and tempts you, you must resist, even if it means your death. This is what it means to be a true disciple of Christ."

"So, this Reverend Nelson believes that true Christians should be prepared to die for God?"

"Yes."

"Well, we are here, we will have to ask the Rev, about what else is in the book." Sonia parked the car, and they walked up two flights of stairs. The two of them, in unison, knocked on Reverend Nelson's office door.

"Come in!" A voice behind the door bellowed.

Park and Sonia entered the door and stood in front of a middle-aged, handsome, tall man with salt and pepper hair, cut meticulously. He was wearing a cardigan sweater and khaki pants.

"Reverend Nelson?" Park asked.

"Yes. How can I help you?"

"I'm Detective Jacob Parkerson and this is Special Agent Sonia Brambilla. We called…"

"Oh yes, you wanted to talk about my book. Please sit down."

They sat in the two chairs in front of his desk.

"Now, what do you want to know?"

Sonia and Park looked at each other, not knowing where to start. Sonia turns towards the doctor and asks, "What did you know about the murder of Christopher Reed?"

"I didn't know him if that is what you are asking."

"No sir, I asked what you knew about it," Sonia said curtly.

"Well, it was about 10 years ago. He was a student here."

"That's all you know?"

"Yes."

Park interjected, "So, is it just a coincidence that the victim was bound to a St. Andrew's cross and your book," He held up Reverend Nelson's book, "has a whole chapter about it?"

Reverend Nelson smirked. "Detective, many people have written about St. Andrew, especially at a Christian College. I'm sure many of my colleagues have. Would you like me to ask them to join us?"

"That won't be necessary. Can you help me understand what your book is about?"

"You haven't read it?"

"Bits and pieces, not my cup of tea." Park retorted.

"Well... in layman's terms, my book is about how humans can strive for the perfect ascension into heaven. I postulate that we, Christians, must emulate the apostles. We must be tested; we must overcome temptation. I discuss that the perfect ascension is when we pass an appropriate trial, and we are sinless in the eyes of God. I also hypothesize that young men and women are the best candidates for ascension because they haven't gone through adulthood and all its temptations.

For today's world, the mid-twenties is the prime age for ascension. The young Christians, who have dedicated their lives to doing good for humanity, who lead sinless lives, and who have been tested, are ready for ascension. It is adulthood that takes them on an alternative path. If humans only lived until they were thirty, God would have more souls at his side. My main point is that Heaven is empty, and we must do something about it."

Park and Sonia looked at each other with wide eyes, indicating to each other that they understand the motivation behind the murders and why the Reverend's book has relevance.

Sonia interrupted, "But can't you just ask for forgiveness and ascend into heaven?"

"That is a popular misconception. The Bible does state that God is forgiving and merciful, but it also tells us that you must believe in your heart, just asking for forgiveness isn't enough. You must be remorseful and a true believer. Furthermore, Matthew 7:21, says that those that do the will of the father will be saved. We must do God's will, walk the earth as Jesus and his apostles did. Most Christians, in this modern world, enter a Church on Sunday and are perfect for 2 hours. The rest of the week, they are sinners."

Park nods in agreement. The Reverend continues.

"John 14:12, states that if you believe in God, you will mimic Jesus and how he lived, but you must be even better. You can't sin all your life and then just ask for forgiveness and have eternal life, you must walk the walk. Nowadays, we Christians are disadvantaged, especially in America."

"How's that?" Sonia asks.

"Well, the temptations, the lifestyles, the stress, and the influence is much greater than the will of most Americans can handle. Technology, greed, narcissism have led us astray. We are losing the battle against evil, and in my book, I surmise that there aren't many Christians getting into heaven. The Gospel of Matthew says, *but small is the gate and narrow the way that leads to life, and only a few find it.* In today's world, the road gets narrower as you age. The more temptations you will find. The road is becoming less traveled, to reference Robert Frost. So, like I said, the perfect time for a Christian to die, would be in early adulthood, before our modern society corrupts them. We can protect our children up to a certain point. Then, when they are more independent, they will be tested, and only if they pass will they ascend."

Sonia and Park sit in silence, not knowing what to say.

"Detective? Special Agent? Is everything OK?"

Sonia shakes herself out of her trance. "Are you familiar with the murders in Nashville 30 years ago? The victims were also bound to a St. Andrew's cross. Mary Bronson and Gretchen Dorian? It seems to me, Reverend, you would have been attending Vanderbilt at the same time."

The doctor swallows hard. "Yes, I am aware of those murders, but I didn't know those women."

"So, it is just a coincidence that you were in Nashville and Colorado at the same time as these murders, **and** you wrote a book that describes the exact way in which they died?"

"Yes, it is a coincidence." His nervousness was evident by the way the chair, he was sitting in, was becoming more and more uncomfortable.

"Help us understand why we shouldn't bring you in, right now?" Park stood up.

"Do I need a lawyer?"

"You might if you don't start talking."

"My book was part of my graduate work. It started back

when I was a student at Vanderbilt. I remember talking to some friends and other classmates about the idea that Heaven is empty and fading, and that dying young is a gift that would guarantee ascension. I wrote my senior thesis on St. Andrew. Anyone who knew me could've used my hypothesis as some type of inspiration to kill young people. I remember just before those deaths occurred, there was this guy in my Religious Theory class that was enthralled with my hypothesis of an empty heaven, obsessed even. He was much older than most students, a non-traditional student, probably in his mid to upper 30s. He told me that he knew the two women. I remember something he said that sent a chill up my spine. One day before class started, he sat down next to me and said, *Those girls were lucky.* When I asked what he meant, he said, *They can now sit with God in heaven, whoever killed them gave them a perfect ascension, like the one you talk about.* I told him that he misunderstood what I meant, that it was a critique of our modern society, not instructions on how to get into heaven. He just laughed and then walked away. I never saw him again."

"What was his name?" Park, sitting down again, asked.

"I don't remember. Mike or Mark, or something. I didn't know him; he just took that one class with me. I think he was a law student."

Again, Park and Sonia looked at each other. Sonia asked, "Do you know a Gerald Miller?"

Reverend Nelson turned white. "Yes, but I don't understand, what does he have to do with your visit?"

"You go first, how do you know him?"

"I don't know him, know him. I mean, we aren't friends or anything like that. He visited me about 10 years ago and has written letters and emails to me ever since."

"What did he want 10 years ago?"

"I just published my book, and he wanted to know more about it. He stopped by my office and said that he agreed with what I wrote. He kept referring to himself as a *serpent*, and that he must help Christians who are worthy to ascend. Then he asked me if killing someone after they *passed their trial* was sinful or merciful? This started to creep me out, so I asked him to leave. What he said shook me. My book was being bastardized, taken out of context. He mentioned to me that he was a lawyer, and he was using his career to help find those he can save. I looked him up, and I found out that he went to law school in Nashville, at Vanderbilt University, at the same time I was there, and that he knew the girls who were murdered.

Park shut his eyes and shook his head in disgust. He thought to himself that he screwed up by not doing a better background check on Gerald Miller. If he did, he might have connected the murders in Nashville to the current ones in Norman and been on Jerry Miller's trail before Rebecca was murdered. He felt sick to his stomach.

"Why didn't you go to the authorities?" Sonia asked.

"What would I tell them? That a man likes my book?"

Park responded, "What she means is, don't you think you should've gone to the authorities after the murder of Christopher Reed? You must've thought that Mr. Miller might have had something to do with it. Not to mention your connection to the other murders."

Reverend Nelson looked down at his hands and balled them into fists. He cleared his throat and, in a whisper, said, "I was scared."

"What was that Reverend?"

"I was scared." Reverend Nelson said in a louder voice but still reserved.

"Scared of what?" Sonia jumped in.

"Well, I thought my book and the fact that Mr. Miller visited me, that I would be tied to it somehow."

"Reverend Nelson, you do realize that the murder was never solved, and you had pertinent information about it. Now 10 years later, we have three dead people."

"Yes. I feel awful about it, but I didn't know about the three people until you told me. I didn't know, and I still don't know if, Mr. Miller murdered that young man."

"You tell yourself what you need to." Sonia chided.

Park was staring at Reverend Nelson's book. He looked up from it and stared at him. "So, what you are saying is, Jerry Miller, put the three young adults from Norman through trials, and after they passed, he murdered them, so they could have the perfect ascension," Park said the last two words with air quotes, "before they were exposed to more temptations. He then bound them to an X-shaped cross to symbolize St. Andrew's sacrifice. Is that what you are saying?"

Reverend Nelson nodded. "That would be my guess that Mr. Miller used my book as an instruction manual."

"What would the trials be?" Sonia asked.

"I don't know. Some sort of temptation."

"Like sex?"

"Yes, temptations of the flesh could be a trial."

Park and Sonia stood up in unison, both knowing they got what they needed. Park handed Reverend Nelson his card. "Call me if you think of anything else, like the identity of that classmate from Vanderbilt."

"I will. I'm sorry."

Park snapped at him. "Don't tell us that. Tell the Millers and Williamses. I wouldn't leave Colorado if I were you. We will be in touch."

They walked out of his office.

CHAPTER 57

Sitting on the plane, Park was still commiserating about not doing a more in-depth look into Jerry Miller. His face was tense and pained with anguish.

"What is it, Park? What's bothering you?" Sonia asked with concern as she placed her hand on his.

"Jerry Miller went to law school in Nashville. I could've done a better job in getting his background. That might have led me to those other two murders, and Jerry Fucking Miller would have been on my radar 6 months ago. Rebecca would be alive if I just did my job."

"Stop. You had zero reasons to suspect him of anything 6 months ago. You didn't know about the other murders at that point, so where he went to school wouldn't have mattered at the time. Stop torturing yourself about every little detail that you miss. I hate to break it to you, but you aren't perfect, and you aren't a psychic. Hell, I should've immediately checked his background, but instead, I found out about where he went to school from good ole' Reverend Nelson, and I'm an FBI agent! HA!"

He smiled and relaxed. For just that moment, he felt his guilt dissipate and give him some relief from the weight of it all. They sat in silence for a while until Sonia turned to him and asked, "Do you think it was Jerry Miller who was dating Rebecca Williams?"

Park considered this and answered, "Well, that would make sense. I am not sure why Rebecca would date an older man, but I mean, it happens all the time. How does Cameron fit into all of this?"

It was Sonia's turn to contemplate. "Hmm...what happens if you don't pass the trials?"

"What?"

"Well, we have an answer to what happens if someone passes their trial, but what happens if you *don't* pass your trial."

"How does that fit into this?"

"I don't know. What if Cameron was forced or manipulated into helping Mr. Miller because he failed the trial?"

"Interesting. That would explain his behavior. But how could they have forced him? I mean, could they really have manipulated him into helping murder someone?"

"I don't know."

The rest of the trip home, Sonia and Park remained quiet but pensive. Their thoughts swirled around the new information they received. As they drove back to Park's house, Sonia looked at him and could see on his face the fear of failing again. They were close; she wanted to give him this win so badly, that she almost teared up thinking about it. Over the last week, he went from being a stranger to someone she deeply cared for. She preferred not to think about the case ending and them parting ways. She reached for his hand but pulled it back before touching it.

"Park?"

He turned to her, "Yeah?"

"What are you thinking?"

"That we don't have enough to arrest Jerry Fucking Miller, we need to place him with Rebecca on the night of her murder."

"Ok. Let's get to your house and let's look over all that we have."

"With Cameron's confession and everyone, including my Lieutenant, wanting to close this case, I don't think it matters anymore."

"We can't stop working the case. We are so close."

Park pulled into his driveway, shut off the engine, and turned towards Sonia.

"Close? How the fuck can you say that? All we have is an alias of Jerry Miller on some dating site, that we can't prove was with Rebecca Williams. Not to mention, his alias could have been concocted in my head. We have a book that is the blueprint to these murders but doesn't prove guild for anyone. We have Reverend Nelson, who is connected to the other three murders and who had contact with Mr. Miller at the same time as one of those murders. Unless you can find the weird classmate in Nashville, we have squat. Circumstantial bullshit is what we have." He slapped the steering wheel.

"Park... I didn't mean..."

"What did you mean?" Park barked.

"Hold on right there." Sonia turned her whole body towards Park. "You will not talk to me like that. Who do you think you are? I could've left this case at any time, but I convinced my superiors that I should stay. I'm putting my reputation on the line for you..."

"I didn't ask you..."

"Shut up. I put my reputation on the line because I believe in you. Do you think I sleep with every local I consult? I'm going to see this through with you. I am not going to let Cameron Anderson take the fall for this. Now stop feeling sorry for yourself. You aren't responsible for those deaths or for solving every mystery in this town. You can only do so much."

Park was speechless. Whatever he was feeling for Sonia, it multiplied in the few minutes they were sitting in the car. This is what he needed. Julie just withdrew, leaving him alone. Park required someone to slap him out of his self-indulgence.

"Are you listening to me?"

"Uh…yes ma'am."

"Good. Now let's get in the house, and I'm going to fuck the stupid out of you, and then we will nail Jerry Fucking Miller to the motherfucking wall."

DAY TWELVE

CHAPTER 58

The morning sun-drenched the living room in its warmth. Sonia sat on the couch drinking a cup of coffee, wearing only a man's large white T-shirt. In front of her, on the coffee table, was all the information that they had gathered on the murders. She was leaning back on the couch with her eyes closed, one leg stretched across the documents and her other leg bent with only her toes grasping the edge of the table. As she sipped her coffee, a memory shot through her. She placed her coffee on the table and darted towards the bedroom. She bounded into the room and shook Park awake from one of the deepest nights of sleep he has had in years.

Park slowly opened his eyes to Sonia hovering above him. She shouted at him. "Get up! We forgot about the fucking flash drive!"

"What?" Park sat up and rubbed his eyes and face, willing his body to wake up.

"The flash drive! The last victim's flash drive, the one we found in the hidden pocket."

"Fuck. Holy shit!" Park leaped out of bed, threw on a pair of jeans and a t-shirt, and ran into the living room.

"Cameron's journal distracted us. Where did you put it?"

Park had to think for a second and remembered he placed it in his home office on the desk before they flew to Colorado. He scurried to the office and returned with it in his hand like he found the last clue in a scavenger hunt.

"You probably should've brought your laptop."

Park grinned and ran back into his office, grabbed the laptop, and now held both objects over his head. He placed the laptop on top of the paperwork, pressed the power button, and waited. Sonia returned from the kitchen with a fresh cup of coffee in her hands for Park, "Here, I make it just the way you like it, black like your soul. HA!"

Park laughed, grabbed the mug, and sipped. "AHH" The computer finished booting, and he placed the flash drive into the USB port on the side of the machine. On the screen, a window popped up asking if they wanted to open the files on the F: drive. In the window, there were several folders. Each folder was titled.

Documents

Recipes

Bible Studies

Volunteer

School

Work

Jen :)

As both their eyes see the folder named *Jen :)*, they then turned and looked at each other as Park double-clicks the laptop pad.

Inside the folder was a journal and some links. The links opened the dating site, *Cross my Heart*, the same site where Rebecca Williams met Thomas Scaggs. They scrolled through Mark's profile, and then they clicked on the picture of a young blonde girl named Jennifer Sullivan. Unfortunately, it wasn't a good picture of her, her face was obscured by her hair, and it was taken from far away. As they tried to zoom in, the picture just got grainier. "I can have my people try and make sense of this," Sonia said. Park felt like she looked familiar, but couldn't place her, not without seeing a clear picture of her face. There was nothing in her profile that would help identify her.

Park moved the cursor over the document named, *My journal - Jen*. After double-clicking, the document opened to 20 pages of journal entries, all about a woman named Jen. They began to read.

Well, I think I met someone online tonight. Dating has been hard. Finding the right Christian woman has been daunting until I found the perfect Christian dating app. After about a week, Jen popped up in my matches. She was beautiful with her long blonde hair and her blue eyes...

Park and Sonia read all 20 pages. It explained their courtship. The one word that kept popping up that made them both uneasy was the word *testing*. The journal described Mr. O'Brien explaining how he felt tested by Jen. He wrote about her testing him about drinking and sex. According to the journal, Jen pushed enough for him to vehemently reject her advances, but then she would apologize and be *cool*. He disclosed being a virgin and felt like Jen made him feel good about his choices. The last entry described him buying her a copy of *Misery*, their first movie they watched together. He was preparing for their date, their last date.

"Well, it seems this Jen woman is working with Mr. Miller in some way. It is obvious that she was putting Mr. O'Brien through his trials." Park broke the silence.

"He obviously passed," Sonia answered.

"Looks like it. So, it would only make sense that all three victims were tested and passed. This Jen and Mr. Miller were the ones that tested them. Do you think Cameron was testing Rebecca Williams?"

"I don't know. What are you thinking, Park?"

"I think Cameron was saved by the church and to repay them, he had to test Rebecca or, at a minimum, help them with their project."

"So, you think the whole church is in on this?"

Park paused. He squinted and pursed his lips, moving his mouth back and forth as he thought about her question.

"No, not the whole church. I think the Pastor gets informed of these wayward souls that the church embraces and then contacts Mr. Miller, so he can use them in his mission, quest, thing."

"Lord of the Rings!! Nice. HA!" Sonia laughed, "but why would the Pastor want to hurt the Williamses by killing their daughter?"

He rebutted. "Why would Mr. Miller want to hurt his nephew? Remember, Mr. Miller and possibly the Pastor believe they were helping Anthony Miller and Rebecca Williams ascend to Heaven before they were corrupted. They don't think they were hurting anyone; they believe they were saving them."

"So, the Pastor is informed of people who are flawed from local law enforcement, maybe including your Lieutenant. The Pastor, and possibly other religious leaders in the area, then contact Jerry Miller, so he can use these unworthy souls to do his bidding. Two of these people are Cameron Anderson and this unknown woman who goes by Jen."

"Don't forget about Maria." He added.

"Right. They use a dating app to meet potential Christians worthy of a perfect ascension. They put these Christians through trials. If they pass, they murder them and then display them on a St. Andrew's cross. Is that where we are at?"

"That is what it looks like." Park agreed. "Only one thing is wrong with this. Why would these troubled people help Jerry Miller? What are we missing?"

Sonia pondered this. "Hmm. Good question."

"We need to link Jerry Fucking Miller to these murders."

"Who do you want to talk to next?"

Park scoffed. "You're the F.B.I. agent." He enunciated each letter in FBI, like Keanu Reeves in *Point Break*. "What do you think we should do next?"

"I trust your judgment Park, but if it were me, I would try and figure out how Cameron went from a great kid to a druggie, and then be helping a cult murder young men and women. I would also go talk to the Pastor, the Williamses, and Jerry Fucking Miller. Let's bring him in."

"What if we won't cooperate?"

"Well, there is one thing I have learned from being an FBI agent investigating serial killers and the like. They want to talk. They think they are smarter than us, they want the challenge."

"Well, right now, he may just be smarter than we are."

"We'll see."

CHAPTER 59

As predicted, Jerry Miller accepted the invitation to speak with Sonia and Park. He walked through the front door like royalty, smiling with his shoulders back and head held high. He was wearing an expensive suit, and overpriced leather, shiny shoes. His tie was tied with a wide knot and a pretentious dimple under the knot. He was an attractive man who looked years younger than his age.

"Good afternoon, Officers, thank you for your service!" Mr. Miller greeted the precinct, wanting all eyes on him, and he accomplished his goal. Lieutenant Gregory walked out of his office and stared at him. Jerry Miller nodded at him as he remained motionless and slack-jawed. The Lieutenant marched over to Sonia and Park.

"What the hell is he doing here?" The Lieutenant angrily whispered.

"We are interviewing him regarding the Anthony Miller case. You know, the case that is still open and has nothing to do with Rebecca Williams. Do you know Mr. Miller?"

"Everyone knows Jerry Miller. He is a well-known and respected lawyer in Oklahoma. He grew up with me in Norman. We weren't close, but we traveled in the same circles. That doesn't matter. This man shouldn't be interrogated. Cameron Anderson confessed to killing Anthony Miller, that case is closed."

"We just want to ask him questions about his nephew. Maybe it will help us solve the other three cases." Park insisted.

"Those aren't our cases."

"No, but they're mine. Since the three cases in this town are closed, I have to see if I can find any leads for the other three. Mr. Miller is a person of interest for the FBI. I need Detective Parkerson to assist me on this."

Tread lightly, Park, Mr. Miller is here to assist. At no point will you treat him like a suspect. Do you hear me?"

"Yes sir."

Park walked over to Jerry Miller and held out his hand. "Thank you, Mr. Miller, for coming in today. I know you are a busy man. Would you follow me?"

Jerry Miller made sure he showed his strength by strangling Park's hand. "Of course. Whatever I can do to help this community." He looked around the room full of staring eyes with a grin on his face.

Park and Sonia led him into a room with a two-way mirror. The Lieutenant stood on the other side of the mirror.

"What can I do for you, Detective Parkerson?" Mr. Miller leaned back in the metal chair and crossed his arms.

"Tell me about your nephew."

"Didn't we already go over this after his death? A murder in which you haven't solved yet," he said, smirking.

Park paused, trying to stay in control and not let this man manipulate him. "Well, we think we might have further information about that. We would like to ask you about that information if that is ok with you?"

"Fire away!"

Sonia pulled out *Perfect Ascension* by Reverend Daniel Nelson from her briefcase and slid it across the table towards

Jerry Miller. "Do you recognize this book?"

Jerry Miller uncrossed his arms and leaned towards the book, looked at it, pushed it away, and then returned into the defensive posture. He cleared his throat. "Never saw that book before."

"Look again, are you sure?" Park interjected.

"Yep. Positive." He insisted.

Sonia took the book back and returned it to her briefcase. "Then, can you explain why you visited Reverend Nelson in Colorado Springs?"

He uncrossed his arms and put his hands on his thighs. Leaning in, he smiled wide, showing all his teeth in almost a challenging grimace, and quietly laughed. The look on his face was of shock and amusement. He was impressed, as well as nervous, as to what Park and Sonia knew. "Well, I guess you caught me in a lie. Yes, I know that book. Looks like you two have been busy." He glanced at Sonia, and then his glare landed on Parks. Jerry's jaw was set firm. "I was a fan of the book, so I wanted to meet the author."

Park felt uneasy. He sensed that if they poked too much, they would unleash something they wouldn't be able to contain. He thought of being bound to that cross in his house. Furthermore, he thought of Julie and Mia. Sonia reached into her briefcase again and pulled out a manila folder. She opened the folder and showed Jerry Miller three pictures: two women and one man on St. Andrew's crosses, bound with rope. Mr. Miller looked at the pictures lazily, like he was browsing a Sears catalog, and then pushed them back towards Sonia. He stayed silent. His demeanor changed from a man with all the power, to one that was afraid of losing it. It was subtle, but both Sonia and Park felt the room change. Jerry Miller swallowed hard and, in a menacing, quiet voice growled, "What am I doing here?"

"Can you explain for us how you are connected to 4 different murders committed in the same way over 20 years?" Sonia pushed the picture of a young blonde woman towards him. "You knew this woman, didn't you?" Jerry didn't flinch. Then Sonia pushed the other young woman's picture towards him. "You knew this one too." Jerry stayed motionless with his palms on the table, leaning back in the chair. Sonia pushed the last picture of the young man towards him. "This man was murdered around the same time as when you visited your favorite author." Sonia slid her hand into her briefcase for a third time and pulled out a picture of Anthony Miller bound to a cross, sliding it towards him. Still no reaction. Jerry Miller didn't move a muscle. His pupils didn't move at the sight of his dead nephew. Park was now on high alert. A person with no emotional response towards death, especially the death of someone he claimed to be close to, was what Park feared the most. A sociopath and, even worse, a psychopath, were obviously the most dangerous of criminals. In that instant, he knew they had their guy. Sonia continued, "Can you explain any of this to us, Mr. Miller?"

Jerry Miller let out a maniacal laugh. His mask fell, and his transformation was almost demonic. Park envisioned him with red glowing eyes. "You two and your outlandish theories. I came here to help find my nephew's killer because *you*," He pointed his large finger at Park, "are incompetent. Maybe you are missing the bigger picture here. Did you ever consider that there are others in Norman that have the same connections? Maybe even some folks you didn't even think of considering. I have no recollection of those girls in the photos you showed me. Don't you think there would be a record of the police interviewing me if I knew them? If you want to accuse me of murder because of coincidence, good luck with that. Next time you want to talk to me, it will be with my lawyer." He stood up angrily and let himself out of the room.

Park and Sonia sat in silence for a few seconds before Sonia blurted out her patented "HA! He so did it!"

Park look at her thoughtfully and responded less confidently. "He's right, there is no record of him being interviewed. Do you think Reverend Nelson lied to us? I think he is involved, but maybe we should cast a larger net. Based on what he said, we need to look deeper into the Nashville murders."

"I couldn't agree more, but he is definitely a main suspect. That, my handsome partner, is **not** how innocent fellas respond. To your question about Reverend Nelson, I'm not sure if he lied, or he was misinformed. We need to circle back to that."

"Agreed on both points," Park replied.

Lieutenant Gregory entered the room. "Did you guys have your fun?"

"Lieutenant, we barely asked any questions. How can you deny how guilty he looks?"

"What tangible evidence do you have?"

Park looked down. "There is something bigger here, Lieutenant. We just need more time, sir."

Sonia jumped in, "Lieutenant, I have been working solely as a consultant until now. However, due to the nature of these murders and their potential ties to other murders in other states, spanning two decades. I am considering making this a matter solely for the Federal Bureau of Investigations moving forward."

"No. You can't." Park barked. Sonia patted his arm and continued.

"I would hate you to find out that your red herring, Cameron Anderson, didn't murder the Norman three. You wouldn't look very good, Lieutenant."

"Special Agent Brambilla, Cameron Anderson, is responsible for all three of the murders. I am sure of it. I have let you two play out your theories, and they have amounted to nothing but conjecture and coincidence. Although they may be compelling, this community needs to move on. You obviously can do what you want with those cold cases, but here in Norman, we are going to move on." The Lieutenant looks at Park. Park was shaking his head in disgust but kept his anger to himself. "Park, let this go. You are done with these murders. I'm ordering you to take some time off. I don't want to see you here or investigating these cases or any other cases for two weeks, or you will be suspended, do you understand?"

"Yes sir."

The Lieutenant left the room. Park slams a fist down on the table. "Fuck!"

Sonia stood up, put her hands on both his shoulders and squeezed. "Come on, let's get out of here."

Park looked up at Sonia. "He's involved."

"I know." Sonia agrees.

On the other side of the two-way mirror, the Lieutenant watches as Sonia consoles Park. He pulls out his smartphone, opens his text app, chooses a recent conversation, types, and sends the message, *It's done.*

CHAPTER 56

"What are we going to do?" Park asked as he paced around his living room.

"Well, it sounds like **we** aren't going to do anything. I will continue to work the other cases now that we have a lead. I'm going to look into the Nashville and Colorado murders some more. If I can get closer to solving those cases, that might give us more information to reopen the cases here. I'm leaving in the morning to go back to Oklahoma City."

"What the fuck am I going to do?"

"Relax? HA! Well, if I know you, you will probably drink some bourbon, stew on your couch, pace a lot, and then you are going to disregard your Lieutenant's orders and keep investigating these cases on the down-low. HA!"

Park laughed. He was awed by her. "Down low? Really?"

"Yeah, I'm hip. HA!"

"Well, I think you know me pretty well, Special Agent Brambilla." Park approached her and wrapped his arms around her, gently kissing her, before they both pulled away and just stared at each other, not saying what they each wanted to say. Shaking her head, Sonia took his hand and guided him towards the bedroom.

DAY THIRTEEN

CHAPTER 57

The next morning, Park woke up in an empty bed. He rose, put on a pair of jeans, and threw on a T-shirt. Before he entered the living room, he knew she was gone. The air was different, the energy dull. Melancholy filled into the spaces; she left a void. He sat on the couch with a cup of coffee with a splash of bourbon and stared at the files in front of him. Sipping his coffee, he savored the heat and the warmth of the bourbon in his throat.

Park picked up a folder and started to sift through it. Something was gnawing at him. *Maria Burrows. When Sonia asked her who she thought killed Rebecca, she thought of someone. Who was it? What was she doing at Cameron's house; did she plant the journal?* He grabbed a pad of paper and wrote three names on it. *Maria Burrows. Pastor Morris. The Williamses.* He then wrote a question under each name. Under Maria's name, he wrote, *How is she involved?* Under the Pastor's name, he wrote, *How is **he** involved? What's his connection to Jerry Miller?* Lastly, under the Williamses, he wrote, *What do they know about Maria? Do they know Jerry Miller or recognize him as someone Rebecca knew? Do they think Cameron did it?* After getting himself together, putting some breakfast in his stomach, and planning his first stop, Park quickly put on his jacket and bolted out the door.

After knocking on Maria Burrows' apartment door for five minutes or so with no response, he got back into his car. He didn't know where to go next. He looked at the time and saw it was just before noon. Before his Lieutenant found out that he was ignoring a direct order, Park knew he needed to get as much done today as possible. Sorting through the evidence he had, he needed a game plan for when he approached the next person he intended to revisit. Grabbing a legal pad from his front seat, Park started to write down what he still needed to find out to fill in the multiple puzzle pieces.

Is Maria working with Jerry Miller?

Is the Pastor working with Jerry Miller?

What do the Williamses know about Maria and Jerry Miller?

Did their daughter know Jerry Miller?

Did they have any issues with Maria?

Do they think Cameron did it?

Do any of them know of the book, **Perfect Ascension***?*

Does the Pastor have any connection to Nashville or Colorado?

After writing the last question, Park hurriedly took out his smartphone and typed the Pastor's name into Google. He clicked on the Church's webpage and then clicked on the About section. Jackpot. The Pastor's biography was laid out perfectly under a picture of him and his wife, smiling.

As the Pastor of the Seventh Day Adventist Church in Norman, Oklahoman, Pastor Morris provides teaching, leadership, and guidance for our community. Following a vision God gave both he and his wife Dorothy for a different life path, he became a Pastor in 1996. Moving from New York shortly after, he has served God and the Lord Jesus Christ in Norman since 2008. He and Dorothy have 3 children, John, 16; Mary, 14; and Sarah, 12.

Park grimaced. Dead end. To cover all bases, he typed in "Pastor Jim Morris and Nashville, Tennessee" into Google. He scrolled through dozens of James and Jim Morrises, but none were a Jim Morris of Norman, Oklahoma. Exiting the search, he then typed Jim Morris, Colorado Springs, Colorado. The same zero results flashed onto his screen. He blacked out his screen, tossed the phone onto the passenger seat, and let out a long sigh. Another question wormed its way to the front of his cerebral cortex. Picking up the legal pad again, He wrote, *Who is Jen?* Which triggered more questions: *Does Maria know Jen? Jerry Miller? The Pastor? The Williamses or the Millers?* Something about the name Jen bothered him, as he knows her somehow. It had some relevance to him, but like having a word on the tip of your tongue, this revelation was on the tip of his consciousness.

Park flipped the page of questions over the top of the legal pad and started to draw on the new blank sheet. He drew three circles and named them, Nashville, Colorado Springs, and Norman. Under the Nashville circle, he wrote the 2 victims' names. Under their names, he wrote Jerry Miller and Reverend Nelson with question marks next to their names. Underneath the Colorado Springs circle, he wrote the victim's name and then, again, Jerry Miller and Reverend Nelson with question marks. Pausing, he tapped the pencil on his lips, then he wrote *Perfect Ascension* under the Reverend's name. Moving to the third circle, he wrote Anthony Miller and then Jerry Miller, Cameron Anderson, and Jen with a question mark. After Rebecca's Name, he wrote Cameron Anderson, Maria Burrows, and then Jerry Miller with a question mark. Finally, under Mark O'Brien's name, he wrote Jen, and then Cameron with a question mark.

He stared at it like a work of art, trying to garner any meaning out of it. Park squinted his eyes, looking at the page, seeking the artist's message or motif. *What did it all mean?* He then wrote *Perfect Ascension* at the bottom of the page. He then wrote Pastor Jim Morris and Lieutenant Gregory, with a question mark next to each of their names. Then, Park remembered what Reverend Nelson said about another classmate of his from Vanderbilt. He wrote down *The guy from Reverend Nelson's Religious Studies class, Mike, or Mark.*

Park was tapping the pencil again on his lips when a knocking on his car window startled him. Maria Burrows was standing outside his car, looking at him inquisitively. He rolled down his window.

"Hi, Ms. Burrows."

"Are you watching me?"

"Uh… No… I went… I knocked, and you weren't home, so I was about to leave."

"Oh. What do you want?"

"Can I come inside, so we can talk?"

"I don't… I thought the case was solved, Detective. Why would…"

"I just have some follow-up questions, you know, tying up loose ends."

"Um… I don't think I can help you."

"Sure, you can, Maria." Park's tone changed from polite and patient to brisk and accusatory.

"How?"

"Just answer some of my questions, so I can fill in the gaps of these murders. I mean, your best friend was murdered, don't you want to know the whole story?" Park exited his vehicle as Maria backed away from his door. He didn't like her standing over him; he needed to be standing up for her to feel his authority.

Maria moved to the sidewalk as Park followed. "I know the entire story, Detective. Cameron Anderson was a psycho who was obsessed with Rebecca, killed her and any guy she came in contact with romantically. He killed himself because of it; how much more do you need?" She wiped a single tear from her eye. Park wasn't buying the act. He could tell the difference between crocodile tears from real tears easily.

"Sure, but there are still some," Park paused to find the right word, "*inconsistencies* that I want to figure out, so I can close this case forever and leave you alone."

"What inconsistencies?"

"Do you want to do this here?"

"Yes." Maria looked around to see if anyone else was around them. They were alone.

"Fine. What were you doing at the Anderson's the other day?"

"I... I went to get a book back that I'd let Cameron borrow."

"Was it **that** important that you bothered grieving parents? Couldn't that wait?"

"I... didn't want them to throw it away. It was significant to me. Mrs. Anderson was fine with me being there."

"What book was so significant that you couldn't just buy a new one?" Park pressed. He could see Maria shrink in front of him.

"It was just a book, but it had notes and stuff written in it, so I wanted that one back."

"What book?"

"It is called *Perfect Ascension*."

"Hmm... What's it about?"

Maria shifted her stance and looked over her shoulder to her apartment building across the street. "I gotta go, Detective." She turned and started to walk across the street.

"Before you go, have you given the book back to Jerry Miller yet?" He needed to throw a Hail Mary. Park knew he would probably be suspended, but he didn't care.

Maria stopped. She whipped around and stared through Park. She smirked as she transformed into the same demonic character Jerry Miller did at the station. Her eyes seemed to darken. He knew he pushed the right button.

"You think you're so clever, huh, Detective?"

"Sometimes."

"Well, you're not. You think you are helping the Williamses by harassing me with conjecture and your baseless theories?"

"Yes, I do."

"Well, you're not. You are hurting them and the community they belong to, with all your insane assumptions. Let it go if you know what is good for you."

"Ms. Burrows, did you just threaten a detective?"

She just smiled and shrugged, "I don't know, seems like I was just giving you advice. I need to go." She walked across the street.

Park spoke loud enough for her to hear him. "Tell Jerry I said, 'Hi.' Oh, and tell him I won't let his secret out, you know, about his love for **Man**kind." She paused briefly and then continued walking towards her apartment building.

He knew he went too far, but Park needed to push the domino so the rest of them would fall. He just hoped he wasn't one of them.

CHAPTER 61

"He knows."

"Who?"

"The Detective."

"He knows what?"

"He knows about you and your *friend*."

Silence. After about 30 seconds, Maria broke in, "Jerry?"

"I'm here. What else do they know?"

"Well, that you and I are connected. He asked me about the Reverend's book."

More silence, then, "I guess they aren't letting this go like I was told. They aren't buying the Cameron story," He paused again, then said, "Ok. We know what must be done." Jerry Miller ended the call and then texted the words, "Go."

CHAPTER 62

Sonia sat in the conference room of the FBI building in Oklahoma City. Spread out on the table in front of her were all the documents, pictures, and evidence from the Nashville and Colorado Springs murders. The Reverend was wrong. The two women did have boyfriends and the boyfriends were both interviewed and cleared with alibis, but Jerry Miller wasn't one of them. Neither Jerry Miller nor Reverend Nelson was interviewed or identified as persons of interest. The Nashville detectives had no suspects, no physical evidence, and no leads.

She walked around the table, fixing her gaze upon the collage of information, hoping something would pop. *What do we know about the victim, Christopher Reed? Did he have a connection to Jerry Miller or Reverend Nelson? What did Jerry Miller do after he visited the Reverend?* Sonia circled the table until she came across some interviews that were conducted in Colorado Springs. Christopher Reed had some really close friends, none of them understood why someone would hurt him. He was last seen at a local pub. He sometimes went there at the end of the week with his colleagues, according to witnesses. According to one of his closest friends, Christopher never drank, he always ordered a club soda with lime. He always made sure everyone got home safely. Sonia continued to read through all the transcripts, trying to find anything that screamed Jerry Fucking Miller. She read about how wonderful a man he was, how he wanted to become a Pastor to help people in need. He volunteered on the weekends and never partied, as one of his peers put it. *Where did he go after the pub?* Sonia kept reading. Just when she was about to quit for the day, Sonia came across an interview with the bartender. According to the transcript, the bartender, Ethan McMahon, a twenty-something graduate student, saw Mr. Reed in his establishment once or twice a month. He only ordered Club Soda and always drove his friends home. Ethan described Mr. Reed as the epitome of a good guy. Ethan described how he enjoyed listening to his stories, and that he could tell a great joke, always clean, never dirty. The next part is where Sonia paused. Ethan was giving an example of how Christopher refused to drink by describing how an older man tried to buy him a drink, very insistently. Christopher refused vehemently. The older guy was persistent and asked him to sit next to him. A few times it looked like the older man was trying to hit on Christopher. Finally, Mr. Reed stood up and excused himself, went over to his table of friends, and soon exited the bar. The detective asked what the older man did next and according to Ethan, he smiled, shook his head and continued to drink for a few more hours, and then left. He gave the detective a description of a thirty-something tall white man, a description that would identify most men in Colorado. Sonia knew differently: *Jerry Fucking Miller.* She gathered the files, put all of them, except the transcript of Ethan McMahon, back on her desk, and ran out of the building.

Four hours later, Sonia was sitting in a rental car in front of Ethan McMahon's house in Denver, Colorado. With the time zone difference, it was 6:45 pm. She stepped out of the car that she parked across the street and walked up to the front door and knocked. She grabbed her badge and held it up as the door opened. A man in his mid-thirties stood before her. It was definitely Ethan, based on her research of him.

"Can I help you?"

"FBI. I'm Special Agent Sonia Brambilla, can I come in and ask you some questions?"

"What's this about, it's pretty late." From inside the house, another man yelled out, "Who is it, Hun?"

Ethan yelled back, "The FBI." This made the other man join him at the door.

"Gentlemen, I am investigating a serial killer and I just flew in from Oklahoma City. I will only take a few moments of your time. Please."

The two men looked at each other and nodded in unison. They then parted, so Sonia could walk through, guiding her into their large kitchen, then motioning for her to sit down at the counter.

"Do you want something to drink? I'm making tea." The other man asked.

"A cup of tea would be lovely, thank you."

"So, what do you need, Agent Brambilla?"

"Call me Sonia."

"Ok, Sonia, what is it that we can do for you?"

Sonia pulled out a current picture of Jerry Miller and showed it to Ethan. Before a question could be asked, Ethan swallowed hard and sweat started to bead on his forehead. "You know this man, don't you?" This piqued the other man's attention as he meandered over.

"Ethan, what's wrong?"

"I know that man if that is what you were going to ask." Ethan answered, "I don't know his name, but I know him, or I knew him, kind of."

"Explain." Sonia leaned in.

He took a deep breath as the other man rubbed his back out of concern. "I met that man, around 10 years ago, at a bar, I used to work at when I was finishing graduate school. He was sitting at the bar talking my ear off about some book and his faith. At first, I was annoyed, but there was something about him that I was attracted to. He was also tipping pretty well, which always garnered my attention. As I served him about 6 or 7 drinks, I watched him tell stories to anyone that would listen. He even tried to pick up this guy, who was becoming a pastor." Ethan stopped and stared straight into Sonia's eyes, as the realization of her visit became clear to him. "You are here because that man was murdered, aren't you?"

Sonia simply nodded and allowed him to finish. Ethan was afraid now. His voice quivered.

"Well, I went back to his hotel room to, well, you know." Ethan paused as Sonia nodded again. "Well, he was pretty drunk, and he couldn't 'perform,' if you know what I mean. He got a little aggressive. He started to choke me and then started asking questions about Christopher Reed. Like, what was his name, where did he live, what he was like. I was so scared, so I told him. He was so strong that I couldn't overpower him. I thought I had to tell him what he wanted to get him off me. After he got the information, he pushed me out of the door. I went home. A couple of days later, I saw on the news that Christopher Reed was murdered." Ethan was crying. His partner was motionless, staring at him, in shock.

Sonia couldn't believe what she just heard, she swallowed, cleared her throat, and asked, "Why didn't you go to the police?"

Ethan was sobbing in his hands. His partner was now stepping away from him, not knowing what to do. "Mr. McMahon, why didn't you go to the police?" She repeated.

He wiped his eyes, took a deep breath, and replied, "Because I wasn't out yet. I... "

"I get it." Sonia interrupted. "Your family, friends, and even maybe even a girlfriend didn't know you were gay. You didn't want them to find out this way."

He just nodded as tears streamed down his face. Sonia continued. "His name is Jerry Miller." Sonia almost said *Fucking*. "He is a lawyer who lives in Norman, Oklahoma, a suburb of Oklahoma City. I came here tonight because I think he may be involved in the Christopher Reed murders, as well as four others."

Ethan was white as a ghost. His partner was now sitting in disbelief.

Sonia continued. "Is there anything else I need to know?"

Ethan shook his head, but then stopped. "There was one thing. He was talking to someone else that night, a blonde woman. She was young, like in her early twenties or late teens. It was early in the evening and, at first, I thought they were together, but she left after only 15 minutes. I think she may have dropped him off or something. I didn't remember that part, until right now."

Jen? "Mr. McMahon, did you catch a name? Did he call her by her name? Think."

Ethan was now pensive. He wanted so badly to help since he failed almost a decade ago. "I don't know, maybe I recall him saying something like, *I'll catch you later, Maddy,* or *Patty*" or something like that."

Fuck, not Jen. Alias? "Is there anything else, Ethan?" She reached over and touched his arm.

"I'm sorry. No."

"Well, thank you for your time, I am sorry to have had to come and stir up old memories, but you were extremely helpful."

Ethan stood up and grabbed Sonia's hand. "Am I in trouble?"

"No. Thank you for your hospitality. I would take a rain check on that tea, but I hope we don't need to cross paths again, me being a Serial Killer Investigator for the FBI, HA!"

Ethan gave her a fake smile and walked her out.

"I'll be in touch if I need you for anything, Mr. McMahon. Here's my card if you think of anything else." She reached out and touched him on the shoulder and then left.

CHAPTER 63

Park walked up to the Pastor's house and knocked on the door. From inside the house, he could hear Dorothy yell, "Coming!" The door opened, and she stood there dressed like she was about to attend church. "Hi, Detective, what can I do for you? I heard about that poor tortured soul, Cameron Anderson. So sad."

"Is the Pastor here?"

"No, I'm afraid not, he is at the church. He has meetings all day. I can tell him you stopped by, or you can try and talk to him down there."

Park was about to walk away but stopped and thought maybe Dorothy can shed some light on things. "Do you mind if I ask you some questions?"

"Don't mind at all. I thought those murders were solved."

"Just filling in some missing pieces; you know, being thorough."

"Of course. Fire away." She walked out onto the porch and sat in a wicker chair. Park followed suit and sat in a chair across from her. He was surprised at her cooperation.

"Do you or the Pastor know Jerry Miller?"

"Well, of course, we do. He's that big shot lawyer. The Pastor hired him to work on some legal issues for us over the years."

"Do you mind me asking what legal issues?"

"I don't mind at all, but I don't really understand any of that. Some tax stuff, church stuff; you know, normal business stuff."

"The Pastor mentioned a program in which troubled youths were taken in by the church and then some of your wealthier constituents would donate their time in helping them get back on their feet. He mentioned that Mr. Williams, Rebecca's father, helped Cameron and that is how Rebecca met him."

Dorothy put her hand over her chest. "So sad. Mr. Williams must be so torn up, I mean, being the one that introduced his daughter's killer to her. I don't know what I'd do if I were him." Park never thought of it that way. He was thinking how the Williamses must be in such pain and have so much guilt.

"Did Jerry Miller also participate in this program, even though he didn't belong to your church?"

"Oh dear, the program wasn't just created for our church, but multiple churches in the area, mainly the Baptist church that Mr. Miller belonged to, and ours. Jerry was such a giving man; he helped out many youths. Such a tragedy that his nephew died in that way. Cameron was such a disturbed soul who lost God along the way. We thought he turned the corner after his drug addiction."

"Who did Mr. Miller help; I mean, which youths or young adults did he mentor or give his services to?"

"Let me think... Oh, there was that Maria Burrows girl, Rebecca's friend. Something happened to her in college, and he helped her with some legal issues. He also supported her as she got stronger through therapy, and of course, through our Lord and Savior Jesus Christ."

Park did everything he could, not roll his eyes, but he has an official link between Maria and Jerry now. "So, part of this program is to have these young people become a part of your church?"

"Well, yes, that is a condition. I mean, we believe that to have pure penance, you must commit to the Lord. You can't redeem yourself without it. So if you want help from some powerful and connected men, you need to do some work yourself."

"What do you mean work, other than attending and participating in the Church?"

"Oh, you know, volunteer stuff. I heard that some troubled youth help with other youth, like peer support or something."

"That sounds like a wonderful program, Mrs. Morris." Again, he suppressed an eye roll.

"Call me Dorothy, dear. It is an incredible program, thank you. I don't have a lot to do with it, other than keeping some records and doing some research. Stuff to help them get better."

A thought jumped into Park's head that didn't make sense. *If Jerry Miller was involved in this program, wouldn't Rebecca know him?* "Mrs. Morris, I mean Dorothy, would Rebecca Williams and Jerry Miller have known each other?"

"Why yes, they must have. We would meet quarterly regarding Rebecca's program. But I honestly can't say, if they were ever at the same meeting, though. Bless her heart, she started this whole program because of her friend Maria. Jerry volunteered."

Park started to doubt himself. If Rebecca knew Jerry, why would she knowingly date him? Why use a dating site? He regained his focus and asked, "Could you give me all the youths in the program?"

Dorothy's body language shifted from an open and honest interviewee to more of a closed and untrusting one. She stiffened up and leaned back, crossing her arms across her large bosoms. "Mr. Parkerson, I... I think I have said too much, and I don't think I can talk to you anymore without my husband. I'm sorry."

Park knew he pushed too much, but he needed to ask one more question, hoping to get something. "I understand. Dorothy did Jerry Miller do anything that was... I don't know, ... weird or that made you question his motives?"

"Is Mr. Miller in trouble?"

Park knew he had to tread lightly here, but the cat was out of the bag, and he knew that he would be punished for coming here. "No, his name just came up in our investigation, and we want to clear his good name."

"Well, to be honest, sugar," Dorothy was lightening up again. Gossip was the drug that women like that couldn't resist. "I don't like his vibe. He took in a teenager once, she was sixteen. Her parents kicked her out of her house because she got pregnant. Mr. Miller tried to get her to keep the baby, but she got an abortion behind his back. He was pissed, but he took care of her. Since then, she has been like his assistant or something. The rumor was that she was a friend of his nephew's that he'd slept with and got pregnant, but I don't know if that's true or not."

"What was her name?" Park was standing now.

"Well, she used to go by Patty Sullivan, but when she was 18 she changed her name to Jennifer Miller, she even dyed her hair blonde."

All the blood rushed from Park's face. He struggled to

speak but forced out another question. "Where is Jennifer Miller now?"

"Hmm… I don't know. I haven't seen her in over a year or two. Huh, she used to always come around with Jerry, but come to think of it, she hasn't done that in a long time. Weird. Did something happen to her? Is that why you are here?"

Park composed himself. "No, ma'am, like I said, just filling in some gaps to help clear Mr. Miller's name. Thank you for your time."

"Well, I don't think I helped much. I will let the Pastor know you stopped by."

Park swallowed hard. He doesn't have long until the Lieutenant finds out, and then he will be suspended, if not arrested, especially after his next stop, but they would have to wait until tomorrow.

DAY FOURTEEN

CHAPTER 64

Sonia struggled to sleep in her hotel room. She knew that the case against Jerry Miller was building. All she needed is a little more, something she thought their dear author friend Reverend Nelson might provide. The next morning, Sonia revisited Reverend Nelson. "Please sit down. I wasn't expecting to hear from you so quickly since our last visit." Reverend Nelson expressed as he gestured to the same chair Sonia sat in days ago.

"Well, some information brought me back to Colorado Springs and I thought, while I was here, you and I could talk some more."

"Of course, anything to help, but I'm not sure what more I know that would help."

"Let's just see. Tell me more about the student in your Religious Studies class that was so interested in your ideas."

"As I said, he was older than me, by about twenty years. I believe he was a law student and was just auditing the class because, I don't know, he was interested in Religion."

"How did you know he was a law student?"

"He told me."

"You failed to mention that in our last meeting. What do you mean by 'he told you?'"

"I mean that during one of our conversations, not that there were many, he mentioned that he was becoming a lawyer. He wanted to change the world, and he wanted to use the law as his weapon. I remember him saying that being a lawyer, you are around many lost souls that you can help."

"I'm sorry to be curt, but where were these details a few days ago? It seems to me…"

Reverend Nelson cut her off. "Agent Brambilla, I wasn't being obtuse. Since your visit, I couldn't stop thinking about Gerald Miller, Christopher Reed, and the creepy older man. I've been racked with guilt ever since. I haven't slept in days, and during my insomnia, I started to remember conversations with that man."

"Should I feel pity, Reverend Nelson? I don't. What else do you conveniently, remember?"

Reverend Nelson's face hardened. "Nothing else except, I would occasionally see him around campus sometimes. He always had a group of students with him. That seemed weird to me for a nontraditional student. He would see me, and he would always have this smile on his face like we were friends, and we had some sort of inside joke. He creeped me out."

"Do you remember seeing Gerald Miller with him?"

"It's possible, but I can't recall, since I didn't know him back then."

"You told us that Gerald Miller knew the murder victims. We looked into it and he wasn't. Why did you think that?"

"Um… I thought he did. I mean that…"

"Reverend Nelson, you actually said that you checked and found out that he did. What are you not telling me? Who did you check with?"

Silence. Beads of sweat started to collect on his forehead. "I think we're done now." He stood up and opened the door, looking at her, willing her to leave.

"Reverend Nelson, are you in danger? I can protect you."

"I just need you to leave. There is nothing more I have to say."

Sonia stood up and faced Reverend Nelson. She scribbled something on her business card and handed it to him as she walked out the door. As he was closing the door, she turned back and stopped it with her hand. "I'm sorry I upset you. You have been very helpful, and we appreciate your cooperation. Please contact me if you think of anything else."

She walked back to her rental car, sat in the front seat, and waited.

CHAPTER 65

After a restless sleep, Park woke up later than he wanted. He checked his phone and was relieved that he didn't see any calls or texts from the Lieutenant. The absence of Sonia from his phone, though, made him a little sad. He thought of texting her, but the thought of being needy changed his mind. After eating a breakfast of bourbon and oatmeal, he started to think that maybe he needs to quit drinking. He quickly pushed that idea away and retired to his office to prepare for the day.

After preparations for his game plan were complete, Park took a breath and prepared himself for what he knew was going to be a long and treacherous day. Grabbing his jacket and keys, he stepped out of his house with the knowledge that today something needed to happen. After driving by Maria's and Jerry's again, he made his way over to Williamses. He walked up the walkway and knocked on their door. It swung open to the sight of a tired-looking Mrs. Williams.

"Good afternoon, Mrs. Williams. I am so sorry to bother you, but I just needed to ask you some questions. Can I come in?"

"Yes, of course, Detective. What is this about? Didn't Cameron kill my daughter? It's over, right?"

Park didn't want to lie to her. "Well, the evidence does suggest that, Mrs. Williams."

"'**Suggests**?' Lieutenant Gregory told us the case was closed. Cameron killed my daughter and confessed to it in his suicide letter. Didn't Cameron also confess to the other two murders?"

He was concerned about how much Mrs. Williams knew. The Lieutenant shared with them details they shouldn't have had yet. Park knew he didn't have a lot of time and wanted to jump right into his questions. "Yes, Mrs. Williams, that is all true, but there are some lingering details I wanted to clear up, so we can move on from all of this." As he said that sentence, he immediately regretted it. "I'm sorry, I didn't mean…"

Mrs. Williams held her hand up, "I know what you meant. We do need to start to move on, it just may take us a little longer than you." She directed him into the living room, he knew so well. As he sat, he saw the same opened bible on the coffee table that was there the last two times he was there. Park glanced at the open pages and noticed it was open to *Judges 11*. Mrs. Williams pushed her Bible to the center of the table and then sat down. "What can I help you with, Detective?"

He didn't know where to begin, she seemed off. "Um. First, how are you doing?"

"I'm fine, Detective. Thank you for asking, but you didn't come here to see how I was doing." Mrs. Williams tugged at her buttoned collar. She looked uncomfortable. Park knew this was a mistake, but he had no choice but to continue.

"Do you or your husband know Gerald Miller?"

Mrs. Williams adjusted herself in her chair and cleared her throat. "Yes. He is very involved in the program that Rebecca started."

"What do you know about him?"

"Well, he's a big shot lawyer here in town, probably too big for a city this size. He and my husband are, I want to avoid saying, 'friends,' but they are friendly with each other when we get together."

"Get together? What do you mean?"

"At the church during our meetings, and sometimes he will come to a barbecue or other gatherings. As I said, he got to know all of us because of our program for needy teens."

"Yes, I have heard great things about him. Did he work with Maria Burrows? I mean, did he mentor her, help her with her issues?"

"Yes, yes, he was great with her. Rebecca met Maria in college, her freshman year. One morning, Rebecca found Maria, naked and drugged out, on a bench. She came home and we took her in. That's when Rebecca thought of the program. Having a well-to-do father with connections in family law and the financial means to boot, she thought that our church could help young adults like Maria turn things around. So, she talked to John and the Pastor, and they were all for it. Word got around and other churches got involved, but mainly ours and a Baptist church across town. That's when we met Jerry. At first, John was helping Maria, but Jerry took over. He had an assistant, well, more like a ward, her name was Jen, who befriended Maria. So, Jerry volunteered to take care of Maria's legal issues and other things."

Park nodded. He could tell Mrs. Williams was uncomfortable talking to him. She couldn't stay still, her body continuously moved in her chair. He started to regret putting her through this, but he pressed on. "Tell me more about this, Jen."

"I don't know much about her, except the stories and gossip. I heard that Jerry took her in because she was pregnant. Some said it was his, but I don't know. All I know is that he seems to be a wonderful, giving man."

Park didn't like the energy she was giving off. It felt like he was watching a hostage video. The words didn't match the face or the body language. Her movements were mechanical and emotionless. He kept craving eye contact, but her eyes stayed fixated on her hands.

"Mrs. Williams, did your daughter and Jerry ever... um... spend time together?"

Mrs. Williams didn't react; she just lifted her gaze to meet Park's. "Not that I know of... he went to the meetings, but come to think of it, they were never in the same place at the same time."

"You mean they never met? They didn't know each other?"

"I don't think so. Come to think of it, that is weird."

"Weird how?"

"Jerry has been to this house, but never when Becky was home. Jerry was at the church for meetings about her program, but never when she attended." She paused and put her finger over her mouth and looked up, trying to remember. "I don't think, John, has ever talked about Jerry in the presence of Becky!"

Park could sense that this was a revelation to Mrs. Williams. "Why do you think that is?"

He watched her face contort while she was trying to make sense of it. "Knowing John, he was probably being protective of her. You know how dads of girls can be. Even though they were friendly, John knew of the rumors about him. I guess I never realized it. Jerry didn't exist to Rebecca, and yet he was one of the biggest contributors to her program. What are the odds?"

"What are the odds indeed?" Park knew this wasn't just a coincidence, even though he still couldn't see the whole picture. "I've only got a few more questions, then I will get out of your hair."

"Oh, that's OK, I don't mind. Talking about her is nice."

He returned a sad smile and continued with his questions. Knowing his time was running out, Park pressed on. "Did Rebecca ever bring up the name Thomas or Tom to you?"

She made a confused face at him before she replied, "No, not exactly, not directly, but I remember overhearing a conversation between Maria, Cameron, and Becky. I was walking past her room and, as mothers do, stopped and listened. Becky was an angel, but you never know with kids." Park just nodded in agreement, willing her to continue. "Well, it sounded like Maria was trying to convince Becky to *go for it*. Maria said something like," Mrs. Williams altered her voice in an attempt to sound more like a young woman like Maria, "*You should just go for it, Tom seems like a great guy.* I listened for another second or two and heard Cameron say something like, *What's the harm in meeting him?* " I remember smiling because it was obvious Cameron was jealous, even though he was trying to be supportive." Mrs. Williams's face morphed into sadness at the thought of her daughter's killer.

"That's all you remember, Mrs. Williams?"

"Yes. Why did you ask me about this Tom fellow?"

He knew he may have gone too far and needed to scramble, so he lied. "It was a name we found in Cameron's journal, so we were just covering all the pieces, so we can finally put closure on this."

"Oh. I understand. He was jealous of this 'Tom'."

Park needed to talk to Mr. Williams. He may be the link he needed to put away Jerry Miller. Mrs. Williams alluded to Mr. Williams possibly not trusting Jerry Miller and keeping him away from his daughter. "Where is your husband, Mrs. Williams? I would like to follow up with him as well. I want to discuss Jerry Miller with him."

Her face morphed instantly. Fear enveloped her, even though she tried to cover it up. The mere mention of Jerry Miller frightened her, Park knew he was getting close to the information he needed. "He's in his office. He should be there for a while. I should warn you, he's not much of a talker, even less since, well, you know. He can be a little curt at times. Difficult, some would say."

"I'm used to that, Mrs. Williams. Thank you for your time."

She rose from her chair and hugged him. He was taken aback by that gesture, but he leaned into it and let her. She softly spoke as her chin rested on his shoulder. "Thank you, Detective. I know how hard you were trying to help us. I just wanted you to know that I appreciate it." A tear formed in Park's eye. He released her and smiled. She walked him out. They waved at each other as he approached his car. Her eyes were transfixed on him as he drove away, giving him chills.

CHAPTER 66

"Hey Mom, I'm going out."

Julie turned towards her daughter and protested. "No, you are staying here, you know what Jacob said, we are in danger."

"I don't care what that asshole said. I'm not going to be stuck in this house any longer. I'm going out to meet Jen. She just called and wanted to grab a coffee and then a snack. I won't be home late."

"Mia. You aren't going anywhere."

"I'm not a child; I'm an adult. I don't need your permission."

"If you are living in my house, if I still do your laundry and shop for you, then you are not an adult, and you will listen to me!"

"You're a bitch! I wish you never met that loser." Mia stormed off to her room and slammed the door.

Julie was exhausted as she flopped her body onto the couch. She was frightened. Sometimes she thought to herself that she wished she never met him either, but she loved him still. Now, more than ever, she wished she wasn't alone. The responsibility of protecting her child, even though she was an adult, was overwhelming to her, but unconditional love was a drug. She dreamt of the early days when Mia was an infant. When there wasn't any arguing. Mia cried, she gave her what she needed, and then pure joy. Now, with Mia being an adult,

Julie felt like she may have failed her, that she didn't raise her right, and was too easy on her. The guilt of making her daughter a prisoner in her own home got to her. Julie rose from her rest and walked to Mia's room to make amends.

She knocked on Mia's door. "Mia, I'm coming in." As she entered, she already knew that she was gone, she could feel the cool fall air rush through the room and onto her face. Julie raced over to the open window and her heart sank. She screamed out the window, "Mia!"

CHAPTER 67

Sonia's eyes were closed, as her head rested on the car seat. A knock startled her. It was Reverend Nelson. After she met with him, she drove her car a couple of miles away and parked in a dark area off a dead-end street near the University. Noticing the street on her way to the University, due to how secluded it was, she instructed Reverend Nelson, on her business card, to meet her there in two hours. He got in.

"Well, Reverend, now that you are safely away from your obviously compromised office, what do you have to say to me?"

He took in a long breath, closed his eyes, and stared at his hands. "I have been lying to you all along."

"No shit. Continue."

"I've known Jerry Miller since college."

"So, this mystery man, the non-traditional student, was made up?"

"No. He's real. I only met him twice. Jerry told him about my ideas, and he came to me and asked me about them. A few months later, those 2 women were murdered and that's when I saw the man again, where he creeped me out."

"So, what was the first interaction like, you know, the one you seemed to have left out?"

"I don't know, he, well, he said that Jerry told him about how I was writing a thesis on the idea that Heaven is empty based on how humans behave in modern society. I explained my thesis as a call to action for all religious leaders to find a way to help humans reclaim their purity, to dedicate their lives to how God wants us to live. The Bible explains who gets to sit next to God in Heaven, based on those criteria, I don't know many who qualify. Countless Christians believe that deathbed repentance is good enough to punch your ticket to paradise, but that is erroneous. Our response must be surrendering our lives so that God can transform us into people of godly character, prepared for the glorious Kingdom of God. That is from Romans. That is what my thesis was about, my book is about. Religious leaders need to find modern ways of helping people surrender their lives to transform into a person of godly character. This man took away something different from my ideas. He wanted to help people get into heaven before they had a chance to become ungodly. He posited that dying young was a gift that could be given to Christian souls. A religious sect from the 1970s, called The Move, that he and his family belonged to, believed in being born again into sinless perfection. A new movement was started, according to him, that threw away the notion of being born again and that reimagined sinless perfection. He felt like my thesis, and eventually my book, encompassed these ideas. I dismissed him as a nut job until he came back to talk to me **after** the two women were murdered. He spooked me."

"How does Jerry fit into all of this?"

"Jerry and I met through a mutual friend. One of my friends from my hometown went to law school with him. So, we occasionally crossed paths. There was a group of us that started to hang out together, regularly. Back then, I would smoke some pot from time to time, and I would wax poetic about my thoughts around religion and world issues like people do when high. Those conversations continued long after the THC was out of our system. Jerry was the most enthralled. He explained that he was approached by someone who wanted to change the world, and he needed new members, he called them *serpents*. I remember cringing at the sound of the word, *serpents*. This man, apparently, had similar beliefs about the world as I did, so he told him about me."

"So, after the murders, what did you say to Jerry?"

"That's just it, I never saw Jerry again. After that man approached me the first time, Jerry just disappeared. I would see him here and there out in public, but we didn't hang out anymore. After the murders, I didn't see him at all. I know he graduated, but the next time I saw him was 10 years ago."

"Why do you think he came to you 10 years ago?"

"I really don't know."

"Do you remember if he had anyone with him? A young woman in her late teens, maybe?"

"No, I don't think so."

"So, what did he talk to you about?"

"He told me he read my book, that he loved it, and he has read it over and over again. He wanted to know if I wanted to change the world. He explained that ever since he became a lawyer that he has been changing the world and ensuring that Heaven wasn't empty. Two other men were his partners. I'm assuming one of them was that older, creepy man. I stopped him, knowing that he may have been connected to the murders in Nashville, and told him I preferred not to continue the conversation. Explaining how he has misunderstood my book; I did everything in my power to express that I wanted nothing to do with his perverted views."

Sonia could see the fear creep up his face. He feared Jerry. "Continue."

"He stood up and was angry, but instead of yelling at me, it was like he transformed into someone else, someone more diabolical. The persona he brought in with him was just a facade, a mask hiding his true self. He got quiet and in a soft, menacing voice said to me that he was disappointed and wished me luck in my future endeavors. Since then, Jerry has called me and occasionally asked for advice. During one of the calls, he wanted to know, he always said *hypothetically*, about how to put someone through a proper trial. Fearing for my life and the people in my life, I helped him."

"So, neither the creepy older man nor the other man contacted you?"

"One day, right before you and your partner came to visit me, A man called me and simply said, *If anyone asks you about Nashville, tell them that Jerry Miller knew the murdered girls.* I complied because they knew things about my life, and I knew I was being watched. I was scared."

"Why, I mean, I don't understand how they knew we were coming to you."

"Well, they knew, and they wanted me to point you to Jerry Miller, even though I thought it was a waste of time because you could easily have found out he didn't know them."

"Why not just have you tell us Jerry did it."

"Because maybe there is more to the story? I don't know. If I told you Jerry murdered those girls in Nashville, you would have asked more questions about how I knew, questions I couldn't answer."

"True, and once we found out that Jerry was linked to all three locations, he would be in our sights. I guess this mystery man wanted Jerry to be our prime suspect. So, the man who called you was the mystery older man?"

"That's my guess, Agent. It sounded like him."

Sonia's brain was trying to deduce how someone knew

they were headed to Colorado Springs. She went through the timeline, *Thomas Scaggs to Jerry Miller to Perfect Ascension to Colorado Springs. No one knew about our discovery of the book.*

"Agent?"

"Oh, sorry. Why did Jerry want your help?"

"I think weirdly, he worshiped me because of my book, or maybe they all worshiped me." Reverend Nelson slowly turned his head towards Sonia, wide-eyed. "I think I may be responsible for a cult."

"You can't remember the name of the older man? Or the other guy?"

"No, that wasn't a lie, I know I was told it, but all I remember is that it started with an M."

"Do you know of any other murders? The FBI looked into other murders with the same victim profile, and unfortunately, the data wasn't helpful. There were too many other factors. There were a few that didn't have any specific motive known, but there is no way of knowing if they are connected. We looked at any murder within an area around Nashville, Colorado Springs, and Oklahoma City, and everywhere in between. There are a few we are looking into that weren't solved, but they don't fit perfectly into the pattern or timeline."

"You are looking at this the wrong way, Agent Brambilla."

"What do you mean?"

"To have a perfect ascension, you must be pure of heart **and** pass a trial."

"Yes, I get that. So, what am I missing?"

"How many young adults do you think pass the trials?"

Sonia was stone-faced. All at once, she realized she was

barking up the wrong tree, that her research has been skewed in the wrong direction. "So, what does that mean? What should we be looking for?"

"What do you think happens to those who don't pass the trials?"

"I guess they don't get a life of luxury?"

"No. If you don't pass the trials, then you must suffer the consequences. You are destroyed. Everything you were living for is destroyed. These young adults are framed for crimes, drug usage, and other acts so that they have to be dependent on powerful men like Jerry Miller. Based on my phone conversations with Jerry, trials started as just a few questions and maybe some temptations. After my consultation, they started to test them over days and sometimes weeks to ensure that every weakness is exposed and tested. So, Agent, you shouldn't be looking for murders, you should be searching for young people who out of the blue, for no comprehensible reason, threw their lives away because of sex, drugs, and other deadly sins."

"Cameron."

"Who?"

"Nothing. Continue. Tell me, how do they pick the young adults they want to put through the trials?"

"I'm not quite sure, since I have never consulted on that. I would guess, they observe young people in the community. At church, at college, and other places that would show the character of someone."

"A dating app, maybe?"

"I guess that would work, actually that is a brilliant method if you think about it. You could have access to thousands of potential young people without leaving the comfort of your own home. Did you find something pointing to them using dating sites?

"We're uncertain if it is wide-scale usage or just a one-time thing. So, they watch them, decide if they are worthy of the trial, and then if they pass the trial, they murder them and put them on a St. Andrew's cross for all the world to see. If they don't pass the trial, their lives are ruined, and they have to start over as a punishment for failing. Is that right?"

"That's how I understand it."

"So how do you know your office is compromised?"

"Simple. Jerry likes to drop little details of my life during our phone conversations that he would only know if I was being watched, bugged, or videotaped. I haven't looked because I'm afraid of the consequences."

"Well, Jerry seems like a guy who wants people to know how powerful he is."

"Yep."

"We have a theory that some of these young men and women who have failed the trials are recruited to help the cause. What do you know about that?"

"I don't, but that makes sense. A man in his fifties watching college students would be noticed. Also, these kids have no choice but to help, they are powerless. I never really thought about it. How many of these kids are out there?"

Sonia couldn't fathom how many lives Jerry Miller and his cult have ruined. She was sick. *Who was the older man? Who was the other man? Was there more?*

Reverend Nelson interrupted the awkward silence. "Agent, I have to go. I know I'm in trouble, but I'm also in danger, no one can know I talked to you. There are people I love here that Jerry won't hesitate to kill."

"If this information helps me end this, I will make sure they are lenient on you. Meanwhile, I wouldn't go anywhere."

"I couldn't go, even if I wanted to."

"Right. Hey, do you have a picture of you and your gang? Do you think the other guy was part of that group?"

"I never even thought of that. I mean, I really don't know where any of those other guys are now. I didn't know them well. They were mostly Jerry's friends. I think I have a picture, in a box at my house, of us during some party we went to. I will email it to you and send you the names of everyone that I can remember."

"Wonderful. Be careful."

Reverend Nelson left the car and disappeared into the afternoon shadows. Sonia sat in the heaviness of what was just learned. She now feared that this was much bigger than she even thought. She started her car and made her way to the airport for her return flight.

CHAPTER 68

"Hello, what's wrong?" Park answered his phone, sensing something was off.

"Jacob. Mia's gone." Park turned white.

"What do you mean? Where?" Julie was crying and didn't answer.

"Julie! Where is Mia?" Park shouted frantically.

"She... She... snuck out of her window."

Park relaxed. "So, she is OK?"

"I don't know. You told me…"

"I know what I told you, but she just snuck out of the house. Do you want me to come over or look for her?"

"No, I'm sure you are busy, I'm in my car now, I think I know where she is going."

"Ok. Just calm down. She will be OK. Hey. I'm getting another call. I'll call you back in a bit. After I do one little errand, I'll find you, OK?"

"Ok. Thank you, Jacob." She ended the call.

"Hey, you," Park answered his other call.

"Hey, I just got off my return flight and I have to fill you in on what I have found out."

"Me too. I have had a day. So, tell me about what you found out."

For the next 10 minutes or so, Sonia explained how she found the interview while searching through the Christopher Reed case, her flight to Colorado Springs, and her conversation with Ethan McMahon. After she and Park discussed that for a while, she then described her visit to Reverend Nelson and the disturbing information he was withholding. They processed this information for another 10 minutes or so.

"Wow. Do you think we have enough for a search warrant?"

"I do. I will file for one, first thing in the morning. We can search his house and his office and hopefully, we will find something to charge him."

"Let's hope so."

"So, Parky, what happened to you?"

"It started with talking to Maria. Let's just say that after we charge Jerry Fucking Miller, we need to bring in Maria Fucking Burrows. She unfortunately may be one of the casualties of failing a trial, but she still needs to answer for her involvement in the death of her friend. After I was threatened, and I turned the tables and told her I know Jerry has a boyfriend, I decided to pay a visit to the Pastor, but ended up talking to his wife." Park described the interaction and the information about Jen.

"So, this Jen character is the girl who hung around Anthony Miller? Patricia Sullivan? Oh shit, I think she was with Jerry in Colorado, the bartender remembered a girl in her late teens with him. He thought her name was Maddy or Patty."

"So, she must have changed her name shortly after that."

"How did Jerry take this girl in without Anthony and his parents not knowing?"

"That's still a mystery we need to figure out. Maybe she is the one who put Anthony through the trials? We know Cameron was involved, so he could have helped as well."

"Fuck, Park. I think you are right. I mean, getting pregnant and then having an abortion, must be an easy failure of the trials. She was dependent on Jerry Miller; it makes so much sense. She would be a perfect person to tempt Anthony due to their history. What else did you learn today?"

"I went to visit the Williamses. Only Mrs. Williams was home. She was acting weird. I think Jerry Miller scares her. Just mentioning him made her squirm."

"Why do you think she was being weird?"

"Well, she just looked different, not mournful or sorrowful, but nervous. Also, it might not be anything, but she always closed her Bible the two times I visited before. This time, it felt purposeful that she left it open. I don't know, I'm being paranoid."

"Reverend Nelson was sure his office was compromised. Do you think the Williamses are compromised as well?"

"That could explain it, I mean, she was cautious on how she was talking about Jerry Miller. Wouldn't that mean they know who killed their daughter?"

"Not necessarily, but if their house was being surveilled by Jerry or one of his cronies, and they knew about it, it is likely they know something they shouldn't. Maybe Mrs. Williams stumbled on a camera or a bug, like at your house. We also could be just reading this wrong."

"Well, if the Williamses know that Jerry Miller is responsible for their daughter's murder, they are in danger."

"What chapter was the Bible opened to?"

"Why?"

"I'm just curious. Mrs. Williams may be reading a passage that would tip us off to her thinking."

"Judges, I think. Chapter 11. Is that how you say it?" Park laughed at his ignorance.

Sonia returned a laugh. "Yes. I think so. So, what else did she have to say?"

"She just validated everything the Pastor's wife said, except she told me that even though Jerry was around, sometimes, even at their house, Rebecca and he never met, never interacted."

"Odd. Or did Jerry do that deliberately so that he could put her through the trials?"

"That's what I thought. I'm in front of Mr. William's office right now to see if he can shed some light on this."

"Ok. Be careful, if their house is being watched, his office might be as well. I'm just getting into my car at the airport. I will be in Norman tomorrow afternoon. If I get any more information, I'll call."

"Sounds good. I don't have much time left before the Lieutenant finds out about my day, so I may be unavailable really soon. I'll keep you in touch as well."

Park ended the call. He took a deep breath and exited his car.

CHAPTER 69

She's with me.

Jerry Miller responded to the text with, *Ok. Is everything ready?*

Jen replied. *Yes. We are in the park.*

Excellent. I will text you with more instructions.

CHAPTER 70

Sonia was sitting in her car about to drive back to her place in Oklahoma City when she decided to google *Judges Chapter 11*. She clicked on the first link and read the Chapter. "Holy Shit!" She exclaimed. She went to call Park, but he didn't answer. She put her phone down, started her car, and sped away towards Norman, Oklahoma. A torturous 30 minutes until she could be in Norman. She feared that would be too late. After 3 more attempts, she stopped trying to call him and just sped along the highway.

CHAPTER 71

Park stood outside of Mr. Williams's office, giving Julie a call before he came in. The call went to voicemail. "Hey, just checking in, call me when you get this." As he was leaving the message, he heard a double beep in his ear, indicating a phone call was coming in. He takes the phone from his ear and looks at the screen to see who the caller was. "Fuck! The Lieutenant." Park said aloud to himself. He sent the call to voicemail, turned off his ringer, and started to walk towards the office building.

Mr. Williams's office was on the second floor of the building. As he walked into the front entrance, the bell sound resonated throughout the building. Park checked the directory in the lobby of the building. Park saw *John Williams, Esq. 201.* He walked up the flight of stairs to his right and found the office. As he entered the office, it comprised a waiting area with a reception desk that was unoccupied due to the lateness of the day. Behind that desk was the door leading to Mr. Williams's office. It was early evening, so the waiting room was dark. Park could see light coming from the bottom of the door. He knocked.

"Come in."

Park pushed the door open. "Hi, Mr. Williams, it's Detective Parkerson."

"Yes. Hello. I've been expecting you. My wife phoned me to let me know you were coming. So, what is so important that you needed to bother my grieving wife, Detective?"

This will not go well. "I'm sorry to bother both of you, I'm just trying to wrap up some loose ends."

"'Loose ends?' The Lieutenant has assured me that this case should have no loose ends. That boy killed my daughter. Can't we mourn in peace, Detective?"

"Yes. Of course." Park looked around the room, and it looked like every Lawyer's office he has ever been in. The expensive dark wood desk, with a high back leather chair. Behind him were bookcases full of lawbooks. His framed degrees were on the wall to Park's left. Mr. Williams sat in his chair, elbows on the armrest, with his hands steepled and his mouth resting on them. His head tilted down, but his eyes looked straight ahead. This is what Park liked to call, the Attorney Pose. Usually, they would be bobbing their head up and down, but maintaining the steeple. Mr. Williams just stared. Park continued. "I'm so sorry, yes, Cameron Anderson seems to be the killer. We still would like to follow up on some other leads, so we can have complete closure."

"*Seems* to be the killer? Detective, why is it that the leader of your department has assured me that this case is closed, and we can start to move on, but you are continuing to stir things up? I lost my only child, my daughter..." Mr. Williams paused and turned his teary eyes away from Park. "Why are you here?"

"Tell me about Jerry Miller." Invoking this name didn't seem to bother Mr. Williams. Park assumed that he was tipped off by his wife.

"Well-respected lawyer, philanthropist, deeply religious, and an overall decent human being who cares about his community."

"Do you know him well?"

"I know him well enough. He volunteered for Rebecca's program, and he's been over to my house for barbecues and the occasional football game."

"What do you know about the girl he took in?"

"You mean Jennifer?" That was the first time, Park realized, that someone called her Jennifer.

"Yes."

"I don't know, according to Jerry, she knew his nephew, she got into some trouble, her parents were pieces of shit, so he stepped in and probably saved her life. She's like a daughter to him."

"Did you find their relationship odd?"

"What are you implying, Detective Parkerson? Was he abusing her? Using her for his sexual gratification? Wow, do you really think that all of us religious types must be some repressed sexual predators? Is that what your liberal media is telling you?"

"I didn't go there; you did, sir."

"Ah, the ol' detective tricks. Ask a leading question and see where the interviewee goes with it. Touché. Well, you got me. I guess, at first, that crossed my mind too. But, if you saw them together, you would have seen a loving man, trying to be a father figure for a broken and lost girl."

"So why didn't you ever let him be around your daughter?"

Mr. Williams steepled his hands again and spoke softly. "I don't want you to speak about my daughter."

"Mr. Williams, your wife told me that Jerry was never around your daughter, I'm sorry I am upsetting you, but that seems odd to me."

"Is it possible Detective, that my daughter was a busy woman, that maybe it was just coincidence?"

"That doesn't sound like an answer, that sounds more like lawyer-speak. Were you worried about Jerry Miller? Does he have something on you?"

Mr. Williams let out a loud belly laugh and stood up and walked around to the other side of his desk. He sat on the edge and leaned towards Park. Mr. William's big frame made Park seem small, and that is exactly what he wanted Park to feel like. "Detective, no man or woman could ever intimidate me or *have something on me*." He made air quotes. "Jerry Miller knew about his reputation due to Jen. We decided that we didn't want to tarnish her reputation by having her around him. Not everything is a conspiracy, Detective. Your obsession with my daughter is what concerns me, not Jerry Miller."

"But if you wanted to avoid tarnishing her reputation," it was Park's turn to use air quotes, "why have him be a part of her program at all?"

"Are you a religious man?"

"No."

"So, you don't know what it is like to devote your life to being a Christian, do you?"

He wasn't looking for an answer, so Park stayed quiet and let him speak.

"No. No, you don't. We don't cancel people in our world, Detective. We don't destroy their reputations because of innuendo or rumors. But Jerry knew what he could do to Becky in the real world, just by being in the same room as her. He made sure that any interaction with our church or any of us didn't involve Becky." He paused to wipe the tears that were welling up in his eyes.

"You didn't care about your reputation?"

"I'm a lawyer, if my reputation was ruined by the company I kept, I wouldn't be allowed in my church."

Park smiled at that comment.

"You see, Detective, our church is a community, a family. We don't toss aside lost souls; we help them find their way. Any time you would like to join us, I would be the first one in line to greet you. You seem like someone who needs a map."

"I'll pass, but thanks for the invite." Park's phone buzzed in his pocket. He ignored it. The Lieutenant could wait. "Do you think Cameron killed your daughter?"

Mr. Williams stood straight up, and a deep redness crept up his face. His eyes narrowed. "Be careful Detective."

"I'm just curious how a smart lawyer, like yourself, could misjudge that situation and allow a killer around your daughter." Park knew what he had just done and was prepared for what was about to come next. He needed to push to see if Mr. Williams had been playing him the whole time about Jerry Miller or was, he covering for him. If Jerry Miller did have something on him, an emotional Mr. Williams might forget.

As Park predicted, Mr. Williams lost control. He reached and grabbed Park by his coat and lifted him off the chair and pulled him in close to his face. Park grabbed his wrists, but no matter how much defensive training he had, he was at the mercy of Mr. Williams. He was much stronger than Park. Mr. William's face was red and contorted. His anguish and guilt came roaring out as he yelled at Park. "You little shit, who do you think you are talking to? Do you think there is a day that goes by that I don't blame myself for Becky's death?" He threw Park back down in the chair. He turned and walked back around the desk while he slicked back his hair with his hand. As he straightened his clothing, he slowly sat down and took a deep breath, composing himself. "I think we are done here, Detective. If you came here to push my buttons, well, congrats, you achieved your goal. I hope you got the answers you were looking for."

"Mr. Williams, that wasn't my intention. To be honest, Cameron being the killer seems too convenient, too clean." Park's phone buzzed. "I don't think Cameron killed your daughter at all." Buzz. Buzz. Buzz. "He might have been involved, but he didn't kill her by herself. He loved your daughter." Buzz. Buzz. Buzz. Park reached into his pocket and turned off the phone. He knew the Lieutenant was probably on his way. "I think Jerry Miller, with help from his little assistant Jen, or should I say Patricia Sullivan, and Maria Burrows, murdered your daughter and put her on a cross." Mr. William's face slowly transformed from red and angry to pensive. "I also think you may have deduced this yourself but are you afraid of Jerry Miller." Park awaited his response. A smirk came across Mr. William's face. He stayed quiet. Park needed to leave; he did what he came to do. He put things in motion. To what conclusion, Park didn't know. He stood up and made eye contact with Mr. Williams. "If I am right, you know how to get in touch with me, and we can figure out how to bring down Jerry Fucking Miller." He turned around and started walking out. Taking his phone out of his pocket, he saw that Sonia tried to call him multiple times. He put his phone to his ear to listen to the voicemail message she left for him. He then looked at a picture that was sent to him. Frozen, he just stared at his phone.

"Is there something wrong, Detective?" Mr. Williams rose out of his chair, sensing the shift in his behavior. Park slowly turned and looked around the room, saw what he missed the first time, and then slowly turned to face Mr. Williams. The sound of the entrance door chime filled the air. *Somebody was coming.* Park had bigger concerns; he was staring at Mr. Williams pointing a gun at him. Park already had his hand on his gun, but before he could do anything, Mr. Williams spoke. "Ah Ah Ah, ...let's see your hands." Park showed his hands. Behind him, someone was standing in the doorway. *Jerry Fucking Miller,* Park thought.

Park watched Mr. William's eyes move to meet their guest's. Mr. Williams greeted him, "Well, Hello, Lieutenant Gregory."

CHAPTER 72

During her panicked drive, Sonia received a notification of an email from Reverend Nelson. Although she was driving at speeds of nearly 90 miles per hour, she picked her phone up, opened the message, and read it.

So, I found this picture of the group of us that hung out together. Jerry is there, next to him is one of his friends, Sean, and the person he has his arm around is John. The man in the Yankees cap is Darren. I don't know last names. This is the best I can do. If I find anything else, I will send it to you. Good luck.

Reverend Daniel Nelson

Sonia opened the picture and yelled, "Shit! Fuck!" She then dropped her phone on the floor between her feet. Her car swerved back and forth, as she struggled to reach it and keep her eyes on the road. She grabbed the phone and expanded the picture, so she could make sure it was who she thought it was in the picture. As she zoomed in, there was no doubt that she recognized all three men. Lieutenant Sean Gregory sitting next to Jerry Fucking Miller who has his arm wrapped around John Williams. She immediately tried to call Park. Nothing. She tried 9 more times. Finally, giving up trying to call him, she left a voice message.

Park! Answer your phone! The passage from the bible was about a father who sacrifices his daughter to God! Mrs. Williams wasn't scared about Jerry Miller, she feared Mr. Williams! Also, John Williams went to school with Jerry Miller at Vanderbilt! He's part of this! The Lieutenant is also in the picture I sent; he was going to Vanderbilt at the same time! They all knew each other! You are in DANGER! Get out of his office! I'm on my WAY!

She forwarded the picture. Fear consumed her.

CHAPTER 73

"What a nice surprise, Lieutenant. You got here at the perfect time. This man tried to break into my office, so I had to shoot him. He's dead."

"John! Put down the gun. You don't have to do this." The Lieutenant pleaded with John Williams.

"So, Detective, what tipped you off?" Park's eyes moved towards the wall to his left. Mr. Williams looked and shook his head. Laughing, he replied to his own question, "I knew I should've taken down my diploma from Vanderbilt after I was told that you were nosing around the Nashville murders. I never thought you would visit me here."

Park didn't want to tell him the other evidence he had on his phone, so he remained quiet.

"So, I'm sure you have numerous questions, but this isn't a stupid movie, book, or TV show in which the bad guy confesses all his secrets before he kills the hero. You can die not knowing everything. You know, the funny thing is, by you coming here, you have given us an easy way out. I can kill you and it will be self-defense. 'A rogue detective, against his Lieutenant's orders,'" Mr. Williams waved the gun in the Lieutenant's direction, "tried to break into my office. Startled and scared, I pulled my gun out from under my desk and shot the intruder. I won't be charged with anything. Here in Oklahoma, I will be a hero. The sad thing is, we had this other elaborate plan where you would be convinced to stop investigating. I'm not sure what we are going to do with Mia now. You were going to find her tied to a cross in the park." Park's face shrunk, and he was about to speak when Mr. Williams stopped him. "Calm down, she was going to be alive. She would have been naked and tied to a cross, but she would have been alive. Spoiler alert, she didn't pass the trials. See, you were going to have a choice. Either you dropped the case and let Cameron take the fall and everyone goes home the same, or you didn't drop the case and poor Mia would have had her life ruined by a horrible addiction to some drug, and she would have been arrested. The difference is, we wouldn't be there to help her repent and get on the right path. Her life would have stayed ruined. In the extreme situation, we would have killed her, so you would know how dangerous we are."

Park now realized that Mia's friend was the Jen they were looking for, that she was right in front of him at Julie's house. He was fuming, but pushed it down and stayed still and quiet, waiting for a moment to act.

"John, stop, you aren't going to kill him. I won't allow it!" The Lieutenant barked.

"Oh, yes you will, or you know what will happen! You just couldn't be a team player, back then, could ya?" The Lieutenant stayed quiet. "So now I get to kill you, Detective, and Mia can be let go. I don't think Jen has done anything to her yet. After I kill you, I just have to text Jen to stop."

Park didn't know what to do. He couldn't move, he thought that his death may be the right thing to do. It would save Mia. He wanted to try to reason with this man first. "John. If you are part of this, then you either allowed your daughter to be murdered, or you helped her be murdered. Why do you care what happens next? Didn't you achieve what you needed to?"

"You think that was easy? I did it for her, she is saved because of what we did. My selfishness of wanting her alive can't get in the way of our purpose."

"What is your purpose, exactly?"

"We need to save… You did it again, you're clever. Hey Sean, I know why you like this one. Enough talking, it's time to go."

John Williams walked around the desk and settled in front of it, only about 5 feet away from Park. He raised the gun and pointed at Park's chest. The boom of the gun was deafening. Park fell to the ground. His head was ringing, but he was alive. Checking his body with his hands and finding no wound, no blood, he stood up and saw John Williams bent backward over his desk, his arms limp by his sides. The gun was on the floor. His instincts made him kick it away. As he got closer to the lifeless body, he could see the gunshot wound in the middle of John Williams's forehead. Park looked back towards the Lieutenant, he was still in a shooting position, with a tiny amount of smoke coming from the nozzle of his Glock 19. Park pulled his own Glock out and pointed it at the Lieutenant.

"Lieutenant. Sean. Please lower your weapon."

He blinked his eyes rapidly, and he was murmuring something under his breath.

"What are you saying, Lieutenant?

"My girls are in danger." He holstered his gun. "My girls are in danger, Park!"

"Ok. Ok. Explain."

"Maria Burrows visited my house one night. It was right after Rebecca was killed. She sat on my couch and showed me pictures of my daughters in college, doing college stuff. She then showed a picture of them sleeping. I tried to act all cop-like, but they are my girls, Park. So, I listened. She said that all I had to do was allow the case to follow its natural conclusion. She said that I needed to control you and not let anyone else interfere. Every time you guys made a discovery; I would get another picture." He paused, closed his eyes, and then covered his mouth with his hand. "She sent me a picture of my girls engaging in sexual acts. They have access to them; they might be manipulating them. So, that is why I have been trying to slow you two down. When you called Jerry in to question him, one of my daughters called me and told me that she was arrested for possession of marijuana. She insisted that she didn't do it, that they were hanging around some new kids, and they may have put it in her jacket. I made it go away, but I had no choice but to force you to take time off. I knew you wouldn't listen, so I followed you around today. When you were parked in front of John's office, I knew I had to tell you the truth. You didn't answer, so I knew I had to come in."

"So, when you showed up at my house after they tied me to a cross, that wasn't a coincidence, was it?"

"No. I brought the note. They told me what they did and told me to let you down. A text came later saying, ``*Imagine your daughter up there.*'"

"I don't understand. Why did they threaten you in the first place?"

"That's a long story, and we don't have time. The short version is that after Anthony Miller, I put two and two together and visited Jerry and John and questioned them about it."

"So, you knew back then?"

"Yes. I couldn't tell you. You have to believe me. I know that case wrecked you."

"I lost Julie."

"I know."

"What's your plan, Sean?"

"We can't have Jerry know that John's dead just yet; he

still has access to my girls and Mia."

"What are you going to do then?"

"I'm going to call my girls and have them go stay at my mother's"

"What if they are followed?"

"I'll take care of that."

"What about Mia? They have her."

"Yes, but they aren't going to do anything yet. Go get his phone."

Park knew what he was thinking and hurried over to the corpse, once called John Williams, and found his phone in his inside suit pocket. He turned it on, and it asked for a passcode or a fingerprint. As he was pressing John William's dead thumb on the screen, the realization of how sick and twisted these men overwhelmed him. The phone was now opened and ready to be used. He brought it over to the Lieutenant and handed it to him.

"Ok, we need to text that Jen girl and tell her you're dead and to let Mia go home. Then, we will text Jerry and have him meet John somewhere, that is where we will arrest him."

"Sean? Why didn't you have your daughters just leave after Maria visited you?"

"Because, Park, I thought I could find a way to stop them without disrupting my daughters' lives, plus I didn't want them to put them at risk by having them leave. I have no choice now."

Park could see the fear in his face. "I'm sorry I doubted you."

"I would've doubted me too; part of me was glad you were ignoring my orders. I was hoping you would find a way out of this. I'll be honest: you and the FBI agent make a great team; you were able to learn so much about things that were hidden for decades. You were underestimated."

"I have a feeling there is still a lot I don't know or understand."

The Lieutenant didn't say anything. He looked down at the phone and started to push some buttons. "Weird. There are no messages to anyone in here, not even his wife."

"Have you scrolled through his contacts? He might just delete everything."

"Hold on. I found her. Jennifer Miller."

Sean typed the message, *Our problem has been taken care of. Change of plans. No need to continue.*

Park nodded and Sean sent the message. They both watched the phone, waiting for those three little dots to show up. Jennifer Miller responded.

Understood.

"Ok. I need to call my daughters. You go find Julie and make sure Mia gets home. I will take care of Johnny here. I will text Jerry after I am sure my daughters are on their way to safety. Make sure you keep your phone on, I will text you the location where we will meet Jerry."

"Ok. Lieutenant. Thank you."

"For what?"

"Saving my life."

"I shouldn't have put you in this position in the first place. Now go!"

Park left the building and got into his car and drove towards Julie's house.

CHAPTER 74

Jerry Miller was sitting in his library chair reading *Perfect Ascension* when his phone buzzed on the table next to him. He placed a bookmark into the pages and placed it down. He picked up his phone, opened the screen, and then read the communication from Jen on the secure network.

John has been compromised. He contacted me through the regular text app. What do you want me to do?

Jerry shook his head and whispered to himself, "He was always the weak one." He then replied.

Change of plans. Hold on to Mia. I'm sending us someone else to play with. I'll meet you at Rebecca's spot.

Jerry stood up, slicked back his hair, and prepared for a long evening. Making his way downstairs, he yelled out to his companion, who was watching TV in the living room, "I have to go out."

As he walked out of his house, a text buzzed his phone. It was from John on the regular text app. He smiled, knowing it wasn't John. John would only use that form of communication for BBQ invites or talking football. He read the text.

Hey, we need to meet up. We have a problem. Don't want to say anymore over the phone. Meet me at the church.

Jerry nodded, laughed, and said out loud to himself, "Impressive." He then responded.

Sounds important. The church may be compromised. Meet

me where your daughter ascended.

He waited patiently for the response. He figured it was the annoying pest of a Detective. Finally, he saw the three dots appear.

Ok. See you soon.

He then texted Maria over the secure network and gave her instructions.

Jerry then typed in the Lieutenant's name to text and then paused. He was unsure of his loyalty. He wondered if he may be helping the detective even if his daughters may be in danger. You can't stop cops from being cops, he thought. Either way, Jerry wanted him there. The Lieutenant didn't have access to the secure network, so Jerry used the normal texting app against his better judgment. Even though Jerry instructed him not to text details, he was always worried about this method of communication. At this point, he didn't care anymore. He typed and sent,

May need you tonight, meet me at Rebecca's crucifixion.

He waited. Seconds later, a response entered the screen.

What's up? Hope everything is ok. I'll be there shortly.

Jerry laughed excitedly out loud as he walked towards his car. He had a few more people to contact.

CHAPTER 75

Sonia raced south on I-35. Tears filled her eyes. In all her years working at the FBI, she had never felt so scared. Seeing the picture of Jerry Miller, The Lieutenant, and John Williams filled her with dread. Her experience, training, and education set off alarms in her head that they are dealing with a very dangerous cult. She kept thinking about what Reverend Nelson said about not looking at the murders, but at the lives ruined. The mystery older man also haunted her thoughts as the obvious cult leader. *Are we just touching the surface of this thing?* Thirty years is a long time to be an active cult, she thought, is Norman just one location of many? The multiple questions swirled around her brain, distracting her, as she accelerated, again, to over 90 mph.

"Come on, Park, answer your fucking phone!" She screamed as she pounded her steering wheel. She impatiently yelled at her car to call Park again. The car speakers spread the sound of a phone ringing throughout the call. As she was nervously willing the phone to be picked up, she heard two beeps. She looked at her car's display screen to see it was an unknown number. She pressed the green accept button.

"Agent Brambilla."

"Hello, Agent."

Jerry Fucking Miller. "How did you get this number?"

"Reverend Nelson was very helpful, he needed some… motivation, but he helped me get your number. Don't worry, he wasn't hurt, not physically that is." Jerry Miller chortled at his little joke.

"What do you want, Mr. Miller?"

"Oh, well, if you want to save your little detective friend, you will meet me at Lake Thunderbird State Park where Rebecca ascended."

Ascended. The delusional thoughts of a madman. "What do you mean, save?"

"Ah, well, soon he will be on his way here. If he gets here before you, then he has to die. This has gotten out of hand and unfortunately, unless he can be convinced to finally let this go, I will have to kill him. I need you here to convince him. How far out are you?"

"You crazy motherfucker. I will…"

He arrogantly interrupted. "OH, agent, do you think your insult-laden diatribe will change what I'm doing? Don't you realize that only people without the power yell empty threats and profanity? You are better than that. Plus, I've been called names all of my life, and you kind of get used to it; you stop reacting emotionally. I'm sure you have been trained to keep your emotions in check. So, what this tells me is that you love your detective friend, and your training goes right out the window when you throw romance in the air. How adorable. Now, just come and do not talk to him, ignore his calls, or he dies. Oh, and don't call your FBI friends or any law enforcement agency, I'll know if you do, and then he dies. How far out are you?"

"20 minutes."

"Perfect."

The call ended.

She lied. Lake Thunderbird Park was only 10 minutes away. Hoping for the ability to surprise him, Sonia pressed on the gas.

CHAPTER 76

After talking to Julie on the phone, he raced over to her house. She was home waiting for Mia to come home. Park raced up to her door and pounded on her door. Julie whipped the door open and let him in.

"Park, what is going on? You sounded concerned on the phone."

"Sit down."

"Park, what is it? Please tell me."

Park placed both his hands on her shoulders and guided her to her couch. She sat as he did next to her.

"Listen. I think Mia will be fine, but she is in danger. Her friend Jen is part of, well, … a cult and they are using her to get to me."

Tears streamed down Julie's terror-filled face. "Park, you have to…"

"We have a plan and Mia should be fine. Now I have to wait for a phone call, and then I will know everything is fine. Ok? Trust me."

"Ok… Ok." She fell into Park's arms, and he held her shaking body. The guilt he felt was churning his stomach. He so wanted a drink right then. They fell back into the couch and both of them closed their eyes out of exhaustion. After a few minutes of them embracing, Park's phone buzzed. They both jumped up into a sitting position. They looked at each other as

Park reached into his pocket and took out his phone. He opened the text message as the blood drained out of his face.

Hey there, Detective. You need to meet me where Rebecca was on display. I'll be waiting. If you value Mia's life and your FBI girlfriend's, then you will be at Lake Thunderbird Park in 30 minutes. Oh, and don't try to call the police, the FBI, or your dentist. If I get wind of anyone else at the park that shouldn't be there, Mia and Agent Brambilla will be sent to an eternity of fire and suffering. Don't forget I'm watching you. See you soon!

He looked up from the text and met Julie's eyes.

"So, is she ok?"

He sat in silence, not knowing what to say.

"She's going to be. I just need to go get her."

"I'm coming with you!"

"Julie, you can't. I need to do this alone. You have to trust me."

She looked at him, up and down, and into his eyes. Park almost felt like she was scanning him, to see if she should trust him or not. "I do trust you. Bring my daughter home to me."

They stood up together, and she once again fell into him, needing his embrace. He held her and then let her go. Park walked out the door and followed Jerry Miller's instructions.

CHAPTER 77

Jerry Miller arrived at the park. Jen was sitting on the ground next to Mia, who was tied up in Nylon rope, unconscious. A St. Andrew's cross was built in the same location it was just two weeks ago.

"So, are we doing this or not?" Jen asked.

"Well, yes, but not with her."

"Ooh, who then?"

"The FBI agent."

"Isn't that risky, Jerry?"

"Yes, but if we want to get out of this, then this is what we need to do. All we need is a few hours to disappear, and I need to take care of some loose ends."

"You have many loose ends, what are you planning? What does he think?"

"He doesn't know, he thinks we have this under control. Have you heard from John?"

"No. You?"

"No. He's probably dead. Poor soul, not sure if he was able to repent enough to punch his ticket into heaven. I mean, he did sacrifice his daughter, so she could have eternal happiness, but I know about his skeletons."

"What are you going to do about *your* skeletons?"

He laughed. "Yeah, I have to start over, somewhere else. I need to be pure, sinless, and I need to free some more souls if I want to bask in the light of our God almighty. That's why I can't go to jail or die tonight."

"So, what's your plan?"

"The FBI agent should be here any minute. You will hide over there in those trees and point your gun at her. I will have mine drawn as well but pointed at Mia. I will simply give her an option of us killing Mia and the Detective, or she voluntarily gets up on that cross."

"She will never do that. She will fight or try something."

"If she does, we kill her and then put Mia upon the cross and put the Agent's corpse right in front. I also have a contingency plan. Maria will be following her here as well as some other tricks up my sleeve. Hopefully, we can count on the Lieutenant to make all of this go away if it goes to shit."

"Can we trust him?"

"I think so, I mean, would he risk his two daughters?"

"You've been reckless since your nephew's ascension."

"I know. I got sloppy. I didn't count on our friendly neighborhood Detective to call the FBI and for them to put the pieces together. What led them to me? I need to ask the Detective."

"Am I interrupting?" Sonia shouted as she slowly walked towards Jerry with her gun drawn.

"Agent Brambilla, well, aren't you prompt? We couldn't even get into position, oh well, this will work just fine."

After she heard him say *we,* she turned her head and found Jen pointing a gun at her. When she looked back at Jerry, his gun was pointing at an unconscious Mia. She cursed herself, *Rookie mistake!* "Where is he?" Sonia moved her gun from side to side, pointing it at Jen and then back at Jerry.

"First, stop right there, or Mia dies. Second, your boyfriend isn't here yet, but he will be soon."

Sonia knew she was skilled enough to shoot Jerry in the head and then turn and shoot Jen before Jen could get off a shot. However, she didn't know how skilled Jen was and if she missed Jerry even by an inch, he could squeeze the trigger and kill Mia. "Let her go!"

Jerry laughed. He took his foot and moved Mia with it. "She isn't going anywhere for a while, even if I did untie her. I have a proposition for you. Your boyfriend is on his way. To save his life and Mia's here, I will need you to remove all your clothing and then let us put you on that." He moved his head in the direction of a large wooden X that she didn't see as she entered the scene.

"Are you going to kill me?"

"What kind of monsters do you think we are?"

"You killed Cameron."

"Well, that isn't true. Cameron committed suicide. He didn't really have an option, though." Jerry laughed and Jen followed.

"You won't get away with this."

"I think I just might. So, what do you say? No one has to die tonight."

Frozen, Sonia could hear her heart pounding in her ears. She has never put herself in this type of situation before. Her feelings for Park were unexpected, and now she realized, distracting. Breathing deeply and calmly, she was trying to control her heart rate, but it was too late. Her inability to control herself allowed Maria Burrows to sneak up behind her and place her gun at the base of her skull and say, "Drop it."

CHAPTER 78

"Did he buy it? Are you meeting him?" Park asked the Lieutenant through his phone.

"I think so, but he wanted John to meet him at Lake Thunderbird State Park. He thought the church was compromised."

"Do you think he is on to us?"

"Maybe. Park, I can't go until I get word from my daughters that they are safe."

"I understand. I have to go now."

"I will be there as soon as I can. I won't be far away. Be careful. I know this man. He is dangerous."

"Lieutenant, how long have you known about him? Why didn't you do anything?"

"We don't have time for that story Park. What I will tell you is, I had my suspicions for a long time, and that is why my daughters were compromised. I'm sorry I didn't tell you sooner."

"I understand."

CHAPTER 79

Park walked into the secluded spot of Lake Thunderbird Park slowly with his gun drawn. He wanted to see what he was walking into, before making his presence known. Slowly, he shuffled his feet through the leaves. As he maneuvered through the trees, he thought that a rustling sound was less noticeable than the leaves crunching below his feet. He was wrong.

"I can hear you, Detective. Olly Olly oxen-free! Come out, come out, wherever you are! You will want to see this!"

Park could see movement through the trees but couldn't see what he was walking into. He raised his gun and extended his arms, walking slowly towards the clearing, remembering to keep his balance centered in case he needed to fire with accuracy. As he entered the clearing, he immediately saw a naked Sonia bound to a large X. Her eyes were open. Relief enveloped his body. She was staring straight at him with eyes swimming in fear. Her mouth was bound, she was silent. Park kept his gun up, pointed at Jerry Miller who was standing next to the X, slowly moving in front of the scene Jerry Miller constructed. Darting his eyes back and forth, Park was looking for anyone else. He didn't see anyone but doubted Jerry Miller was alone. In front of the X, was a naked unconscious Mia bound by the wrists and ankles. *Jen must be here.*

"Where is Jen?"

Jerry let out a maniacal laugh. "You can come out!"

The blonde girl that Park had met at Julie's house, Jennifer Miller or Patricia Sullivan, came walking out from his left with a pistol aimed for his head. "Hello," she said, "Piece of shit, was it?"

"Detective, put down your gun, and let's talk. You have no moves. Even if a SWAT team came rushing in, I would shoot Mia, then your beautiful FBI agent, and then myself, and I would hope GOD was merciful. So just lower your gun, you can keep it."

Park lowered it. He knew if they wanted him dead, he would be dead already. Jerry kept his pistol trained on Mia. In his peripheral, he saw Jen lower her weapon. "Why not just kill me?"

"See Detective? After all, you're investigating, you still don't get it, do you?"

"No, I think I do. In your screwed-up head, you think the work you have been doing over the last 30 years will get you into heaven. If you murder me, then you will burn in hell with me."

"That's the cliff notes, but yeah, that is about it. I'm doing God's work. He will reward me. I haven't murdered anyone, I simply ensured that sinless young people got to enter Heaven."

Park shook his head. "That is murder."

"You poor, naive soul. The chosen believed in what we did, their fear and instincts were the only reason they fought us. Before they took their last breath, their eyes were at peace, when they figured out what gift we gave them."

"We? As in, you and John Williams?"

"Ah yes, John. Yes, he has been with me since Nashville. He was more reluctant than I when we had to sacrifice our own blood, but she was his daughter and Anthony was just my nephew. For us to ascend ourselves, we had to make the ultimate sacrifice. Waiting for decades was so difficult, but we kept busy making sure my nephew and his daughter stayed on the path. When he watched his daughter slowly pass into paradise, he understood. Is he dead?"

Park had to lie. "Dead? How would I know that? Why do you think Mr. Williams is dead?"

"HA! You are good!" Jerry Miller, saying *Ha*, made Park look at Sonia, who now had tears running down her face. *Control Park, stay in control.* "You think you are so smart. Either he is dead, in custody, or you stole his phone somehow. You think you can pretend to be him, and I wouldn't know?"

Park was relieved that he thought it was him, not the Lieutenant. "He's dead. You use a secure network to communicate, don't you? I should've known."

"Too bad. I loved that man more than you could know. It was difficult for him to let his daughter date me. It took forever to get her to meet me. I spent months on that stupid online dating app. Who would have guessed she was into older men? The things I tried to do with her, wow, any father would be tortured. The good news for her, *and him*, is that she said no, every time. Cameron was supposed to test her, but she wanted a mature, older man. Cameron was also supposed to strangle her at my house, but he chickened out. She almost got away. I had to do it. John was there, too. He wanted to see her ascend, he waited 30 years for it. The last thing she saw was her father's face. Seeing the shock in her eyes, OOO WEEE, that was enthralling. Gives me goosebumps right now. John was weak, though. When those two girls in Nashville were murdered, and we put them on the crosses, he started to cry. Do you know what was funny? Those two girls were probably killed too quickly. The trials were not as difficult back then. Just a little background and that's it. It wasn't until I sanctioned the help of our friend, Reverend Nelson, did I grasp what the trials needed to be."

"I would love to have you explain everything to me, but can we just fast-forward to how no one gets killed?"

"Fair enough. Here is how this is going to go. I am going to throw Mia over my shoulder and walk out of here. Jen is going to hang back and ensure that I'm gone. Then she is going to leave. You are going to wait 5 minutes, and then you can let Sonia down. We will know if you don't wait the 5 minutes and Agent Brambilla will die. You will find Mia, in these woods somewhere. I'll keep her mouth unbound, so she can scream when she wakes up."

There is someone else here, Park thought. "Fine."

"Oh good. You are a smart man. You must love this woman." He gestured his gun towards Sonia. "Look at her, what a specimen. I get it."

"Let's just get on with this." Park snarled.

Jerry Miller put his hands out, indicating he meant no harm. "Jen. Come here."

Jen started walking towards Jerry, but her hands were up, and she didn't have her gun anymore. The Lieutenant was behind her with his gun in the middle of her back and his other hand on her shoulder pushing her forward and at the same time using her as a shield. "I'm sorry, Jerry, he came out of nowhere!" Jen apologetically and angrily grunted.

"Lieutenant! You made it! Well, well, well, I'm guessing you aren't here to help me. So, that means your daughters are safe?" Jerry exclaimed. "Are you certain they're safe going to your mother's?" He roared with laughter.

"I'll kill her! Leave them alone!"

Jerry composed himself and instantly transformed into the demonic creature he was at the station, and a low voice said, "Kill her."

"Jerry!" Jen exclaimed.

"He won't, Jen. He thought he was in control here but he miscalculated his intelligence. Now, as soon as I walk away from here, his daughters will die."

The Lieutenant violently pushed Jen down to the ground. She tried to stop her fall with her hands, but the force was too great, and her face slapped the ground. She was faced down, motionless on the ground. Park aimed his gun at her.

The Lieutenant started to march towards Jerry, in front of Park, ready to shoot. Jerry grinned and lifted his gun towards Sonia's head. Park could hear a whimper come from her.

"SEAN! STOP!" Park cried out. He continued to march towards him, stopping 10 feet in front of Jerry. "He will shoot her!" He pleaded with his Lieutenant.

Tears fell from his eyes, "I have to kill him, or my daughters w..." A loud gunshot rang through the forest. The Lieutenant dropped. Park winced from the pain in his ears. Maria Burrows came from behind him holding a smoking gun. It was now trained on Park only a few feet away. Jen got herself up. She was stumbling a bit but regained her composure. She walked to the wounded Lieutenant and took her gun back. Reversing her course, she returned to Park's left, next to Maria Burrows. Both women had guns pointing at Park.

"Wow!" Jerry yelled. "Well, I guess we are back to square one. The offer still stands, but if your Lieutenant isn't already dead, he will be soon, you only have minutes to decide. So, are you going to let me walk away?"

Park dejectedly nodded. He lowered his gun and looked at Sonia. Her eyes were different. She was trying to communicate with him, and then her head moved slightly to the right. He glanced to the left of Jerry Miller and saw someone lurking in the woods. He recognized the figure in the woods and knew what they intended to do. Park needed to distract Jerry Miller. If he saw them coming, he might panic, and kill Sonia and Mia.

"Before I let you go, I need to know you won't hurt his daughters?"

"Ah, you are such a good man, Detective. You are a better Christian than most Christians. If I am allowed to leave and no one tries to find me, his daughters will be safe."

"How can I trust you?" The person in the woods inched closer. Jen and Maria didn't see them, but if they moved their gaze away from Park, they would.

"You can't, but they are just one of my insurance plans."

"One?"

He just smiled. The figure was getting close but hesitant. Park stalled. "Who else do you have for insurance?"

"Now, Detective, if I tell you, then it will ruin the surprise. Tell me, Jacob, before I leave you and this town, I'm curious. I have to know what led you to me and then to the Reverend Nelson?"

"Agent Brambilla and I figured out that you were using an online dating site to find your next targets. We found a name in Rebecca's account, one Thomas Scaggs. I, too, am a fan of the Steve Miller Band. It was my late father's favorite band." Park continued, hoping the person in the woods would make their move. "Well, when we were in your house, we found Cameron's book, written by our mutual friend, Reverend Nelson. We figured out that the Reverend's book had relevance, and all we had to do was read his bio, and the connection leaped from the page. I think you know the rest."

"Clever. Very clever. I underestimated you, Jacob. After my nephew's ascension, I thought you were incompetent, and I continued without hesitation. I was wrong. Bringing in the FBI was bold. Your dying Lieutenant, my old friend, was supposed to stop that from happening. I guess when a young woman is murdered, rather than a young man, people dig a little deeper for...." Jerry stopped abruptly and turned his head towards a noise to his right, bringing his gun with him. Park lifted his gun and turned it towards Mia and Jen, knowing how this might go down. They also turned towards the sound with their guns. Instantly, the figure appeared from the woods holding a revolver, pointing it at Jerry Miller, and without hesitation, fired the .357 caliber bullet. It missed by inches. Jerry Miller, in shock, hesitated but pulled his trigger at the same time another shot was fired at him. He was struck and went down like his bones folded in on themselves. Jerry's round also landed its target, and they went down as well. Park shouted at Mia and Jen, "Freeze!" The two women, also in shock, turned toward Park with their guns pointed at him. He fired hitting Maria in the chest, then he went down to one knee, as Jen fired her gun missing Park by a foot over his head. He fired and hit her in the head, dropping her to the ground. Park stumbled to his feet and ran over to both girls, kicking their guns away. He knew they weren't getting up. As he approached Jerry Miller, he knew right away he was dead. He could see the hole in his forehead and a larger hole in the back of his head. Making his way over to the person from the woods, he knelt and examined their wounds. Blood gushed out of the hole in their gut. A soft, labored voice got his attention. He placed his hand under the head and lifted it.

"Mrs. Williams? What is it?"

She coughed. Blood trickled out of her mouth. She was dying, quickly. "Forgive me."

"Ma'am, you have done nothing to forgive." He said trying to give her peace.

"I knew." She coughed again. "I knew and I let it happen."

That was the last thing Mrs. Williams ever said.

On his knees, Park was absorbing the events that just occurred in the 10 seconds from the first shot from Mrs. Williams. So much death overwhelmed his senses. A thought lifted him out of his shock. *Sonia! Mia!* Forcing himself to move, he ran to the crucifix, and what he saw took all the air from him, dropping him to his knees once again. Mrs. Williams's first shot missed Jerry Miller but struck Sonia through her right side, through her heart. She was dead, bound to that cross. Tears poured from his eyes as he untied her, took her off the cross, and laid her down next to Mia's unconscious body. He closed her eyes, kissed her lips, and placed his jacket over her.

DAY SEVENTEEN

CHAPTER 80

Three days had passed since that horrible evening and Park, still grieving, had so many questions still unanswered. He approached the door and knocked. Julie threw open the door and hugged Park.

"What's that for?"

"You need it. I know you do. I also can't thank you enough for saving my daughter."

"Well, you have Mrs. Williams to thank for that."

"I don't believe that at all. If anything, she put her in more danger, but you did what you needed to do."

"I just stopped by, to see how she was doing."

"She's ok, still a little traumatized. Thankfully, she was unconscious through the worst of it." Julie paused, knowing how that sounded. "Oh… I'm so sorry, Park. That was insensitive."

"No worries, I understand what you meant. I'm just glad she's ok."

Mia appeared at the door, next to Julie. She saw Park and, without hesitation, hugged him. "Thank you, she whispered."

Park squeezed her back. "You're welcome."

"Why don't you come in and have lunch with us?" Julie interjected.

"Thanks, but I am on my way to see the Lieutenant."

"How's he doing?"

"He's going to be fine. His lung collapsed, and he broke some ribs, but the bullet missed his heart, and the surgeon thinks he should be fine, eventually. He was lucky. If he laid there just a few minutes longer, he would've died."

"Well, give him our love."

"Will do, and I will take a rain check on lunch."

Julie smiled and gently closed the door as Park ascended from her porch and headed to the hospital.

Park knocked on the hospital door as he peeked his head in. "Good time?"

"Jacob, come on in. I hear I owe you, my life."

Park walked to the empty chair to the right of the bed and turned it to face him before he sat down.

"Well, it was also Mrs. Williams."

"Yeah, I was told. What a sad story. All three Williamses are dead."

"That's just it, I don't think I understand the whole story. Do you mind if I tell you what I know, and could you fill in the gaps for me? I don't think I can move on from this without it."

"Of course, I at least owe you that. Go ahead and tell me what you know."

Park took a deep breath and spoke, "Jerry Miller and John Williams believed they needed to find young Christian adults, put them through some trials, and if they passed they would murder them to have them ascend to Heaven without sin. For an extra bonus, Jerry wanted to place these lucky individuals on a St. Andrew's cross. This was due to Reverend Nelson's book, which they believed was their instruction manual. The next parts are just guesses. Jerry and John would then take those who failed the trials and turn them into soldiers, somehow. This is how Jen, Maria, Cameron, the blonde fellow we caught watching Julie, and the two men we caught following your daughters got involved." The Lieutenant, with pain in his eyes, just nodded along. Park continued. "At some point over the last 30 years, they used a website called, *Cross My Heart*, to find their next lottery winner. Jerry, John, and maybe the rest posed as potential Christian suitors to put individuals they found on the dating app through trials. This is where it gets hazy. Years ago, Rebecca started a program to help troubled youths. This was run by the Pastor and included Jerry Miller and John Williams. This allowed them to control Maria, Cameron, and the like. How am I doing?"

"So far, you have hit all the high points."

"Ok, so when did you know about this?"

Clearing his throat, the Lieutenant shifted his position to sit more upright, wincing in pain, and then replied, "I was friends with John, and to some extent Jerry, as kids. They were a few years ahead of me, but John and my parents knew each other through our church. Jerry was John's friend. We all went to Vanderbilt University. When they were later in law school, and I was an undergrad in my third year, I sensed a change in them. It was night and day. Shortly after I noticed their behavior change, they introduced me to this man. He was an older man in his thirties, a non-traditional student auditing religious and law classes. He seemed to be wealthy, at least there was this air about him that indicated such. There was this charisma about him. After a while, there was a group of us all hanging out, and this man seemed to have garnered some influence over all of us. He would preach about *sinless perfection* and argue its merits. Then he spoke of this thesis he read that talked about an empty heaven and that the lucky ones were those who died sinless, for only those souls would enter the kingdom of God. I started to feel like it was getting a little culty, but I still hung out with them because of John and Jerry." Park suppressed a comment about how all religion was culty and instead nodded along. "One night, John asked me to help him with a project but swore me to secrecy. When I refused, he dismissed me. Two days later, I learned of those two girls being murdered and crucified. I confronted John about it, but he denied knowing anything about it. I should've done something, but I wanted to believe him. After that, I separated from the group and finished out my last year. I barely saw them. I stopped going to church. The next time I interacted with them was about five years ago when John showed up at my door and convinced me to find my way back to my religion. So, I took my family to church, and John and I became friends again. Jerry was around, but he went to another church, so we didn't cross paths that often. I never forgot about Vanderbilt, but John assured me he had nothing to do with the murders. I was then told about John's daughter wanting to create a program to help troubled youths, so I joined, as did John and Jerry, among others. At first, It seemed like a great idea, but I saw Maria Burrows transform in front of my eyes, from this scared girl into, well, something different. She reminded me of how John and Jerry looked around that older man at Vanderbilt. That cult vibe returned. I then stopped participating in the program. Months later, I found out that the program wasn't Rebecca's idea, but John's. Rebecca put it in motion, but John suggested it to her. Jerry and John needed a better way of, well, they wouldn't say it like this, but a better way to brainwash the unworthy. Do you think it was a coincidence that Rebecca found Maria? I'm getting ahead of myself."

The Lieutenant grabbed the cup of water and took three sips from it before he continued. "Where was I? Oh, yeah. Everything changed for me when Anthony Miller was found in the same manner as those girls in Nashville. I immediately went to John and expressed my concern and told him that I couldn't ignore the connection. He just smiled at me with this evil undertone, and said, *How are your daughters doing in college? Are you keeping tabs on those girls? Because girls like that can get into trouble if you know what I mean?* I was scared. The next morning, I gave you the case, my best detective. I needed you to figure this out, and I couldn't tell you anything. When you didn't solve the case, I thought my daughters would be safe, as long I kept my mouth shut. Then Rebecca happened six months later. I wanted to vomit. I never thought John would do that to his daughter. After Maria visited me with the pictures of my daughters, and before I could even confront him, John picked me up in his car and drove me to a cabin in the woods. It was creepy, like weird cult creepy. It had an altar and three chairs. Jerry Miller was waiting for us there. They showed me new pictures of my daughter that I couldn't even look at. They went on to explain how they needed to sacrifice their own blood to redeem themselves and to be able to continue saving souls. It was their penance, but at the same time, a gift. I saw no remorse or even pain from either of them. What you saw at the station, from John, was an act. I was told that if I help in any way with this case, my daughters would be *judged*. If I allowed you to get too close, my daughters would suffer. I'm so sorry, Park, I didn't know what to do." He paused, trying to keep his composure. Park patted him on the arm.

"It's ok. I understand. Continue."

"There is not much more to say, other than you and Agent Brambilla were a remarkable team, even with the barriers I put up. I am so sorry, Park, I know you cared for her."

Park just nodded, holding in his tears now. "Thanks. I'll be ok."

"What about Colorado Springs?" Park asked.

"I don't know. What I think happened is that Jerry went rogue and killed that man because he just wanted to."

"According to Sonia's notes, Jerry was a bisexual. He hooked up with a male bartender in Colorado to find the man he murdered."

The Lieutenant's face scrunched up, he remarked, "Really? Huh?"

"What did you know about Reverend Nelson? He is being investigated as we speak, but what did you know about him?

"Only that Jerry was obsessed with him and his book. I read the book because they referenced it so often. I understood the hypothesis, but I could also understand how a deranged person could use it to serve their psychotic needs."

Park summarized what he just heard. "So, they find men and women through a dating site, if they pass the trials, they get killed. If they don't pass the trials, their lives are ruined, and then Rebecca's Program is used to brainwash them into repeating this cycle."

The Lieutenant nodded.

"So, Cameron did he…"

"No. He didn't. My heart broke, seeing that kid hanging there, knowing I could have stopped it. Cameron was tested by Maria and failed. They injected him with heroin and dropped him in the middle of nowhere. Then, John Williams saves the day, and they force Cameron to help with Anthony Miller and seduce Rebecca and put her through the trials. That's how Cameron got the community service gig with Rebecca. His mistake was that he fell in love with her. He couldn't manipulate her like they wanted him to. Rebecca only saw him as a friend. They made him befriend her and encourage her to join the dating app. Maria, also, helped with this. They didn't have another brainwashed male to sweep her off her feet, so Jerry Miller did it himself. Come to find out, Rebecca was attracted to older men and Jerry knew exactly what to do to seduce her. Finally, Rebecca was strangled at Jerry's house and then brought to the park. Cameron was there, helping them set up the crucifix. After that night he started to break, he just couldn't deal with her death. After they forced him to break into your house, and he was almost caught, he wanted out. He was now a liability. You know what happened next."

They both sat in silence for a while until Park asked one more question.

"Why only the six murders? Five if you count the planned ones."

The Lieutenant paused, but then replied, "I don't know. My guess is that either they couldn't find the right candidates, or they just didn't crucify them. I don't know. All I know is after they killed their own blood, they moved on to Mark O'Brien. If you didn't sniff them out, they may have killed dozens more. I guess Mrs. Williams found out what Mr. Williams did. She must've followed you or me to the park, looking for Jerry and John."

Park's face saddened as he explained to the Lieutenant about his last conversation with Mrs. Williams. "Mrs. Williams confessed to me with her last breath that she knew. She knew and either didn't or couldn't stop her husband from killing her daughter. She took her husband's other gun from the house and followed one of us out to the park. Overhearing Jerry's confession about killing her daughter, and her husband's death, she just snapped. That would explain an interaction I saw between her and Maria Burrows." He paused and gathered himself. "I don't blame Mrs. Williams for Sonia's death. She was a victim too. I wish I could have heard her story." He stood up. "Well, you need your rest. I'll come by tomorrow and bring some bourbon."

"That sounds perfect." He smiled, but then his face turned remorseful. "Hey Jacob, I am sorry."

"I know."

He left the hospital and headed to the Anderson's home.

DAY EIGHTEEN

CHAPTER 81

Sitting on his couch, participating in his favorite pastime of sipping bourbon, Park was decompressing from all the events over the last few weeks. Talking to the Andersons, yesterday, about their son's innocence, not only with the Rebecca Williams murder but with his drug usage and his arrest, gave him a sliver of joy. That feeling of closure for a family, even if their lives are forever altered, is necessary for any semblance of a life. He was able to give that to them. Thinking of this case and the puzzle in front of him, he saw the picture of religious fanaticism turning into a cult with serial killers. A few pieces were missing but the picture was clear. Slowly falling into the alcohol's warmth, he was shocked back into reality by his phone buzzing. He pulled it out of his pocket and looked at the number and answered it quickly.

"This is Jacob Parkerson."

"Hello Detective, this is Special Agent Craig Evan from the Oklahoma City FBI office. We need you to come here, right away."

"Why would I want to do that?"

"Agent Brambilla's work on this case has shed light on something much bigger, that we would like you to help us with." The mere sound of her name hurt his heart.

"What do you mean?"

"Well, without getting into much detail, she asked us to look into similar murders to the ones you had in Norman, and although we found some that were sort of similar, nothing stood out. So, she then asked us to look into situations in which promising young adults, for no discernible reason, destroyed their lives. This was much more difficult, but after we surveyed local police departments from Tennessee, Colorado, Oklahoma, and surrounding states, we started getting numerous reports spanning over 40 years. We also found some murders within those clusters that are similar to the ones from your town. You need to see this, we need your help."

Park was overwhelmed by the depth of it all. They've only scratched the surface. Terror shuddered him, as he thought of all those lives ruined and taken away, once again, by religious extremism. Without hesitation, and with Sonia in his thoughts, Park responded gallantly, "I'll be there as soon as I can."

"You will want to pack a bag. You will be here for a few days. We will send you more details through your email. Thank you, Detective Parkerson. Agent Brambilla was a remarkable agent, and an exceptional person. We are going to miss her."

Park started to tear up. He choked down his sadness and simply responded, "Yes sir. I'll see you soon," and ended the call. This is exactly what he needed. His phone rang again. This time it was an unknown caller. He picked up.

"This is Jacob Parkerson."

"Why, hello there, Detective." A raspy voice said with an excited tone.

"Who is this?" Park has heard this voice before. His detective brain doesn't forget people's faces or voices very often, but he couldn't place it.

"My name, well, the one I go by now, is Merrill Thompson."

He immediately recognized the name, but still couldn't figure out from where.

"Do I know you? Have we met?"

"Why, yes, we have. I've been watching you. You didn't get all the cameras."

Terror crept into Park. "Who are you?"

"It'll come to you. It's just the bourbon blocking your memories. I want to thank you, and Mrs. Williams, for removing Jerry Miller from this earth. He wasn't following the rules. He was reckless. Our mission is crucial for the salvation of humanity, and he was threatening it. I can't thank her, so I wanted to call you. I am impressed by you, Mr. Parkerson."

The caller's face shot to the front of his brain. Nauseousness overwhelmed him. "Lake Thunderbird Park. You were the one who called in Rebecca's murder."

"There you go, Detective. I was. I had to. Jerry and John put her body in a place no one would find for days. Again, with the crucifix. I think John wanted it that way, he had a hard time with his sacrifice. So, I moved things along. As a bonus, I got to meet you. The only detective to get this far down the proverbial rabbit hole."

"You're the man at Vanderbilt!"

"There you go. Smart Detective, Parkerson. Reverend Nelson said too much. I'll deal with him soon."

"Why are you calling me?"

"Because I like you. What happened to Agent Brambilla was unfortunate and shouldn't have happened. I wanted to send you my condolences. I also wanted to warn you. As I said, you have gotten farther than all the other detectives, mostly because of Jerry and his bumbling ways, how do you say it?

Oh, yeah. Jerry Fucking Miller. I knew from the moment I saw the eagerness in his eyes, he was going to be trouble. I thought John would have kept him in line. You live, you learn. Oh... sorry, I'm rambling. Let's get back to your warning. Do you know how they say not to corner a wild animal?"

"Yes."

"I'm a serpent."

"Is that a threat?"

"Take it as you will. I just need you to know, I bite. Our purpose, our mission from God is the only thing that matters. We will do... I will do, anything for my God Almighty. We underestimated you. Now you are being called up to the big leagues. I prefer not to bite you, but I will."

"I guess we'll just have to see who has the bigger bite. How are you different from Jerry, then?"

"Jerry was driven by lust, by power, by his vanity. The crucifixes, the guns, the sex, and everything else about him, was a symptom of his weakness. The Devil never let him go. He was a problem for me, I knew it. I just hoped he would finally see the light. He wanted to kill, not help our passengers ascend. I think he liked it, and I provided the outlet. He once told me, when he was in high school, he killed a younger boy. Jerry was confessing his sins to me. After he had sex with this younger boy, he chased him into the woods and struck him with a rock out of shame and regret. How am I different, Mr. Parkerson? I'm not weak. I don't threaten you out of a power struggle. Simply, my mission from God won't be threatened by the likes of you."

Park was physically sick. He started breathing deeply to keep himself from throwing up. After all these years, he finally found out what happened to that boy. Jerry Miller was responsible for who Park was. He gathered himself and asked, "While

I have you on the phone, how did you get Jerry Miller and John Williams to kill their own flesh and blood?"

"Ok. I'll give you a little more. This is exhilarating. It wasn't that hard. I seek out the most righteous of us all to join me on my mission from God. I slowly teach them sinless perfection, the way I was taught, and they eventually become serpents in the midst of wolves. For them to become purely God's children and to fully commit, I wait and find their weakness, exploit them, and then use their guilt and shame. By convincing them of a larger purpose and showing them the path to redemption, over time they believe in God's plan."

"So, what was Jerry and John's weakness that you exploited? Was it Jerry's bisexuality?"

"Oh detective, you have it all backward, or sideways. Jerry wasn't bisexual. He was a homosexual, and he thought he was in love with John and vice-versa. You see, I caught them defiling themselves with each other. Fearing exposure, they were more open to God's ways and teachings. I simply had to put them on a righteous path, and all they had to do was present their pure and innocent children for sacrifice. John was able to cure himself of his affliction and marry a wonderful woman. They created a beautiful child together. Jerry tried, but he struggled with his disease of homosexuality. Satan has, or I should say, had, his claws in him. He kept trying to lay with women, but he would always give in to the temptations of his affliction. Once, he impregnated a young woman, you know her as Jen. He was finally going to have his child to sacrifice. She went behind his back and got an abortion. Long story short, she failed our trials and became one of our serpents. It was she who put Anthony through his trials, allowing him to ascend. Giving Jerry a sacrifice of his own."

Park was overwhelmed with the final, heavy, pieces of the puzzle. He interrupted. "If they had to wait until they had children to sacrifice, why did those two girls die in Nashville?"

"You really want me to tell you all my secrets, don't you? That's ok, I'm enjoying talking to you. They didn't kill those girls. They just had to watch, to help. Jerry was the one who wanted to put them on crosses. He can be very convincing. Those fucking crosses. He became obsessed with St. Andrews. I warned him about having a calling card like that. The only thing they had to do was wait, help out with other trials, and find some serpents of their own. Only until they sacrificed their own flesh and blood, could they have their own chapter. They would then be in charge, without my guidance. Waiting, almost 30 years, was part of their penance. After they have their chapter to run, they can ascend themselves. Their sins have been forgiven."

"So where does Reverend Nelson fit in?"

"Let's just say, he was offered a seat at the table. His ideas around the narrowing road to Heaven were insightful and validated our quest for sinless perfection. I shared with him our ideas, and how similar our beliefs were. After the two girls ascended, he was spooked. I'll give him credit for one thing, his idea for trials was brilliant. Before, we had no real way of knowing, or putting people's faith to the test. I mean, we looked into people, watched them, and interacted with them, but we had to use our best judgment when deciding if they were passenger-worthy. I'm sure we sent some poor souls to hell mistakenly. When I read in his book about putting Christians through actual trials, I was overjoyed. It took our cause to another level. He was right, the road narrows the more we are exposed to this ungodly world. So, we developed dating apps, and other methods, that I won't share, to help us find worthy passengers to put through trials. So much easier than stalking graduate students. I am saddened that I can't save more souls."

"Are you saying that you have created other chapters, that may have committed other murders and atrocities, for 30 years?

"Oh, Detective. 30 years? You don't see it, do you? I was given a chapter 30 years ago in Nashville after I sacrificed **my** son. He was 20 years old when I gave him the ultimate gift a parent can give a child, a seat next to God in Heaven. I just hope one day, my sins will be forgiven, and I can reunite with him. I wish I could continue with your enlightenment, but I have to go now. We will meet again. Cross my heart!" Merrill Thompson laughed and then ended the call.

Park fell onto his couch and poured himself another drink. As Merrill Thompson's face became clearer and clearer in his mind, Park knew he had a new ghost to haunt his dreams.

"What have you gotten yourself into, Park?" He said out loud. "Ha!" He smiled, then sadness crept in.

After a few minutes of absorbing the gravity of what he just learned, and mourning Sonia, Park stood up with new vigor and packed for his trip to Oklahoma City. As he drove away from Norman, Oklahoma, he made a call.

"Hey, Jake. What's up?" He didn't mind being called that any longer.

"Hey Julie, I have to go to Oklahoma City for a while, but when I get back…um…"

"I would love to grab some dinner with you." Julie finished his thought.

He smiled. "Great. See you soon."

Park ended the call. He pushed down on the gas pedal as he merged onto I-35 North. With Sonia in his thoughts, he needed to finish what they started. There was a larger puzzle out there needing to be put together.

THE END

Made in the USA
Middletown, DE
28 October 2024